WHAT THE DWARF

WHAT THE DWARF

DWARF BOUNTY HUNTER™ BOOK FIVE

MARTHA CARR

MICHAEL ANDERLE

L M B P N

DISRUPTIVE IMAGINATION

THE WHAT THE DWARF TEAM

Thanks to our JIT Team:

Dave Hicks
Deb Mader
Dorothy Lloyd
Thomas Ogden
Diane L. Smith
Peter Manis
Kelly O'Donnell
Jackey Hankard-Brodie
Jeff Goode

If We've missed anyone, please let us know!

Editor
SkyHunter Editing Team

CHAPTER ONE

If the animals hadn't insisted on freaking out so much, Johnny
Walker would have called this a damn fine day. He tried to focus
on the massive new machine in his waterfront back yard and to
put the finishing touches on the concealment panel he'd installed
himself.

*There's only one way to make sure the damn feds ain't spyin' on me
with a gift horse. It ain't hard to improve what they have runnin' on
their end anyway.*

"Luther, you idiot!" Rex barked at his four-legged brother
who raced around the fully built chicken coop. That only added
to Luther's frantic whining, the thump and scrabble of his paws
as he dug a deeper trench in the dirt now that he'd ripped all the
grass up, and the terrified squawking of the coop's current resi-
dents—all eight of them.

"Come on, come on, come on." The hound skidded to a halt in
front of the electric fence around the coop, panting madly. "I'll
get one of them."

"No, you'll get your tongue fried off." Rex snapped at his
brother with a low growl. "Leave 'em alone, bro—"

"No!" Despite his brother's nip at his neck, the smaller coonhound raced away again on his self-made track around the chicken coop and uttered a wild bay.

"For the love of anythin' that ain't the two of y'all right now!" Johnny slammed the concealment panel shut, dropped his welder onto the tarp spread beside his new project, and slapped the visor of his welding helmet up. "Luther! Leave it!"

The hound made another lightning-fast rotation around the chicken coop. He darted away from his brother with wide eyes and a skittering yelp when Rex pounced and snapped at him again. The hounds' high-energy tussle lasted three seconds before Luther sped away again with his tongue lolling out of his mouth and practically slapping against the side of his face.

"Do you have trouble hearin', boy?" Johnny shouted. "I said—"

The electric fence buzzed and snapped when the dog's hind leg brushed against it after a poorly aimed attempt to turn even faster. A crackling orange light skittered across the metal mesh with another loud pop. Luther yelped and scrambled away from the coop. A puff of feathers and dirt and ground shells sprayed up inside the chickens' protective fence. All eight hens completely lost it.

"Ow, ow, ow!" Luther limped away from the fence. He panted and shook his head furiously as he tried to get a better visual angle of the insane poultry on the other side. "Jeez, Johnny. Does it have to be so strong?"

The dwarf grunted. "That's the lowest setting."

"What—like, for squirrels?"

"And hounds."

Rex sniggered and trotted toward his brother. "Why would a squirrel wanna get into a chicken coop?"

"Look at 'em! They keep moving. And clucking. And pecking. And—" Luther raced toward the fence again.

Johnny uttered a piercing whistle and Rex padded obediently toward him. "Luther!"

"I'll get 'em. I'll get 'em, I'll get 'em, I'll get 'em, and I'll...do something!"

Rex sat beside his master and lowered his head with a fearful whine. "This is it. He's lost it."

With a grunt of exasperation, Johnny jerked one welding glove off, dropped it on the ground, and stuck two fingers in his mouth for the mother of all Johnny Walker whistles. The chickens shrieked but instantly fell silent. Luther skidded so far across the dirt that the spray of loose earth pelted his chest, neck, and muzzle.

"Hey! What gives?" The hound snorted and shook his head. "You got something hiding underground, Johnny? 'Cause I'll get that too. Trust me. Whatever it is, I'll—"

"Boy, I ain't playin' around." Johnny snapped his fingers and pointed at the patch of grass beside him. "Come!"

"Oh. Sure, Johnny." After he'd shaken himself vigorously from head to toe and sprayed more dirt across the side of the electric fence—and a few chickens—Luther trotted toward his master and sat at the dwarf's feet. His dirt-dusted tail thumped repeatedly on the dry grass, and he licked his muzzle before he resumed his panting. "What's up?"

"Oh, man..." Rex lowered his head even more and covered his muzzle with a forepaw.

"Hey, when did you get here, bro?"

"Listen up, boys." Johnny folded his arms and only gave Rex a glance before he returned his firm stare to Luther. *At least I ain't gotta worry about* both *of 'em. This one's as bad as two untrained pups all on his own.* "Now, I got work to do on this big hunk of federal metal they call cutting-edge, and I aim to get it up and runnin' the way I want by this time tomorrow. The fella who owns these birds is expectin' to come home to eight hens in that coop and nothin' else. Ya hear?"

Luther whipped his head around to stare at the coop again. "Hey, I counted nine. Where'd the extra one come from?"

3

Rex sighed and lowered himself onto his belly in the sparse grass. "You need help."

"Well, if you wanna help me get some of those birds, bro, I'm down—"

"Hush up." Johnny snapped his fingers again and raised his ungloved hand with a centimeter of space between his thumb and forefinger as he looked fixedly at Luther. "I'm this close to lockin' y'all up inside for the rest of the day, understand?"

"Aw, Johnny…"

"Wait, but we have a dog door."

The dwarf raised an eyebrow and glanced sternly from one hound to the other. "Not for much longer if you keep foolin' around."

Luther gasped. "No…"

"Don't push it." Rex growled at his brother. "I don't wanna be locked inside with you all day. Not even for ten minutes."

"Okay, okay. Yeah. Got it." Luther stared at Johnny with huge puppy-dog eyes. "No foolin' around, Johnny. I can do that. No problem."

A chicken squawked, followed by a violent flap of wings and a round of clucking that sounded more like screams. Luther barked once but managed to remain where he was. The hen fight lasted all of five seconds before it subsided again.

"What about them, Johnny?"

The dwarf grunted and stooped to retrieve his glove and his welder. "They ain't the ones startin' the trouble. Or talkin' in my head." The visor of his helmet dropped into place with a metallic ping. "Now git on."

Rex huffed a canine sigh, stood, and headed toward the swamp.

"But…but…Johnny, what are we supposed to do?" Luther whined.

"Y'all are hounds in the Everglades. Outside and with free rein of the swamps. Y'all can think of something." He turned toward

4

his home improvement project on FBI technology, shook his head, and activated the welder. "I'd better not see you behind me next time I turn around."

Rex barked once. "Bro, that's warning number one."

"Yeah? When's number two?"

"It doesn't exist."

"Huh." Luther trotted after his brother. "Then why is it called number one if there's only— Hey! Look at the size of that frog!"

"Get it!"

"Yeah, I will. Then I'll be number one!" The hounds bounded into the swamp together, baying and splashing, and finally gave their master a few minutes of relative peace and quiet.

As if the hens knew exactly what was on his mind, half of them began a new wave of clucking and pecking at the coop as they fluttered their wings and squabbled with their closest neighbors.

I can't decide which one of 'em is worse. Maybe it's best to stick with talkin' collars on hounds only.

Finally, he could work on the rest of this damn device dropped like a botched illegal-arms deal almost on top of his storage shed. The welder flared to life in his hands and threw the first few sparks as he finished sealing the concealment panel.

No more distractions. No more talkin'. Only me and my tools and some good old-fashioned—

"Johnny!" Luther splashed out of the swamp and slipped on the muddy bank before he found his footing again. "Johnny, someone's coming!"

"Luther, the frog," Rex shouted after him.

"Screw the frog, bro. Wait. Don't do that. But for real, there's someone—"

Johnny cut the hound off with a whistle and pointed firmly at the muddy water and the reeds and the thick foliage of the overhanging branches in late August. "Out."

"What?" Luther skidded to a halt and dripped sheets of swamp water all over the dry grass.

"Go on."

"But Johnny, it's her. Don't you wanna—"

"I ain't sayin' it again, hound."

"Shit, Luther. He called you hound. Get back here."

The sound of tires crunching across dirt and sparse gravel reached Johnny's ears now too and he grunted. Luther's head whipped from the side yard to his master and back again, his ears flapping against his face. "But—"

When his gaze finally settled on Johnny's face and the hound had enough time to take in the seriousness beneath the welding mask, he sighed and turned toward the swamp.

Rex poked his nose out from behind a stand of reeds and stared at the dwarf. "Hurry up, man. He's about to blow."

"He's about to lose out on the best hound of his life."

"Okay, drama queen..."

The hounds splashed away and disappeared behind the reeds again. Johnny grasped the front of his helmet and recentered it against his sweat-slickened face before he returned to his work.

I ain't got it in me for all this at once. Don't matter who has shown up here. It could be anyone at this point.

The welder hissed and threw a constant wave of sparks as he drew it down the seam of the panel. For a blissful thirty seconds, it drowned out even the calmer clucking of hens and the drone of the cicadas and the birdcalls. When he'd completed the weld, he slapped his free hand against the panel with a hollow metallic clang.

That'll do.

"Wow, Johnny."

His hold tightened instantly on the welder's handle and he spun to where Special Agent Lisa Breyer stood between the chicken coop and the house. "At least he got somethin' right."

"What?" Lisa pointed to her temple and shook her head. "You're all muffled."

He dropped the welder onto the tarp again and lifted the helmet off with both hands. It joined the rest of his tools as he inclined his head and regarded his visitor somewhat blankly. "How's that?"

"Well, besides the fact that I can tell you're not all that thrilled to see me here, it's better. I think."

"Naw, I ain't—" He cleared his throat. "Okay, I wouldn't use the word thrilled but I ain't unhappy—"

With a sharp laugh, Lisa folded her arms and studied him with wry amusement. "And you keep digging."

"Huh?"

"A hole. For yourself, Johnny." She laughed again and scanned the yard. "You know, putting your foot in your mouth. Saying all the wrong things—"

"Yeah, yeah. I know what it means." He tugged his heavy gloves off, tossed them onto the tarp, and stuck a finger in his ear and wiggled it around. "I guess I had a little too much noise around."

Like hounds and hens and sweatin' in this damn heat.

"What if I told ya you're a sight for sore eyes, darlin'?"

"That might fill the hole a little."

"Uh-huh."

With a grin, Lisa turned slightly to examine the chicken coop, then trailed her gaze slowly to the metallic monolith that took up a third of the dwarf's back yard. Her smile faded a little beneath a curious frown. "I'm sorry I missed your call but I did get your voicemail. It was very vague, by the way."

"Oh, yeah? How's that?"

She scowled in her best Johnny impersonation and wiggled her eyebrows. "'Got somethin' to show ya, and I ain't fixin' to say what's what on the phone. So...come on by. If you want.'"

He snorted. "That ain't what I sound like."

"No, you're right. Only you can capture the full essence of Johnny Walker." That drew a short chuckle out of him, and she nodded toward the metal contraption behind him. "Do you wanna tell me what the hell you're doing with a spaceship in your yard?"

"Spaceship? Darlin', the feds couldn't build a spaceship the right way if they hired NASA to do it for 'em."

Lisa frowned. "I can't tell if that's a burn on the Bureau or NASA."

"Maybe both. But this baby makes all that fancy gadget tech of yours look like... Hell. I'll show ya. Come on." He waved her forward and walked around the metal hulk until he disappeared.

CHAPTER TWO

"Oh, so it's a giant cell phone." Lisa followed Johnny slowly to the other side. She peered at the odd angles of the contraption the size of any of the shacks on the unmarked roads in this part of the Everglades. Honestly, it was almost as big as the bounty hunter's house.

His snort echoed with a metallic ting. "Better—and completely different. Where are ya?"

She stepped around the curving side of the contraption and jolted when his thick hand and forearm covered in wiry red hair jerked out of a hidden doorway and almost smacked her in the face. "What are you—"

"Come on, darlin'. I ain't gonna bite'cha.'

"Not yet."

"Margo might, though." He chuckled and his hand disappeared inside.

"Margo, Johnny?"

"That's her name, darlin'. It fits like a glove, and I ain't talkin' about those beaters out with my tools, neither."

"He named another machine," she muttered as she stepped into the dark doorway. It took a second for her eyes to adjust to the dark and when they did, she realized it wasn't completely dark in there at all.

Thousands of tiny, blinking lights lined most of the interior walls and even the ceiling. A control panel had been installed at the opposite side, complete with one swiveling chair with leather-upholstered cushions bolted to the floor in front of it. Five huge monitors spanned the wall above the controls, each of them dark but for a rendered image of a crossbow, its bolt drawn back and tipped with glowing yellow.

"Like I said." Johnny smirked and nodded slowly as he gazed around the inside of his contraption. "It fits. And any pretty little thing who has as much power in her as Margo does deserves a name."

"Okay, I take it back." Lisa rubbed her hands down the sides of her Bermuda shorts and shook her head. "This looks more like the first processing computer."

He whipped his head toward her and grinned. "You were around already for that too, huh?"

"No." With a self-conscious smile, she shook her head. "But I've seen enough pictures—wait, were you?"

"Forget computers, darlin'." He waved her off and gave the control panel a loving pat. "Forget cell phones and fancypads and any of those iCouldCareLesses. This might be the best thing I ever had a hand in bringin' to life. Ain't she pretty?"

"Hmm. Maybe she would be if I knew what she was." Despite his confusing allusions to absolutely nothing, Lisa couldn't help but chuckle. "What does it—she—do?"

Johnny winked at her. "It'll be a minute still, but I tell you what. When I have her all fixed up and rarin' to go, Margo will have somethin' real special for what comes next."

"Johnny…"

"Naw, I ain't spoilin' the surprise, darlin'. You'll have to wait and see. But damn, she's somethin'."

Lisa peeled her tank top away from her torso and fluttered it in the still, muggy air. "Will she have AC?"

He wiggled his eyebrows. "The works. But you look ready to drop, darlin'. Come on."

She laughed as he caught her hand and hauled her out of the metal structure. The gentle albeit muggy breeze felt like heaven after the stifling heat inside. "So this is what you called to talk to me about, huh?"

"What?" He released her hand and rubbed the back of his neck. "Naw, this is extra. The big kind, if you get my drift."

"No, not even a little."

"All right. Well, listen. Here's the thing." Johnny scuffed the heel of his boot against the dirt and sniffed. "I know we ain't exactly had the chance to hash all this out, but it's somethin' I—"

"Johnny!" Rex howled and leapt out of the swamp with a massive spray of water. A heron took flight on the other side of the back yard, but the hound ignored it completely. "Someone's here. Someone new!"

Luther stumbled out of the water next. His howl choked off in confusion when he saw Johnny and Lisa standing together in front of Margo, and his ears flattened instantly against his head. "Does...this count?"

The dwarf cleared his throat when he heard another car approaching too, then nodded toward the side yard. "You're good. Go on."

"Yes!" Luther darted forward, stopped again, and barked at Lisa. "Hey, lady! Tell him not to lock me in the house, huh?"

He raced after Rex and added his howls and yapping to the noise as both hounds raced toward the newcomers.

Lisa chuckled. "Is he doing okay?"

"Who the hell knows? Come on, darlin'. It's time for a meetin'."

"A what?"

"You don't wanna be late for the first one, do ya?" He took her hand again and pulled her forward past the chicken coop and toward the side yard.

"Whoa! Hold on." She tripped in the ditch Luther had carved around the coop, regained her footing, and laughed far more uncertainly this time. "Johnny, I thought I was the one you had meetings with. And Nelson, but you'd never be this excited to see him."

He released her hand and slowed before he cleared his throat, hooked his thumbs through his belt loops, and strode down the side yard toward the front. "I ain't excited. You only got one of those things right."

"Now I'm confused."

"You'll have to hustle up and see then, won'tcha?" He wiped his sweaty forehead with a forearm and smirked as they rounded the corner of his house to find an old, extremely dilapidated Honda Civic parked six feet from Sheila.

The man who shut the driver's door wheezed a chuckle as Rex and Luther darted around him. They jumped and whined and wagged their tails like lunatics. "Come on now, boys. Y'all know better'n that. Git. Go on. Y'all ain't—ah!"

Johnny whistled shrilly and Luther instantly released the leg of the man's already torn and stained jeans. "It's Dale, boys. Leave the old geezer alone, will ya?"

"Johnny." Luther sat at Dale's feet and stared at his master. "This two-legs has something in his pants."

Rex trotted around their guest and snorted. "Do you even hear yourself anymore?"

"What? I'm trying to see. I can smell it."

Johnny grinned and stopped halfway across the end of the drive. "How's the leg?"

"Oh, this old thing?" Dale chuckled and kicked the side of his leg against the door of his Honda. Even through his jeans, the clank of metal against metal was clear. "Shit, Johnny—oh. Pardon my French, ma'am."

Lisa smiled at the short man with a mop of thick white hair. He was so thin everywhere else that it made the belt tightened halfway across his surprisingly round belly look like he'd stuck a basketball up his shirt instead.

"You know them docs out in Homestead," Dale continued with a shrug. "They always have some fancy new thing to add to the list of parts ain't meant to be attached."

The dwarf nodded slowly. "They gave you an upgrade, huh?"

"That's what they call it, sure. If you ask me, this damn thing makes me wobblier than when all I had was a crutch."

"He smells like motor oil, Johnny," Rex muttered.

"Yeah, and stale fries." Luther forgot all about the man's leg and sniffed around the bottom of the driver's door instead. "Is that what he meant by French?"

Johnny snapped his fingers and both hounds trotted toward him although they continued to cast glances over their shoulders at Dale.

"Oh. Here I am forgettin' all the partic'lars. Gimme a minute." The old local opened the door again and stretched far inside the car with a grunt.

Lisa leaned toward Johnny and muttered, "He's not talking about your kind of upgrade, right?"

The bounty hunter chuckled. "He lost his leg way back in the military. It sounds like they got him one of them newer prosthetics."

"It sounds like he doesn't like it, either."

With a shrug, Johnny wiped a bead of sweat out of his eye and waited patiently for Dale to finish whatever he was doing in the car.

When the man finally emerged, he held a crumpled, stained brown bag in one hand that looked suspiciously like it held a liquor bottle inside. He shut the door, turned, and hobbled slowly toward them. "Ready when you are, Johnny."

"Sure. Why don'tcha step into my office, then?"

"It's the best place to do business, ain't it?" Dale followed the dwarf toward the front of the house and winked when he passed Lisa.

Agent Breyer barely noticed. She stared at Johnny, who'd now picked up one of the Adirondack chairs in front of the screened-in porch and turned it to face the other. "I didn't know you had an office."

"'Course. Any workin' man—or dwarf—needs a place to put his feet up and get down to business." He gestured toward the chair closest to Dale and waited for the man to sit first before he joined him. They both turned slowly to look at Lisa with knowing expressions, and Johnny gestured at the space between them. "And this is it. Pull up a chair if it suits ya, darlin'. There's no tellin' how long this old bastard's gonna try givin' me the runaround before he finally gets to the point."

Dale wheezed a long laugh and slapped his thigh. "You talk a big game, son."

"Not as big as yours." The dwarf chuckled with him and nodded at Lisa.

Not knowing what the hell he was up to, she stepped hesitantly toward the small plastic lawn chair that hadn't been here the last time she'd visited and drew it closer to complete the small circle for their impromptu and ridiculously casual so-called business meeting.

Sure. Save the cracked plastic chair covered in mold for the half-Light Elf who has no idea what's going on.

As soon as she sat, Johnny leaned back in the Adirondack chair and folded his arms. "All right, Dale. What can I do ya for?"

"Right. Right." The man nodded and stared at his lap, where he'd nestled the paper bag of liquor between his thighs. "Here's what I'm lookin' at. Now, I ain't fixin' to assume you can make things right with this one. Hell, I got no idea what to do myself. That's why I came down here when I heard what you're doin'."

Lisa leaned forward in her chair and felt it wiggle precariously beneath her. "What did you hear, exactly?"

"Hmm?"

"Never mind that now." Johnny waved her off gently. "Go ahead, man."

"Yeah. So it's like this, Johnny." Dale rubbed his wrinkled chin and sagging neck. "You met my niece Patty a while back."

"The one with all tattoos on her face? You bet."

The man winced. "It puts a knife through my heart every time I hear about her like that. She keeps comin' on down to visit me and every time, she's got one more o' them damn things on her skin than before. Now, I ain't askin' you to magic those things off o' her, Johnny. I'm sure it don't work like that anyway."

The dwarf raised an eyebrow. "Uh-huh."

"But see, what I think is Patty has some kinda negative influence on her, ya know? Like some fella she's been runnin' round with and ain't told me 'bout him." Dale tapped absently at his thigh and smacked his lips. "So I reckon I'd come to you and see what you could do."

"You want me to track Patty's fella?"

"Sure. I ain't sayin' I know better'n you, Johnny. You're the businessman. But I wouldn't make a fuss if you found this good-for-nothin' and gave him the ol' what-for. Everyone knows who you are. It might be that seein' your mug will knock some sense into him—both of 'em." The man sighed despondently. "And that's 'bout it."

"Huh." Johnny frowned, cleared his throat, and rubbed his mouth. The rasp of his rough palm over his wiry red beard cut through his "office" over the drone of the insects. "I can't promise nothin', Dale."

"Aw, I know."

"But I'll see what I can do. Maybe I can shed a little more light than you're used to on the situation. Who can tell, right?"

"Right, Johnny. You're damn right about that one." Dale's gaze flicked toward Lisa, and she waved off the apology brewing behind the man's puckered, wrinkled lips.

"Anythin' else?"

"No. Not a thing. You, uh...you won't go talkin' 'bout this down at Darlene's or anythin', yeah? 'Cause it's somethin' of a sensitive—"

"I ain't sayin' bub." Johnny nudged the man's leg with his fist. "Come back in a week. I'll have somethin' for ya then."

"Thanks, Johnny." When the local noticed the dwarf's raised eyebrow, he jolted in his seat and grabbed the paper bag. "And here's your payment."

"I appreciate it."

"It's the least I can do, huh?" Dale slapped his hands on his thighs and groaned with the rest of his body as he stood. "I like what you done with the office, too."

"Yeah, I reckon it has that special somethin'."

The man chuckled and turned toward Lisa with another gap-toothed grin, his previous discomfort completely forgotten. "You keep an eye on this one, sweetheart. I reckon that's why he keeps you 'round anyhow. Good to see ya."

He didn't wait for a reply before he shuffled toward his car. It didn't matter anyway. Her mouth had fallen open and she couldn't think of anything to say.

"By the by, Johnny." Dale tossed a hand in the air but didn't bother to turn. "I love the show."

"Hey, this is a safe space and all that shit," Johnny called in response. "Leave that in the damn car."

With another wheezed laugh, the man slid awkwardly into his vehicle and started the sputtering, coughing engine. He waved a hand out the window as he steered his rickety old Honda down the road and disappeared in a thick cloud of dust.

Lisa finally found her voice and laughed. "He paid you in whiskey."

"It's the best damn transaction I ever made."

"And he called you the businessman."

"Uh-huh."

"Johnny, what is going on?"

He cleared his throat, then turned to stretch over the side of the chair and grasp a small, lightweight plastic container from the ground. He popped it open and retrieved two red plastic Solo cups from the stack inside before he replaced the box.

"Okay, now I'm very confused. You told Dale you'd track his niece's boyfriend and rough him up because the man doesn't like her tattoos."

"I ain't gonna find her with a fella."

"Wait, what?"

"Patty's bad influence ain't a man. And I ain't here to judge."

"That's...huh. That's one of the most tolerant things I've heard you say."

"Aw, don't let it twist you up, darlin'. Hold this." He handed her one cup, nestled the other between his thighs, and slid the bottle of Johnny Walker Black Label from the paper bag to open it right there in front of his house. He gave her a two-second pour first, then did the same for himself. With a shrug, he added another heavy splash into his cup and placed the bottle beside his chair. "Now, I ain't made a toast to somethin' like this in a while, so bear with me."

"A toast." Lisa peered at him over the edge of her cup and raised her eyebrows. "Well, this should be good."

He cleared his throat and raised his cup. "To us. Johnny and Lisa. Partners in baggin' bounties and business."

A wide grin split across her face. "Oh, really?"

"Sure enough." He tapped his cup against hers even though she hadn't lifted it from her lap and took a long, slow sip. "Ah... There's nothin' like the first pour out of a spankin' new bottle. Come on, darlin'. It ain't a toast if you're not drinkin'."

"Johnny, I have no idea what I'm drinking to."

"Are you serious?"

"You haven't explained a thing to me."

"Huh." The dwarf scratched his head and his eyebrows moved in and out of a frown as he scanned the front yard of his property. "I thought it was fairly obvious. All right. Business. This. A new one."

"Are you feeling okay?"

"I'm fine." Johnny sighed. *How the hell am I supposed to spell this all out when the rest of it oughtta tell her everythin' she needs to know?* "Look, here's the thing. I ain't fixin' to keep workin' for the department for the rest of my long life on this planet. I assume you ain't either. Hell, it might be the FBI don't even last as long as the two of us. But I ain't steppin' back into retirement neither."

She responded with a small smile. "Because you like it too much, exactly like I knew you would."

"Well, that ain't...here or there. Whatever." He cleared his throat. "The point is, I want stability but on my terms. And that shit with the Red Boar ain't doin' any favors for the department or me workin' on these cases whenever they need to dig themselves out of a goddamn sinkhole of their makin'. So, I'm goin' indie."

A little startled, she leaned toward him and narrowed her eyes. "Going what?"

"Indie. Short for independent." He shrugged. "I read that somewhere. Still, it doesn't matter. I'm branchin' out on my own now, darlin'. And you get to be my partner for all of it—the whole damn kit 'n kaboodle. If you want."

"Wow." For a moment, she couldn't think of anything else to say. "Wow, Johnny."

"Yeah, you said that."

"I only... Okay, let me get this straight. You'll still take federal cases?"

"Only if they tickle me the right way." He grunted and took another slow sip of whiskey.

"Fair enough. I understand where you're coming from with

that one and I won't try to argue that they didn't seriously screw Dawn's case up and drag you around for the last fifteen years."

"Damn straight."

"But if you're not taking the same number of cases from the department...Johnny, where will you find more work?"

"It's simple, darlin'. First, it ain't like I dumped all my connections down the drain when I moved here for good."

"Fortunately." Lisa sniffed her cup, then lowered it slowly to her thigh again.

"And second, that's the business part. I'm goin' solo. Or we're goin' solo. If you want."

"Are you asking me or merely throwing the option against the wall to see what sticks?"

Johnny stared at her for a moment but looked away quickly and scratched his cheek through his wiry red beard. "It's always about how it's done, ain't it?"

"What was that? You're mumbling."

"I said fine. Yeah. I'm askin' if you wanna be my partner in this new venture." *I didn't think she'd make it this damn hard.* "So? What d'ya think?"

"I...still can't tell if this is for real or if you're screwing with me."

"What?"

"What I mean is...you're not exactly the friendliest guy around. Not to strangers anyway, and you want people to warm to you if you're running your own business as a freelance bounty hunter, right?"

"Indie."

"Okay..."

He swung his cup toward her and lifted a finger to point at her. "And it ain't only bounty huntin', neither. I'm addin' private investigator to the job description."

Lisa burst out laughing and leaned so far forward over her lap that her plastic cup tilted with her and almost spilled over the grass. Johnny leaned closer and tilted her cup gently to an acceptable angle before he swallowed another gulp of his drink.

She thinks I'm pullin' her leg. How hard is this to get behind?

When her laughter finally subsided, she took long, slow breaths, chuckled between them, and wiped tears from the corners of her eyes. "Oh, wow. I didn't realize I needed a good laugh until you—"

She froze when she saw the dwarf slumped in the Adirondack chair, his legs stretched in front of him at a wide angle and his arms folded snugly with the red plastic cup resting against his chest. He narrowed his eyes at her and raised the cup slowly for another slow, deliberate sip.

"Oh." Her smile vanished. "Oh, you're serious."

"And you need to work on your people skills."

CHAPTER THREE

Lisa shook her head. "Sorry. I…uh, didn't think you'd want anything to do with investigating. That's a ton of boring work, Johnny. You know that, right?"

"It ain't borin' when it's the two of us."

"That's…it's sweet."

Johnny swallowed thickly and upended his cup into his mouth, only to realize it was empty. "Damn."

"Right. That wasn't what you were going for, was it?"

"Naw. I'm empty." He tried to peer over the edge of her cup, then gave up and snatched the bottle off the ground for a refill. "Listen, darlin', if you ain't ready for this kinda change, I understand. It might be I simply read the signs all wrong, and that's on me. So lemme know. I ain't made of glass or nothin'. I've spent enough time doin' everythin' on my lonesome and it ain't gonna kill me to do it again—"

"Wait, no. Don't put words in my mouth. That's not what I'm saying."

He looked at her quickly and squinted, a little surprised. "It ain't?"

"No, Johnny. I'm flattered that you'd want to do something

like this with me. Truly." Lisa leaned back in her chair and gestured toward the rest of his yard and the gravel drive that stretched toward the frontage road. "I'm merely not sure how it would all pan out, you know? Not that I doubt your ability to run your own business—"

"Good. That ain't in question."

"But I don't think I'm ready to step down from my current job and turn in my weapon so to speak. And I certainly don't have time to juggle both. And it's…" She cleared her throat. "To play devil's advocate here, what if it doesn't pan out? It takes considerable investment to build something like this from the ground up. It can be a huge risk, you know?"

Johnny pressed his lips together beneath his thick red mustache. Finally, he simply couldn't help himself. A chuckle burst through his nose, then transformed into a wild laugh that startled Lisa into almost spilling her drink again.

She caught her cup and set it on the ground this time so she wouldn't have to worry about it. "What's so funny?"

"You, darlin'. Only you." The dwarf rubbed his mouth and bristly bearded chin with a thick hand and snorted. "Sittin' here, tryin' to lecture me on monetary investment and buildin' and risk. Of all the—ha!"

She rolled her eyes. "Okay, I get it. You can't teach an old dog new tricks, right?"

"But it ain't new. This ain't my first rodeo and I ain't doin' it for the money."

"Then…why even bother with the headache of it?"

"There's no headache. That's a fact. And if it comes along somewhere on down the road, that's fine." He chuckled again and took another long sip of whiskey. "'Cause any headache it might cause us is a boiled peanut next to how badly the department will be hurtin'."

"Oh, come on. Johnny."

"Lisa. I made my mind up. It's done."

"You're doing this to get back at them? Still?"

"Trust me. I ain't done nearly enough to make things anywhere close to even." He straightened in his chair, watched the hounds sniffing around in the reeds along the side of the gravel drive, and nodded. "And you ain't got nothin' to worry about. If it tanks, it tanks. It won't, but I already took care of all that for both of us."

"It won't?" Lisa smirked at him and only briefly looked away to watch a heron soar over the thick trees and the roof of his house before it vanished into the swamp. "I still don't get it."

"It's part of that deal I struck with the whole damn Bureau." His grin shone brightly through his beard and mustache. "It's all been drawn up and written out, although I imagine they'll make sure to hide it even better than they did Dawn's case files. You get to keep your job, darlin', for however long you want it and with the same salary and same perks. Whatever they are. You can stay at the same hotel for as long as you're workin' on this new business with me. Hell, you might as well take an upgrade while you're at it. There ain't no one gonna give you grief for any of it 'cause I can promise you, they don't wanna see my mug in HQ for another fifty goddamn years. At least."

"You—" Lisa scowled at him. "You negotiated my job for me? Without asking if that was what I wanted?"

"Well, shit." He leaned away from her. *I can't do nothin' right, can I?* "I thought you'd be pleased with it."

"Johnny, I'm—"

"And it ain't like you don't have a choice. You don't have to do this. It's simply an option. I thought you liked options."

"I do, and—"

"We work well together, is all. Maybe too well." He snorted. "Maybe I went too far. You know what? Don't even worry about it. Forget I brought it up. You can take care of yourself. You made that as clear as an empty glass many times before, and I—"

"Will you shut up and let me finish?" Lisa's outburst sent some swampland creature skittering into the reeds. She sighed in frustration and snatched her Solo cup off the ground to take a massive gulp. Her wince and furious grimace would've made him laugh if she hadn't yelled at him.

Drinkin' whiskey. All right. That'll be how I know she's pissed.

Rex and Luther reappeared from the foliage in the side yard and stepped warily toward their master, their heads lowered and their ears tucked against their heads. Luther whined. "Uh-oh. What happened now?"

"Johnny, what did you do?"

"What?" The dwarf scowled at them and pointed toward the swamp. "Git on. This ain't a public show."

"But she yelled at you—"

"Out."

Luther scrambled around and darted into the reeds. Rex followed him but cast a confused look over his shoulder before he disappeared slowly between the stalks.

"Something's happening bro. And we're missing all the action."

"Pshh. You mean all the action's missing. She's the only lady two-legs he hasn't—"

Johnny cleared his throat. *It might be the only time I ain't jumpin' up to fix an issue with the audio range.* He turned slowly toward Lisa and gestured silently for her to continue.

With a deep breath, she returned her cup carefully to the ground, fought not to grimace at it, and looked calmly at him. "I was trying to say thank you."

"Say what now?"

"I think it's a great idea, Johnny. Seriously. I don't make as big of a fuss about my frustrations with the Bureau as you do, but I could honestly use a sabbatical at this point. And you looked at all the angles and already took care of them. So yes. I'll be your partner. Again."

He raised an eyebrow. "In business."

"Yes, Johnny." An exasperated sigh escaped her but it was softened by her smile. "Your business partner."

"Hmm. Good." He snatched the whiskey bottle off the ground again and lifted it toward her in a silent question.

"Why the hell not?"

"That's what I like to hear." He chuckled and refilled his cup before he added more to what remained in hers. "We're already off to a good start."

"As long as you don't keep talking over me." Lisa laughed as he put the bottle away and she stared with wide eyes at way more whiskey than she was willing to drink. "That might be the most I've ever heard you say in one sitting."

"Well. I guess it takes a little more work to get me invested in somethin'. And I ain't talkin' about the money side either, ya hear?"

"Yeah. I know."

This time, they both raised their cups toward each other and Johnny smirked. "We can start over. To the business."

"To the business."

The plastic thumped anticlimactically, and they both drank.

"Whew." Lisa scrunched her nose up and held her cup at arm's length. "That'll take some getting used to, though."

"Naw, I ain't expectin' you to match me drink for drink."

"Thank God. Okay, so if we're doing this—"

"We're doin' it, darlin'." Johnny froze when he caught her warning gaze, then lowered his head for another sip and muttered, "Sorry. Go ahead."

She leaned back in her chair and gazed at the wide front yard with the tall trees and the grass browning in the dirt. "We should go over the logistics."

"I already covered that."

"No, I mean of the business."

"Oh, come on now. I already started. We met with the first client. Folks know what's happenin' and they know how to bring it up. If I say this is what I'm doin' now, it's what I'm doin'. It's as simple as that. What else is there?"

"Um...a fair amount, Johnny."

"Yeah. You're about to tell me, ain'tcha?"

"Do you have any advertising planned?"

He snorted. "Sure. I told a few folks at Darlene's. The old geezers won't be able to stop talkin' about it. Oh, and I put a few notes at the trading post."

"What trading post?"

"It's a local place. If you don't live around here, you ain't gonna find it."

"Okay." Lisa nodded slowly. "So that's a no. How do you plan to bring clients in, then?"

Johnny waved dismissively. "Naw, that ain't important."

"This isn't exactly an 'if you build it, they'll come' kinda situation, Johnny."

"Sure it is. Dale came today and we hadn't even had this talk yet."

She shook her head and stared at her lap. "What about payment? What will you charge for your bounty-hunting and...PI services?"

It was very hard to keep a straight face for that last addition.

With a frown, he looked from her to the cup in her hand. "You're drinkin' it."

"Wow. So you'll accept a bottle of this for any job?"

"I already told you it ain't about the money, darlin'." With a grin, he lifted his cup toward her and took another sip. "But it sure is nice to have this around."

"Okay. We'll move on. What about a website?"

"You're killin' me."

"Yeah, we have considerable work to do." Lisa swallowed half the whiskey in her cup and almost coughed it all up again. "And I need water."

"Help yourself. You do work here now."

"I thought this was your office."

"Call it a perk of the job."

She burst out laughing, leaned back in the Adirondack chair, and made no effort to get up for the water or anything else. "You're very lucky we already work well together. Otherwise, you'd have a hard time finding anyone to stick around and help you with this."

"That's why I asked you." He stared at the swarms of gnats that buzzed over the gravel drive, stretched over his armrest, and slipped his hand into hers. Lisa darted him a sidelong glance and helped him to lace their fingers together. "We'll do fine."

CHAPTER FOUR

"We are not doing fine, Johnny." Lisa paced behind the Adirondack chairs as the wizard who'd come to see them pedaled down the gravel drive on his thick-tired mountain bike. "It's been three days already. What are you doing?"

"Bringin' the customers in." Johnny gestured toward the wizard's disappearing dust cloud. "We have the numbers comin' in."

"Yeah, and we might have had a full plate with new cases—if you can even call them that. But you're turning everyone away."

"It ain't my fault if they don't wanna hear the truth."

"Johnny, you don't even know if it's the truth you're giving them."

"Sure I do. Eloise came out here lookin' for her lockbox of cash from the 1940s. Where the hell could it be? Oh, I don't know. Maybe she dug herself a new hole in that little vegetable patch of hers in the middle of the night when her husband was dead asleep."

Lisa stopped pacing and thrust her hands on her hips. "You told her raccoons dug it up."

"Naw, she did it. The woman's been sleepwalkin' for thirty

years. There was dirt caked all over the bottom of her dress. You ain't seen that?"

"Then why the raccoons?"

"Well, I thought she'd feel better hearing some vermin stole all her secret cash than if I told her she already spent that money on a new tractor about…oh, five years ago. 'Cause believe you me, darlin', she ain't likely to believe that half as much."

"Oh, boy." Lisa sighed and pinched the bridge of her nose briefly. After a moment, she straightened her shoulders and walked around the Adirondack chair to sit beside him. "Do you know what this is like?"

"A damn fine business, if you ask me."

"No, Johnny. This is like you putting yourself out there as a gruff, southern, dwarfy Sherlock Holmes."

He snorted. "Yeah, he's good too, ain't he? Not that I need any pointers from the guy, mind."

"You know he's not real, right?"

"Yeah." He grunted and shifted in his chair. "'Course I do."

Lisa stared at the now independent bounty hunter—and private investigator, although that still made her smile—and waited for him to finish counting the collection of full, unopened whiskey bottles beside the chair. *He's going slow on purpose.*

Shaking her head, she sat in her chair and gazed at the last of their previous client's dust cloud filtering into the muggy, sweltering heat. "Okay. So what other appointments do we have on the schedule for today?"

"Appointments?" Johnny folded his arms and stuck his legs out in front of him to cross one boot over the other. "Naw. That ain't how this works. Folks get the word around, and they simply show up. Open-door policy and all that."

"I can't imagine that works well for a new business."

"It does in the Everglades. And it ain't the business they're comin' for, darlin'. Down here, I'm as established as hell."

The next so-called client was a little girl named Agnes who'd dragged her mother with her to the dwarf's property to ask if he could find her missing baby doll. "I sleep with her every night and now she's gone."

Tears streamed down the child's face, but she ignored them to swipe the back of her hand across the river of snot running from her nose instead.

Johnny raised an eyebrow and glanced at the girl's mom—Candace, or Candy, or Candalyn, he thought. The woman's lips were pressed tightly together beneath a warning glare aimed directly at him. *She ain't happy to be here but she wants her kid to stop cryin'.* "How long?"

The girl sniffed and wiped her hand on her sundress. "Two days. I think. Right, Mommy?"

"Three days, honey."

Agnes smiled briefly when Rex and Luther trotted around her and sniffed the girl's sandals.

"Hey, they have hounds too," Luther muttered and moved to sniff her mom next. The woman shooed him away.

"Johnny. You should tell them to bring their hound," Rex added. "We could have a party."

The dwarf shrugged. "Do your hounds dig in the yard?"

"Yeah…" The girl looked at him with wide eyes.

"I don't see what that's got to do with anythin'," Candy said. "Sweetheart, it's time to forget about that doggone doll, all right?"

"Hey." Luther snorted, sat, and stared at the woman. "That's offensive to some of us, you know."

Johnny nodded at the girl. "Go check the holes they dig. If your dolly ain't there, look in the trash."

"What?" Candy's eyes blazed.

"The trash?" Agnes' lower lip trembled again.

"Sure. Pickup day's on Wednesday for y'all too, right? I'd go check before tomorrow—"

"You can't tell my little girl her doll's in the trash," the woman fumed.

"Sure I can. You ain't gonna."

She snatched Agnes' wrist and tugged her behind her. "This was a waste of time," she blustered.

"Mama, you threw her in the trash?"

"I'm not talkin' about this here, Agnes. Get in the car." The woman opened the back door for her daughter, then spun and pointed at Johnny. "You're a monster, sayin' that to a little girl."

He shrugged. "If you say so."

"And I am not paying you."

"It suits me fine. Maybe try tellin' your kid what's up next time."

With an angry exhalation, she stormed around the car, slid behind the wheel, and accelerated down the drive.

"Johnny—"

"Yeah, yeah." He waved Lisa off and poured himself a small shot of whiskey. "You're gonna tell me I gotta be gentle with the kid, huh? Hell, if her mama wants her to grow up so much, she should quit tryin' to protect the girl and tell her the truth herself. I ain't fixin' to back up a liar 'cause she thinks we're on the same team."

Agent Breyer glanced at the sky and swiped her hair away from her face. "What team is that?"

"Team Adult." Johnny swallowed the shot and pointed down the drive. "I tell you what. Some grown folks ain't any better than the kids they're raisin'."

They had at least another two visitors an hour as the sun climbed in the sky. Lisa busied herself on her laptop between glasses of iced tea and occasionally asked Johnny's opinion on the layout or a particular phrase. He shrugged her off every time and focused on moving between working on Margo, checking on the constantly clucking hens, and coming out front for the next consultation.

Ernesto—who had the boiled peanuts stand five miles down— wanted the bounty hunter to go after his competition, another local named Terrance who had seemingly added a secret spice that suddenly made his peanuts that much more attractive.

"I'm fixin' to go right outta business, Johnny."

"Where do you get your peanuts?"

"What?"

The dwarf spread his arms. "You're importin' 'em, ain'tcha?"

"Well, I—"

"They taste like dirt, Ernesto. Everyone around here knows it. It ain't Terrance's secret spice, man. Only you cuttin' corners."

The man gaped at him, glanced at Lisa, then hung his head and handed his whiskey payment over. "You're good, Johnny. It's not what I asked for but there ain't no two ways about it."

"Buy local, man. You'll see what happens."

The dwarf's responses to the locals who came to the middle of nowhere ranged anywhere from blunt to downright disturbing. A woman from Everglades City wanted to know where her husband was going when he took their fishing boat out every evening at sunset with a six-pack of beer, fishing rod, and tackle box. "I think he might be seeing someone."

"Yeah. The fish. Give the man a little space, huh?"

Twins from the trailer park behind Darlene's asked Johnny if he'd tell the woman they'd both been dating that there was only one of them so she wouldn't run away screaming.

"What? Come on. That's the dumbest thing I've heard all day. Get outta here."

Keith walked down from his property a mile northwest of Johnny's. He shuffled and looked everywhere but at the dwarf's face when he said he thought someone was stealing his crops.

"What kinda crops?"

"They're, uh...of a sensitive nature, Johnny." The old farmer shoved his hands into the pockets of his overalls and glanced at Lisa. "It might be somethin' your cop friend ain't exactly keen on lettin' slip by if you catch my meanin'."

Johnny snorted. "She ain't a cop."

"Then what is she?"

"My partner."

Lisa took a deep breath and forced herself to not say anything.

"What kinda crop, Keith?"

"Aw, hell, Johnny. I picked it up as a little extra side venture, you know? My cousin's son lives out in Miami. You might call him somethin' of my partner if you gotta hear it."

A smile spread slowly across the dwarf's lips. "You growin' marijuana at your place, man?"

"What? Naw. That ain't it."

"Well, I can't help you if you don't tell me what's bein' taken from ya..." Johnny's attention was drawn away by Luther slinking off across the front lawn toward the reeds at the side of the house.

Rex lay in the sun beside the Adirondack chairs of Johnny's office, panting gently. "Hey, Luther. Where are you going?"

The smaller hound paused, his head low and one forepaw suspended in mid-step. "Um...the swamp?"

Keith cleared his throat. "Fine, but I need to find the bastard rootin' through my stuff. I still got a lotta costs to cover, you know?"

Johnny narrowed his eyes at Luther, who now looked slowly over his shoulder to shoot a wary glance at the meeting. "Uh-huh."

The man leaned forward and whispered, "Mushrooms, Johnny."

Rex licked his muzzle and uttered a low whine. "Uh-oh."

"Mushrooms."

"Yeah, you know. The...magic kind."

Lisa cleared her throat, took a sip of tea, and returned her focus to her laptop.

"Uh-huh." The dwarf glared at Luther. The hound turned in a

tight circle before he leapt through the reeds and disappeared with a splash. "I tell you what, Keith. This one's on me."

"No, I can't let you do that—"

"You can and you will." The dwarf slapped his thigh and nodded. "I'll make sure whoever's sneakin' into your crop knows what's what about private property."

"Wow. Man." Keith responded with a long whistle and removed his wide-brimmed hat to wipe his sweaty forehead. "Johnny, I appreciate this. More'n I can say."

"Sure. And a piece of advice, man. Quit growin' shit people wanna steal from ya, huh?"

"It's hidden—"

"Not that hidden."

The man nodded solemnly, tipped his hat at Lisa—who only briefly looked at him with a thin smile—and shuffled down the road.

Johnny glanced at Rex. "When was the last time Luther went down there?"

"What?" The hound looked at his master and his tail thumped once in the grass. "How should I know?"

"Y'all are always together."

"Not always."

"I didn't do it, Johnny," Luther shouted from the other side of the reeds, followed by a sharp yip. "I swear!"

Rubbing his mouth, Johnny sighed heavily. "Next time I see you stumblin' around like a drunk on St. Patrick's day, boy, you'll spend the night on the other end of a lead. You hear me?"

The reeds rustled but Luther didn't reply or emerge.

Halfway down the drive, Keith turned and shouted, "What was that?"

"Nothin'." Johnny waved him away. "See ya around."

The man raised his hand in farewell and soon turned off the gravel drive.

With another pointed glance at the trembling reeds shielding Luther, the dwarf added, "A short lead."

"Hey, Johnny." Rex lowered his head on his forepaws and sighed. "It's time for food, right?"

"Huh. I guess it is around lunchtime anyhow." He stood from the chair and headed toward the porch, and Rex bounded up to hurry after him. "Are you hungry?"

"Yes!" Luther bounded out of the reeds and darted toward his master. "Food? Are you kidding? You're the best, Johnny—"

He skidded to a halt when the dwarf stopped and looked at him. "I was talkin' to Lisa."

"Me?" She looked up from her laptop and turned in her chair to face him. "Sure. I could eat."

"Long workdays have a way of buildin' up an appetite. I'll see what I can rustle up inside." Johnny opened the screen door to the porch, slipped inside, and turned to point at both hounds. "Y'all been eatin' too much of everythin' that ain't yours."

"Aw, come on, Johnny. It's been forever—" Luther yelped when his brother nipped at his face. "Hey, what gives?"

"You. You're the one who ruined snack time for everyone."

"Well, not for Johnny—hey! What—jeez!" The hounds snarled and snapped at each other in a quick scuffle before they raced down the side yard toward the swamp. "Quit chasing me, bro! I didn't even—"

"You're still talking!"

CHAPTER FIVE

When Johnny emerged from the house with neatly arranged plates of pulled pork with vinegar-based barbeque, coleslaw, potato salad, and brined green beans, Lisa was on her way to the porch to refill her iced tea. "Hey, that looks good."

"It's all I have inside right now. I ain't exactly the best cook." He handed a plate to her and proffered one of the forks stuck between his fingers. "Now there's an idea."

"I'm not cooking." She took the plate and fork and slipped past him through the screen door.

"I wouldn't dream of it." He watched her disappear inside, then snorted and let the screen door slam shut behind him. "I was thinkin' about a caterer. Like Darlene."

He returned to his chair and had wolfed half the pulled pork before Lisa returned to join him. "Do you know what we need?"

"A caterer?"

"What? No." She hurried across the lawn and sat beside him, her drink fully refilled. "I think we need an office. You know, with real furniture."

"The front lawn's a fine office, darlin'. We're stayin' right here."

"What if it rains, huh? Do you want people inside your house?"

"Naw, we'll close up."

"Johnny."

"Every day we gotta go over this again?" He crammed a forkful of potato salad into his mouth and stared at her. "I ain't gonna change my mind."

"Fine." She set her plate down and picked her laptop up. "Then take a look at this. If you want the business to be real—"

"It is real."

"But you're not getting any actual cases that require you to leave your front yard."

The dwarf glanced pointedly at the plastic tote he'd dragged outside, now filled with eighteen bottles of Johnny Walker Black Label. "That's kinda the point."

"Well, do you want to be busy enough to tell Nelson you can't take a flimsy case like the last one in Baltimore? Without lying? Or do you want to simply sit here all day playing detective?"

He frowned at her before he stabbed a forkful of green beans. "Why are you bringin' Nelson into this?"

"He called me this morning and wanted to know why you won't answer his calls."

"If he ain't worked it out by now, that's on him." He grunted disdainfully. "What did you tell him?"

"That you were working on a side project and no, I wouldn't play secretary by taking a message or forwarding your calls." She turned the laptop to face him and raised an eyebrow. "Which, by the way, I want to make perfectly clear. I am not your secretary."

"Of course not. You're gettin' paid way too much for that."

"By the Bureau."

"Exactly." He glanced from her to the laptop screen. "What are you doin'?"

"I want you to take a look at the website and tell me what you think."

"Darlin', we've been over this. I ain't interested in all that hustlin' and scramblin' to make a name for myself on the damn Internet. That shit's already been done enough on the dark web."

"Okay. Fine. I'll give up on the website and go call Nelson. Let him know your side project's finished and you have all this time on your hands—"

"Whoa, whoa. I never said you gotta do all that." Johnny reached for the laptop. "I'll take a look. But don't expect me to have some kinda professional opinion about it."

She grinned and handed him her computer. "I'm simply looking for your personal opinion. This isn't my first time building websites."

"Uh-huh." The dwarf placed his plate on the armrest and jerked the laptop open even more—ignoring Lisa's grimace at the rough treatment of her device—and squinted at the screen. "No."

"No?"

"What is this? Johnny Walker Investigations? Come on."

"Well, you didn't want to come up with a business name, so I had to do it."

"It should simply be my name, darlin'. That's all anyone needs to know."

She snorted. "Then it looks like you simply made a website for yourself as a public figure."

"A public—dammit. What's all this up here? 'About Us.' 'Resume.' 'Contact Us.' Are you kiddin' me? That's the last thing I want. Did you put my address on this damn thing?"

"I know what I'm doing, Johnny. It's merely an email form where people can send us a little more information before we schedule a call or meet them in person."

"I ain't checked my email in…months."

Lisa leaned toward him with wide eyes. "Well, it's a good thing I set it up to email us both."

He darted her a sidelong glance and tugged on his beard. *Not a secretary, huh? I think she's been one in another life.* "I don't want my number all over this."

"Too late."

"For cryin' out loud!"

"Johnny, you're the one people want to talk to when they find out this is what you do. That's the point. And again, I'm not your secretary."

"And this ain't—what?" He shoved his head toward the screen for a better look. "You put the goddamn TV show on here."

"It's called branding, Johnny."

"I ain't brandin' a damn cable network. That has to go."

"Well, we don't exactly have customer reviews to put on here as proof of your ability to do your job." Lisa whisked her laptop out of his lap. "It's not like you've given any of these new clients a reason to sing your praises. I think it looks great."

He grunted and snatched his plate up again to shovel a giant forkful of pulled pork into his mouth.

"And you hate it." She watched him scan the ground in front of him before she offered him her glass of iced tea. "I can tell."

The dwarf's eyes narrowed when he took the glass from her, and after a quick chaser to wash down all his angry eating, he uttered a low, conceding growl. "It ain't what I'd do."

"What you'd do is run your business into the ground." She took her glass from him and drank thirstily before she set it aside. "This is how websites work these days so if you don't have anything constructive to say, it's staying the way it is."

"Or you could scrap the whole thing and—"

"Done. Published." She smirked victoriously, closed her laptop, and slid it into its sleeve before she placed it under her chair. "JohnnyWalkerInvestigations.com. You're official."

"Shit." He grasped the whiskey bottle he'd been nursing over the last four days, realized it was empty, and couldn't quite reach the plastic tote of unopened bottles without getting out of his chair. "Well, I ain't sittin' around answerin' emails all day. That's for damn sure."

She returned her attention to her lunch and picked at the pulled pork with a small smile playing on her lips. "That's fine. I set your phone up to send you notifications when you get an email forwarded from the site."

"You what? I didn't give you my phone."

"No. You left it here when you went to play with Margo."

"It ain't playin'. That's real work. Unset it."

"What?"

"My phone, Lisa. I don't want the damn thing going off all the time when I'm in the middle of enjoyin' my life. What? What's so funny?"

Lisa raised a forkful of coleslaw to her mouth and shrugged. "There are so many perks to running your own business. And a few headaches."

"Aw, come on, now."

"It's all part of the process."

His nostrils flared as he watched her enjoying her lunch of premade and prepackaged cookout spread he'd stocked in his fridge. *She knows damn well I ain't got a clue how to take that shit off my phone.* Wrinkling his nose, he picked at a piece of pulled pork and grumbled, "It's better than dealin' with Nelson's desperate ass. At least there's that."

"There's the positive outlook."

"No, you're the one who does that."

She pursed her lips in an attempt to hide the growing smile there. "It looks like I'm finally starting to rub off on you, then."

Despite how much he hated the website and the official administrative bullshit of the whole process, Johnny managed a laugh. "You're havin' yourself a time with this, ain'tcha?"

"So far, yeah. Maybe I'll stick around for a while. Hey, while we're simply sitting here with nothing to do, why don't we go over the stuff Dean brought over yesterday?"

"What stuff?"

"You wanted his phone records."

"Huh?"

"So you could take a look at his son's—seriously? All of that went in one ear and out the other?"

Johnny pursed his lips. "I know what Dean's worried about and it ain't that he thinks someone stole his Eli's phone."

"How do you know that?"

"Because his son's a grown-ass man and ain't fixin' to talk to his pops on the phone every day like he's away at summer camp."

With a sigh, Lisa leaned in her chair. "Then why didn't you simply tell him that?"

"The guy's a friend, darlin'. He's a good man. I ain't gonna be the one who breaks his heart about it. If his boy wants to say it to his face, he will."

"You don't want a real case."

"Sure I do. I merely haven't found one that—"

"Hey!" Rex splashed out of the swamp at the back of the house and raced down the side yard trailing soggy reeds and splashing water the whole way. "Johnny! Who's up there?"

The dwarf turned to watch his hound race down the gravel drive. Luther sprinted behind his brother, slowed when he noticed the plates on their laps, then licked his muzzle and darted off again. "Save some for us, Johnny! We got company."

"What kind?"

"The hound kind!" Rex shouted as he disappeared over the rise.

"Let me guess." Lisa chuckled. "Someone's here."

"Not the kind we're aimin' to see." Johnny frowned after his hounds' dissipating dust clouds and wiped drips of barbeque sauce out of his beard. He almost wiped his hands on his black jeans next, but Lisa cleared her throat and handed him a paper towel. "Where the hell are you hidin' a roll of paper napkins? 'Cause I know it ain't in those shorts."

42

She rolled her eyes. "Your kitchen."

"Huh. Thanks." He used that instead and was about to ask her why she cared so much whether he wiped his hands on his damn pants but the hounds interrupted.

"Johnny!"

"Johnny, you better come see this!"

"Yeah, she needs our help. Like in more ways than one."

"Well, come on, then," the dwarf shouted in response. "Bring her to the office, boys."

"Right. Right." Rex appeared over the rise of the gravel drive, trotting quickly as he glanced over his shoulder. "It's a good thing his office is outside. Don't worry. Johnny's very good at finding things. Especially two-legs."

"Yeah, you came to the right place," Luther added. "That's for sure. Hey, what did you say your name was again?"

"Nice name," Rex said.

"Real nice, like you."

Johnny tilted his head and waited for their next visitor to appear.

"What's wrong?" Lisa asked.

"I have a feelin' this ain't the usual customer."

"Why's that?"

"'Cause they're talkin' to my hounds and I can't hear it."

CHAPTER SIX

When Rex and Luther crested the rise in the long driveway, they were accompanied by a surprising visitor.

Lisa leaned forward in her chair and frowned. "That's a dog."

"Uh-huh." Johnny scratched the side of his face. "And don't tell me you put out some kind of ad in the canine paper, darlin'. I might not be a fan of the crap y'all call fancy tech these days but I know I'm the only one who can talk to his hounds like—"

"Johnny, we could seriously use some help here!" Rex shouted.

"Whoa, whoa. Hang on, okay?" Luther yipped. "Johnny! Hey, it's okay. He's coming."

The dwarf set his plate down and stood. "I'd best go check it out, then."

"The dog?"

"The boys say they need help. So yeah." He strode down the drive.

Lisa stared after him, then pushed out of the chair and followed quickly, muttering, "I will not take an independent case from a dog. What would that be? Help me find the bone I buried?"

Before the bounty hunter got even halfway to the hounds—

who'd stopped in the road and now stood at high alert on either side of their new canine friend—he knew something was wrong. There was no mistaking the fact that the third hound looked like she wouldn't last another five minutes.

The Blue Heeler would have been a beautiful dog. She had a black mask around both eyes with a strip of the mottled black and white fur that made the "blue" color running cleanly from the tip of her black nose and up between her ears. But now, patches of that fur were missing. A large wound along the side of her belly was crusted with days-old blood that had also matted and dried in the fur around it. Her ribs showed more through her once shiny coat than they should on any healthy hound.

"Here he is." Luther licked the Heeler's mouth and sat beside her. "Johnny will help."

"Oh, boy." The bounty hunter stopped in front of the hounds and held his hand toward the newcomer. "Hey, girl. It's all right. I ain't gonna hurt ya."

"Yeah, she already knows that," Rex added and sniffed their visitor's forepaw. "That's why she's here."

"Oh, my God." Lisa jogged the rest of the way toward them when she finally saw the animal's condition. "Poor thing. What happened to her?"

"She doesn't know," Luther said. "Johnny, her master's been gone for days."

The Heeler licked her muzzle and whined.

"Oh. Maybe longer."

"Yeah, it's hard to tell, Johnny. And she's hungry."

Luther stretched his neck toward the female. "Not like we're always hungry, either. She hasn't eaten since her master got up and left."

"And she's not an outside hound like us," Rex added. "I don't think she even knows what hunting is."

"All right." With his hand still extended, Johnny nodded. "You got a name, beautiful?"

"Boots," Luther said.

"That's her name, Johnny. I like it."

"Yeah, me too."

The dwarf pressed his lips together. *Why do folks always gotta give their hounds dumb names like that?* "All right, Boots. Come on. Let's take a look at you."

The Heeler took two feeble steps toward him, then stopped with another whine and lowered herself shakily to the gravel. The whole time, she stared at him with shimmering, pleading eyes.

"She's hurt, Johnny," Lisa muttered.

"Yeah, I see that."

"Maybe she needs to rest."

The dog panted heavily, her sides quivering not with heavy breath but fear and weakness.

Rex sniffed the female's ear. "Come on. That's our house right there."

"Naw." Johnny stepped toward the starving animal that looked like hell and reached toward her so she could smell his hand. "She's beat. Come on now, Boots. We'll getcha inside and have a better look at what's going on."

He stooped slowly beside her and scooped her into his arms.

"Maybe we should call a vet instead," Lisa suggested and frowned in sympathy for the trembling dog held against his solid chest.

"What's a vet gonna do, darlin'? Run a few tests, draw blood, stick her a cage in the back, and pretend they know what's wrong with her?"

"It's their job to find out what's wrong."

"Sure. But a vet ain't gonna be able to ask her questions and get an answer. I got two interpreters right here."

"Where?" Luther spun around and searched the empty drive. "I don't see anyone."

"He means us, bro."

"Oh. Right."

Johnny carried Boots toward the house. "I might need a hand openin' the doors."

"Of course." Lisa hurried after him.

The hounds trotted dutifully behind their master and stretched their necks to sniff their visitor's limp paws.

"Whoa. That's a long way," Rex said. "No wonder you're tired."

"How far?" Johnny asked.

"Twelve miles. Not that big a deal when you're…you know." Rex whined. "Fed every day and not freaked out of your mind."

"Bet you could go farther than that on a good day, couldn't you?" Johnny met the Heeler's gaze as she trembled in his arms.

The hounds burst out laughing in Johnny's mind.

"She's funny, Johnny." Luther yipped and wagged his tail furiously as Lisa opened the screen door for them and held it open. "I like her."

"Yeah, she may be starving and too weak to walk, but at least she hasn't lost her sense of humor."

I don't even wanna know what someone else's hound thinks is so funny.

"She's right, though," Rex added. "You couldn't do half of what she's done in the last…however long."

"Uh-huh." Johnny nodded at Lisa when she opened the front door of his house and he carried Boots to the living room in the back before he placed her gently on the cool hardwood floor.

"I'll get some water." The agent hurried into the kitchen.

"Yeah, good idea, lady." Luther joined his master and the new hound and lay beside Boots to heave a massive sigh. "We have very good water here."

Rex snorted. "Way better than the swamp. We learned the hard way not to drink the stuff when—oh. You too, huh? Hey, lady! Make it an extra-big bowl!"

Johnny sat on the floor with all three hounds and turned over his shoulder to call, "Use the giant mixin' bowl to the right of the sink, darlin.'"

Cabinets opened and closed before she shouted, "Got it," and the kitchen sink turned on.

"Man, oh man, Johnny." Luther panted and stared at his master. "She's been through the wringer, all right."

"I don't even wanna think about what would happen if you left us locked outside all by ourselves, Johnny."

The dwarf frowned at his hounds and extended his hand for Boots to sniff him again before he scratched gently behind her ears. "I wouldn't."

"Yeah, that's the thing. Boots said her master wouldn't either. But it happened anyway."

"All right. We'll get the story soon enough."

Still trembling, the Heeler stared at him as she panted in agitation. He had the strangest feeling that she tried to get through to him like the hounds did. *Maybe I should make an extra collar for the odd hound who comes staggering onto my property. But not until I find out how to turn the damn thing off again first.*

"Okay, here we go." Lisa joined them with the huge metal mixing bowl of fresh well water straight from the tap. "Look at her. If she's been outside half as long as we have today, she must be dying of thirst."

Luther sniggered. "Yeah, and a dozen other things. Go ahead, Boots. That's for you."

Johnny scooted out of the way to slip the bowl under the newcomer's nose. She pushed herself up to crouch over the water and drank greedily.

The bounty-hunter team and two coonhounds sat in silence and watched her drink her fill. Water splashed over the side of the bowl and Boots uttered a weak little grunt now and again but she continued to drink with barely even a long pause for breath.

"Damn." Rex lay on the other side of Johnny, his head raised and ears erect as he looked from the top of Boots' head over the bowl to the rapidly growing puddle of water on the floor. "She's got it bad."

Luther bowed his head almost gravely as he stared at their parched guest. "The Thirst."

Johnny forced himself to not laugh. "That's a thing, huh?"

"You don't know The Thirst, Johnny?" Luther whined softly.

"Only for whiskey," Rex added. "And that's not anywhere close."

"No way. It's the stuff of nightmares. It makes a hound do crazy—"

Boots' snort was amplified by her muzzle buried in the metal bowl and it launched another spray of water over the sides.

"Sorry." Luther lay down and rested his head on his forepaws. "I'll shut up."

Even when the Heeler had lapped what had to be at least a gallon and a half of water, she continued for another moment before she finally lifted her head out of the bowl. She licked the water off her muzzle and stared at the dwarf.

"Damn," Rex muttered. "She wants more."

"Let's hold off for a minute." Johnny pushed off the floor and sat on the couch instead. "There is such a thing as too much all at once."

Luther sniggered. "Sorry, Boots. We say please all the time and it hardly ever works."

Lisa tucked her hair behind her ears and squatted in front of the Heeler, who had once again laid down, now with a full belly. She stretched her hand out for Boots to take a quick sniff, then scratched behind her ears. "She has a collar."

"Oh, yeah?"

"Yep. And updated tags from what I can see." She slid the collar around gently and studied the engraved information on the tags. "Nina Williams."

"That's it," Luther said. "That's her master."

"Nina…" Johnny scratched his cheek through his rough beard.

"That the Wood Elf who runs the nursery about a mile past the produce market?"

Both hounds stared at Boots as everyone waited for an answer.

"Oh." Luther lifted his head. "Johnny, what's a nursery?"

"Not the place where they farm pups, right?" Rex added.

"What? Y'all got some crazy ideas floatin' around in those heads. No. The plant nursery. Flowers and bushes and tiny little trees. Come on."

"Huh. Why would anyone wanna work at a place that grows plants? It's not like the swamp doesn't have enough."

"She says yes," Rex added. "That's her master. Lady two-legs with the small limp. I guess."

"Yeah, I've seen her around." Johnny nodded. "Does that collar have a number?"

"Yeah." Lisa took her phone from the back pocket of her shorts. "Do you want to give her a call or should I?"

"Go for it." He leaned back on the couch and folded his arms. *I'd be more than an asshole about it. No hound deserves this.*

When Lisa made the call, it only lasted five seconds before the recorded voicemail picked up. With a frown, she waited for the beep and left a message. "Hi, Nina. My name's Lisa Breyer. I have your dog Boots with me. I found your number on her tags, so give me a call when you can." She gave her number and repeated it, then hung up. "It went straight to voicemail.'

"And she's been missin' for days." Johnny rubbed his mouth thoughtfully and tugged his beard. "Can you get her to tell the full story, boys?"

"Probably." Luther belly-crawled toward Boots until their noses touched. "If you tell us what happened, we can tell Johnny. Then he can help you."

"What?" Rex jerked his head up off his paws. "No, that's not what he does."

"Well, kind of…"

"Sorry, Boots. Johnny's not a...magical kinda guy. Well, technically—"

"Boys!"

Boots started at his snapped interruption and stared at him with wide eyes as she seemed to shrink into herself.

"Sorry." He pointed at his hounds. "Tell her I ain't tryin' to scare her. Then get to it without all the little side chats, understand?"

"Got it, Johnny."

"Yeah, we'll get everything you need to know. We're on it. No problem."

Lisa pressed her lips together to hold a laugh back as she leaned toward Johnny and muttered, "It's weird, right?"

"What?"

"Only hearing one side of a fairly important conversation."

He sniffed and folded his arms. "I get it. You wanna hear my hounds talkin' in your head too? Sure. I'll whip up another injection."

She laughed again. "No, thank you."

"Good. Half the shit they say ain't worth hearin' in the first place." *Especially to her. Plus, that'd take a whole day of runnin' around tryin' to get the right gear all over again.*

"Okay, Boots," Rex began. "Start from the beginning. What? No, not of your life. The last time you saw your lady master. Yeah, yeah. We're listening. Oh."

Both hounds turned to look at Johnny.

He frowned at them. "What?"

"She's...hungry, Johnny."

"Says she's too weak to tell the story without something to eat. Like that meat you had outside in your office."

"Wait, you had meat and didn't share?" Luther stood and shuffled from side to side. "I'll go get it, Johnny. Bring it back here to share with—"

"Y'all stay right where you are." Johnny pointed at his hounds and stood. "And then she starts talkin'."

"What now?" Lisa asked.

"She's hungry." He strode out of the living room and down the hall toward the kitchen. *And if she weren't half-starved to death and still shiverin' like that, I'd say I had a third hound tryin' to shake me down now too.*

CHAPTER SEVEN

Boots wolfed the helping of pulled pork Johnny brought her—the only thing he had on hand without onions or spice that would mess up her already damaged stomach. When she'd finished it, she sniffed around the floor in front of her for another full minute and licked the puddle of spilled water around the bowl.

It took them almost half an hour to get the full story out of her, only because she seemed able to understand half of what Johnny asked her, and most of what she relayed through Rex and Luther was interspersed by their canine jokes. These inevitably made no sense and provided far more commentary than the interpreted conversation warranted. At least three times, the dwarf seriously considered stepping outside simply to calm his frustration.

But his hounds had an infuriating habit of leaving out useful information when asked for a recap, and he didn't want to miss anything important.

Eventually, something that resembled the full story emerged —or as full as it could be from the mouth of any hound in as bad a shape as Boots was. Her owner Nina was an incredible owner and always took good care of her. She let the dog out into the fenced back yard, and when she heard Nina head out the front door, she found the dog door sealed for the first time. There was no way into the house or out of the fenced yard, and she was left completely alone.

As far as Johnny could grasp, the hound had been out back for three or four days without food or water. Finally, she was desperate enough to dig under the fence and it had fortunately not been buried so deeply that she couldn't eventually squeeze under it. That was where she'd injured her side and from there, she'd wandered to the front of the house. The front door was locked as well and there were no signs that Nina had returned.

"So she's very scared," Rex said when the patched-together story finally came to a close. "Can't blame her."

"Good thinkin' comin' out here," Luther added. "How'd you know where to find us anyway?"

"Oh, you're that hound." Panting, Rex stretched his rear legs out behind him. "Yeah, I remember you. And your fence."

"You have all those chew toys in your yard, right?" Luther whipped his head toward his master. "We should get chew toys, Johnny. I never had one."

"We ain't talkin' about rawhide, boys."

"Yeah, but that's how we know Boots. At least, we've run past her house often."

He raised an eyebrow. "Twelve miles away?"

"Sure. We go farther than that all the time—"

"Shut up," Rex snapped. "You wanna get us in even more trouble?"

"What? We always come back—"

The bounty hunter squeezed his eyes shut and drew a deep breath. "All right. Ask her if she thinks she can take us back to her place."

"Sure she can. But it's a long walk, Johnny."

"Yeah, I don't think she'll make it. And you only have two legs."

"Well, it's a good thing Sheila has four wheels, ain't it?"

Both hounds leapt to their feet, their tails wagging furiously. "Ride! It's time for a ride!"

Luther's tail whipped against the side of Boots' face. She recoiled and leaned away from him, then settled her head on her forepaws with a snort.

"Hey, Rex? You think we could beat him there if we went straight through the swamp instead?"

"Probably."

"That defeats the point." Johnny stood and snapped his fingers. "We'll all go together."

"Go where?" Lisa asked.

"Nina Williams' house."

"Oh, good." She stood and hurried after him. "So you know where she lives."

"Nope. But her hound's gonna tell my hounds how to tell me how to get there." He shook his head and stepped into his bedroom to retrieve his oversized first-aid kit. *After only half an hour listenin' to them talk around each other, I'm dumber than the day I was born.*

Rex and Luther chatted in their one-sided conversation until he returned with cotton pads and a bottle of hydrogen peroxide. The canine chatter stopped the second he returned to the living room.

"Johnny? What's that?"

"Shit. We should make a run for it, bro. You see that look in his eyes?"

Boots began to pant again as she stared at the peroxide bottle.

"Y'all need to relax. I'm cleanin' that big ol' gash in her side." He knelt in front of the Heeler and let her sniff the bottle.

"She's fine, Johnny. Look at her."

"Yeah. Fed and watered and lying down in a cool house. Come on, you don't need to do surgery or anything."

Johnny snorted and undid the cap. "This ain't nothin'."

"But you can't—what?" Luther stared at the Heeler, then sat. His tail thumped rhythmically against the area rug. "Oh, okay. You're better than us then."

"Yeah, we've never had to dig ourselves out under a fence." Rex walked a large circle around the coffee table, his brother, and his master kneeling in front of their new hound friend. "Boots says go ahead, Johnny. She trusts you."

The dwarf smiled and placed a gentle hand on the female's back as he tipped the peroxide bottle over her dried wound. "And I ain't gonna give you a reason not to, girl. You have more sense than either of these yahoos."

Both hounds sniggered. "Yeah, she didn't understand a word of that."

"Nice try, Johnny. Hey, wait a minute. Yahoos?"

Boots stared at him as he washed her cut and cleaned it as best he could with the cotton pads. She didn't flinch once or try to stop him, and when he finally screwed the cap on the peroxide bottle, the Heeler surprised him with a flurry of canine kisses across his mouth, beard, and up to his eyes.

Rex and Luther burst out laughing and stood when their master stood and wiped his face with the back of a forearm.

"She likes you, Johnny."

"Yeah, that means—"

"I know what it means." He put the bottle on the side table and gave Boots another good scratch behind the ears. "You're welcome. All right. Let's get this damn circus on the road."

Rex and Luther bounded after their master but circled a couple of times to coax Boots off the floor. "He's gonna find her. Promise."

"Yeah, Johnny finds everyone. Even if it takes him fifteen years."

"It's a whole lifetime for us."

"But he still did it! You can do it too. We can't get there without you, Boots. Come on."

Johnny had reached the front door by the time the Heeler finally found enough strength to gain her feet. He held it open for all three hounds and Lisa brought up the rear.

"So this is your only plan to find that poor animal's owner, huh?" She stepped onto the porch and opened the screen door for the dogs. Rex and Luther let Boots go through first, then caught up to her and escorted the female, one on either side, toward Sheila.

"Best plan and only plan. It's the same thing at this point, darlin'." The screen door slammed shut behind them and they hurried across the yard. "The way I heard it, that little Heeler might be lookin' at somethin' bigger than a neglectful owner who can't take care of a good hound."

"Like what?"

"Dunno. But we're about to find out, though." He flashed her a wide grin and opened the swinging trunk door of the red Jeep. "Get on up, boys."

Rex and Luther leapt into the back and scrambled around on the bare plastic floor. "Come on, Boots. We've seen you jumpin' around your yard. This is nothing!"

The Heeler looked at Johnny slowly and whined.

"Oh, boy."

"Johnny, she can't even jump."

"Yeah, I'm pickin' up on that." He scooped Boots into his arms again and deposited her in the back, then swung the door shut carefully and gave her head an understanding pat. "Y'all make sure she has enough space to see where we're headed. And Luther ain't the one gonna be translatin' directions."

"What?" Luther thrust his head out over the side of the Jeep to stare at his master as the dwarf strode to the driver's door. "What'd I do?"

Rex snorted. "Dude, you don't even know left from right."

"Sure I do." With a loud yip, Luther rested his front paws on the back of the seat in front of him. "This is left." He yipped again and hopped down on all fours. "This is right. See? Easy."

"And wrong."

Boots responded with a sharp bark and Rex burst out laughing.

"I have no idea. That's what I keep trying to tell him."

"Hey." Luther spun in a circle when the bounty hunter started the engine. "I know you like being the funny female and everything, but seriously. Not cool."

"Yeah, he'll get over it."

Lisa clambered into the passenger seat and buckled up quickly. "You know, out of all the things we've done together, I can honestly say this is a first for me."

"There's a first time for everythin', right?" He strapped himself in, slipped on his dark sunglasses, and accelerated, careful not to lurch forward this time with an abandoned, injured hound in the back. "I tell you what, darlin'. This is the case we've been waitin' for."

"Our client's a dog."

"The best kind. Loyal to the end and they simply don't give up." He glanced in the rearview mirror to where Boots' snout appeared over the edge of the back seat. Rex and Luther already had their heads thrust over opposite sides of the Jeep and their tongues lolled and ears flapped against their heads as Sheila increased speed.

It took them almost an hour to reach Nina Williams' house. Twice, Boots had directed them down the wrong unmarked road and told them to turn when the wind shifted. Once, Luther had shouted the wrong direction at the intersection, and Johnny had to use all his willpower to not pull over and send one hound home while he kept the one who still had a brain.

After five minutes of driving at a snail's pace down the road the whining Heeler was "almost positive" was hers, Boots barked sharply and tried to leap onto the back seat for a better look but was too weak to keep her forepaws in place. She dropped to the floor and continued to bark as she spun in circles between Rex and Luther and shoved them one after the other against the side of the Jeep.

"Okay, okay. Jeez. We get it."

"This is it, Johnny."

"The double-wide up here?"

"Um...not sure what that is but that's her fence."

"Yeah!" Luther started barking with Boots now too. "I know that fence!"

"All right. Keep it down a little, huh?" Johnny proceeded at a relatively normal speed as the rest of the double-wide trailer came into view. *If anyone's tryin' to hide out here, they sure as shit know they have company now.*

Boots' frantic barking died into a low whine, and she stood perfectly still at the Jeep's back door and waited to be let out.

Lisa opened her door slowly and stepped out to gaze at Nina's property. "This doesn't look like the kind of place that comes to mind when you imagine an abandoned dog."

"It sure don't." Johnny closed his door and hurried to the back to release the hounds. Boots licked his hand feverishly and leapt out on her own before he had a chance to try to help her. Rex and Luther bounded after her. "But looks on the outside don't always show what's on the inside."

"I know. But it seems weird that a Wood Elf who keeps her home looking this nice would simply up and leave without her dog. Especially a sweet one like that."

Boots played with the coonhounds now. She yapped and crouched low before she chased them around the well-manicured yard with the brightly colored flowers planted in the front garden. The grass was intensely green, cut short for the most part with a few wisps of taller blades that had grown faster than the others and a handful of dandelions about to turn from yellow to seed.

"That's why I'm interested." Johnny waved Lisa forward and nodded toward the house. "It looks like Nina loved her garden, but I imagine she loves her hound even more. Let's go take a look."

The chain-link fence around the back yard jingled when Luther jumped against it and bounced off again. "Hey, Boots! I found your chew toys. Think we can get 'em from here? What? Oh, come on. Everyone likes to share."

Johnny snapped his fingers and pointed at the hounds. "Start lookin' around, boys. Ask her if there's anythin' that don't feel quite right."

"Um..." Rex glanced from the Heeler to his master. "Everything?"

"Get to sniffin'." Johnny and Lisa climbed the four steps to the wooden front porch and the side rail hung with a row of planters bursting with colorful flowers. The container closest to the front door had been knocked askew to dislodge two flowers that now dangled halfway over the side and had already begun to wither with sun exposure to the roots.

He looked at the dirt strewn across the porch in the same direction. It looked like someone had collided with the railing before they continued down the stairs.

Or it could've been the damn squirrels. It usually is.

"I don't see a car." Lisa turned from her careful scrutiny of the yard on both sides of the porch. "Who's knocking on the door, then?"

"Go ahead." The bounty hunter gestured toward the door. "If we do it my way, I'll simply break in."

"Yeah, let's save that as a last resort." She stepped toward the door and knocked briskly three times.

She still knocks like a fed. Or a cop. I think we should fix that.

"Ms. Williams?" Lisa called. "This is Lisa Breyer. I left you a message earlier."

Her brisk greeting brought no reply. The only sound was the

scuffle of a dozen hound paws and a few short yips from around back.

"Nina?"

"All right." Johnny stepped toward the door. "I guess we'll do it my—"

The door creaked open slowly and Lisa released the handle. "It's always a good idea to check the locks first. Right?"

"Huh." He sniffed. "But not nearly as much fun, though."

She shook her head and peered into the dark entryway of the double-wide trailer. "Ms. Williams?"

"It don't look like anyone's here, darlin'. After you."

She rested her hand on her service pistol in its shoulder holster and stepped through the door. "Try claiming probable cause when you get your information from a starving canine."

"Well, we ain't claimin' nothin," the bounty hunter muttered as he stepped in behind her. "This ain't a federal case. The second-best thing about it is no paperwork."

"And the best thing?"

"It ain't a federal case."

CHAPTER EIGHT

The interior of Nina Williams' house was completely dark, although the curtains just inside the door were open and spilled natural lighting into the entrance area. The slightly sweet odor of moldy fruit filled the air. Lisa turned toward the kitchen on the left and nodded.

"The bananas and strawberries went bad. They were left out on the table. This doesn't look like the home of someone who forgets to put things away. I don't think anyone's been here in a—"

She stopped at the wet squelch beneath her shoe and lifted her foot. The half of the moldy strawberry she'd stepped on peeled away from the surface. She stooped to flick it off the sole of her shoe but her gaze caught on the dozen other strawberries scattered across the kitchen floor, as well as shattered fragments of a pale-blue porcelain plate.

"Or maybe she left in a hurry."

"I'd say that's right on the mark, darlin'." Johnny backed away from the front door and pointed at the hallway on the other end of the trailer. "It still counts as leavin' in a hurry if someone dragged her out."

Lisa turned and frowned at the huge claw marks slashed across the corner of the wall into the hallway. Plaster, insulation, and even a huge chunk of the standing wooden support beam had been ripped out of place and were now scattered across the carpet. "Oh, no."

"Yep." Johnny headed to the hallway and switched the light on. The space illuminated with brilliant intensity to highlight the evidence of a serious struggle in Nina's house.

Slash marks gouged the walls and the floor was littered with plaster chunks and dust. The second overhead lightbulb had been shattered, and the bedroom door at the end of the hall hung askew on its hinges. Interspersed between the claw marks were charred craters in the walls and even the ceiling, left by what could only have been magical blasts.

"It looks like some kinda struggle." The bounty hunter scowled as he voiced the obvious.

"Yeah, a big one." Lisa gestured toward the living room, where the small light-pink loveseat and matching armchair had been flung onto their sides. The bookshelf lay on the floor with a few loose books scattered around it, and the half-curtain that covered the back door had been shredded, the curtain rod barely teetering on the supporting hooks.

"And whoever tore the hallway apart got their hands on the livin' room too. Or claws."

"Right. Nina's a Wood Elf, though." Lisa peered around the overturned armchair to scan the other side of the room. "She has no claws."

"By the looks of these, I think she had an unexpected visit from a—"

"Johnny!" Both hounds bayed wildly as they darted toward the front. "Johnny, we got something."

Claws scrabbled up the wooden porch stairs toward the front door.

"Yeah, we were sniffing around on the other side of the

house and picked up the—" Luther skidded to a halt in the entry and stood frozen, sniffing madly. "Damn. We should've come inside."

"Shifters, Johnny," Rex added as he trotted inside behind his brother. He snorted and shook his head. "Whew. We thought it reeked of them outside. But this smells like walking into a whole den."

"Yeah. The claw marks gave that one away, boys." Johnny gestured toward the destruction and frowned when Boots stepped warily into her house.

The Heeler's ears were pressed flat against her head as she looked around slowly.

"Maybe not such a good idea, Boots." Luther started after her but Rex nipped him in the hindquarters. "Ow. What's that—"

"Her house, bro. Give her a minute."

The Heeler crept away from the scattered mess of plaster, although she stopped to sniff at the overturned furniture in the living room.

Johnny headed down the hall and the shattered lightbulb glass crunched softly between his boots and the carpet.

"What are you doing?" Lisa asked.

"I don't want three hounds walkin' around with their paws all cut. Sit tight." He disappeared into the bedroom.

Lisa ran a hand through her hair and studied the trailer. Loud sniffing and lapping came from the kitchen.

"Dude." Rex stared at his brother. "Do you know how old those are?"

Luther craned his neck to reach a sludgy, rotten strawberry beneath the kitchen table. "Old enough to make 'em smell like heaven, bro. Only a little farther…"

Johnny's loud whistle carried clearly from the bedroom. "Whatever it is, y'all drop it right now."

"Not me, Johnny," Rex called. "I'm standing right here."

"Luther!"

The smaller hound jerked his head up and thunked it against the underside of the kitchen chair. "Ow. Crap. Why?"

"'Cause you're an idiot, bro. That's why."

Johnny crunched down the hallway again with an airy, flowing woman's blouse in one hand and a pair of black heels in the other. "Come on. I got what we needed."

Luther hurried toward his master, stopped, and raised his muzzle. "Um… Those aren't for you, right, Johnny?"

The dwarf stared at him in what might have been disbelief before he faced Lisa and nodded at the front door. "Let's get goin'."

"We don't care, Johnny," Rex added as he sniffed around the entry. "Whatever you're into."

"Yeah, we're with you to the end, Johnny. But I'm very sure your feet won't fit in those stabby shoes."

The dwarf grunted and headed to the door. "Where's Boots?"

Right on cue, a series of low, chuffing whines came from the far end of the living room.

Rex spun and cocked his head. "How much blood?"

"What?" Johnny brushed past Lisa and moved around the overturned furniture.

Boots crouched low in the far corner of the living room, her small black nose almost touching the large bloodstain that had soaked the carpet but was now dry. Another long, low whine escaped her, and Johnny rubbed his chin. It was a considerable amount of blood.

"One of y'all come over here and check this out, will ya?"

Rex and Luther both raced through the trailer. Luther couldn't avoid the side of the toppled armchair in time and thumped his back end against it before he corrected. In moments, they both sniffed madly at the bloodstain. "Shit, Johnny. That's from her."

"Yep. Wood Elf all the way."

"Damn."

Lisa cleared her throat as she stared at gruesome evidence with a grimace. "Whose is it?"

"Nina's. Unless there was another Wood Elf in the house."

"Boots says no, Johnny."

"Yeah, only her lady master here." Rex sniffed the protruding legs of the loveseat. "I only smell one too."

"All right. Let's head on out, then." Johnny pointed at the Heeler and nodded slowly. "If you can understand me, we'll find her."

"Yeah, she has the gist of it, Johnny."

"Smart and funny." Luther inched behind Boots and sniffed her backside. "I like that."

She turned and snapped at his face, still crouched beside her owner's dried blood.

"Okay, okay. Jeez. I'm not the only one being sensitive."

"Dude." Rex snorted and padded silently toward the door. "Show a little respect."

"It's blood. Not a body."

Johnny snapped his fingers and headed to the open front door. "Let's go, boys."

Boots looked from the dwarf's receding back to the stained carpet. Another whine escaped her.

"That's exactly what we're gonna do." Luther licked her muzzle. "You don't wanna stay in here all by yourself, right?"

"She makes a good point," Rex called as he stepped out after his master. "But I don't think your lady master's coming back on her own, Boots. Plus, we have tons of food at our house."

The Heeler whipped her head toward the door, then trotted past Lisa and headed outside.

Luther snorted and hurried after her. "Gets 'em every time."

"Gets you too, dummy."

The agent took a final sweeping glance around Nina Williams' destroyed double-wide trailer, then left and pulled the door shut behind her. "So what's the plan now?"

Johnny reached for Boots but straightened quickly when she jumped into the back of Sheila on her own. "Shifters were here, darlin'. And unless they didn't pipe up and say somethin', the hounds ain't smelled any other kind of visitor. Right, boys?"

"Nothing but one Wood Elf and tons of shifters, Johnny."

"Yeah, real smelly ones. Like they've slogged through the swamp for two days straight."

The bounty hunter held back from commenting on Luther's smell after a full day in the swamp and shut the back door. "So we'll take the fun to the shifters."

"Which ones?" Lisa slid into the passenger seat and watched him walk toward the front of the Jeep.

He got in, started the engine, and cleared his throat. "All of 'em."

"Wonderful." She buckled up hastily and braced herself against the door.

This was Johnny's first good reason—and hopefully his last— to drive down the muddy, bumpy, barely-there road that was hardly a road to begin with. He'd known where the closest Everglades shifter pack had made their den for years. Now, he intended to waltz right into it.

"Johnny." The agent pressed herself back against the passenger seat as hard as she could, grasped the side of the door with one hand, and dug the fingers of her other into the seat cushion near her thigh. "Do you think you can—"

Sheila lurched across a massive pothole in the unmaintained road, and the Jeep's passengers bounced wildly. Rex and Luther scrambled across the plastic floor in the back, and Boots uttered a startled yelp.

"You're not going anywhere," Luther said as he tried to regain his footing.

"Yeah. Keep your head down and your tail tucked," Rex added. "That's how you don't get thrown out."

Johnny accelerated, and they lurched forward over another jolting series of smaller holes.

"Seriously?" Lisa grimaced as they jostled repeatedly. "Can't you—ow!"

"It wasn't that bad."

"No, only if you bit a huge chunk out of your tongue." She licked her lips and dabbed her hand against her tongue to check for blood. "Which I did."

"Sorry about that. Although it's one of the fastest-healin' muscles in the body."

"Oh, that's comforting."

"Sure. For humans, at least. And you're half a one. I assume you have some of those genes in there somewhere—"

The next huge pothole made the Jeep dip dangerously toward the edge of the road on the passenger side, where the verge dropped four feet, not into a ditch but into the swamp itself. Lisa slapped the dashboard with both hands to stop her forehead from connecting with it instead. "Slow down!"

"It's worse when it's slow. Trust me." He pressed the gas and kept the painfully bumpy ride at as much speed as Sheila could handle. "And the last thing we wanna do is get—"

The front tires dipped again and the vehicle lurched to a violent halt on the mud-slick road.

Frowning, he pumped the gas pedal a few times. The engine revved, the tires spun, and a spray of mud kicked up on the front passenger side. "Damn."

Lisa leaned away from the splashing grit and sighed. "You were going to say stuck, weren't you? The last thing we want to do is get stuck."

"No. I was gonna say the last thing we wanna do is get stuck outside swamp-shifter territory. Especially this close to their den."

"Oh, of course. It could get worse and it did."

He shifted into park, unstrapped his seatbelt, and got out.

"What are you doing?"

"What has to get done, darlin'. How are you with takin' directions from the driver's seat?"

She smirked at him. "You want me to get behind the wheel. Of Sheila."

He grimaced, scratched the back of his head, and cleared his throat. "'Course I don't. But that don't change what I need you to do, so go on." Slowly, he met her gaze and shrugged. "Please."

"Because you asked nicely…" She clambered over the center console and slid behind the wheel, then waited until Johnny turned away to slop through the mud before she eased the driver's seat back by an inch to give herself more legroom.

"Hey, Johnny." Luther stuck his head over the back of the Jeep as his master approached and his tail thumped repeatedly against the interior wall. "Aren't you supposed to be driving?"

The dwarf ignored him and planted his feet squarely in the mud slightly to the right of Sheila's center. "When I say go, pump the gas."

"Got it." Lisa glanced at him in the rearview mirror and wrinkled her nose.

"Go."

The front right tire swirled in the mud-filled pothole and sprayed even more sludgy swamp water and silt and whatever else was down there. Johnny pushed fiercely against the back of his Jeep, gritted his teeth, and grunted with the effort.

"We can help, Johnny." Even over the slosh of mud and the rev of the engine, Rex's voice still rang clearly in the dwarf's head. "Maybe we need to dig it out."

"Ooh, yeah. We can dig, Johnny. Like no one's business we can —woah!"

Sheila rocked and lurched forward.

"Stop!" Johnny shouted.

Lisa's reaction time was unfortunately a little too slow. With the front wheels free, she assumed she had the all-clear until the right back tire sank into the same squelching mud trap. The second violent thunk into the pothole forced the already weakened outer wall of the hole to slide away over the edge of the raised road.

Clods of dirt, mud, and a slosh of water spilled over the side and into the swamp as the Jeep's rear tires spun madly. They threw up even more water and mud and splattered the dwarf from head to toe. In the next moment, Sheila started to slide toward the edge as well.

"Lisa! Press the brakes!"

"What?"

"The damn brakes!"

The Jeep rocked slightly when she did as he'd instructed and she turned over her shoulder and grimaced. "It's the same hole, isn't it?"

"Well...mostly." He scratched his head and stared at the slowly crumbling trench the pothole had become. Anyone could see that it might or might not take the whole vehicle with it if any more broke away before they were free.

As if the Everglades suddenly wanted to swallow Sheila, three hounds, and a half-Light Elf Federal Agent simply to prove some kind of point, another large chunk of water-soaked earth broke free and toppled into the swamp with a loud splash.

"Hey, what was that?" Luther practically climbed over his brother to get to the other side of the Jeep. The fifty-five-pound shift in weight rocked Sheila dangerously to the right, and even more of the road sloughed off into the saltwater and the reeds.

"Boy, get back here!" Johnny stretched hastily over the back door and grasped the hound by the scruff of his neck. He hauled him unceremoniously to the side of solid ground. "Don't do that again."

"But I heard a—"

The dwarf snapped his fingers and pointed at what would

have been the back driver's side window if Sheila had any windows. "Out. That way."

"Johnny?" Luther licked his muzzle and whined. "I have no idea how to get home from here."

"Well, I guess you'll find out soon enough. But I ain't sendin' you home. Only outta the Jeep. All y'all."

"I don't wanna die, Johnny!" Rex leapt gracefully through Sheila's open frame and slid across the muddy road. "Luther! It's your last chance. Jump!"

"What?"

"That ain't what I—come on." Johnny waved the smaller hound out of the back as Rex crouched low in the dirt. "Out. See how easy it was? Let's move."

"Johnny. Johnny." Luther shifted nervously and his claws clicked on the plastic floor. "Johnny, is Rex gonna—"

"Now!"

With a yelp, the hound jumped through. His rear paw caught on the frame with a metallic thump, and he scrambled in the mud before he righted himself and immediately shook it off.

"What the—" The dwarf stepped away and spread his arms. "Great. Front and back."

"You've been covered in worse, Johnny."

"Yeah, like exploding goo. This stinks, but not that bad."

He snapped his fingers and raised an index finger. Both hounds sat immediately and their gazes shifted from Johnny to Sheila to wherever they heard movement in the swamp.

"Come on, Boots." Johnny leaned through the back window to reach the Heeler, who'd crouched so low on the tilted vehicle floor that he could barely see her. "Come on, darlin'. I don't want you in here right now. It's okay."

"Johnny?" Lisa called and twisted slowly to lean through the driver's window and look at him. "Do I need to get out?"

"Nope. You stay right there, darlin'. I still need someone to steer while I push."

"Oh, good." She turned away and grasped the steering wheel so tightly that her knuckles popped. "Save the dogs. I'll stay in the tilting Jeep."

"That's right, lady!" Luther yipped. "Like anything that goes down. Get the bitches and pups out first."

"Yeah," Rex muttered and watched his master warily. "You're the bitch."

"And we're the pups."

Rex snorted. "No, we're not."

"Might as well be," Johnny grumbled as he tried to reach Boots.

"Hey…"

"Come on, girl. Time to get goin'." He wiggled his fingers at her but the Heeler only stared at him with wide eyes and wouldn't budge. "It's better than stayin' there, I promise. This ain't the safest place to be frozen to the spot right now."

"Why?" Luther spun in a tight circle and his tongue flapped from his mouth. "Oh, right, because of the shifter—"

As if on cue, a dozen howls issued through the swamp and twisted around each other in a range of rising and falling voices.

Boots scrambled across the Jeep's floor and leapt through the window with a yip. Johnny barely caught her but she bucked and writhed out of his arms before she landed on all fours and skittered toward the hounds.

Luther cocked his head. "Uh-oh."

Rex tucked his ears back and growled. "They're very close, Johnny."

"But we're downwind. Damn, they smell even worse out here than in that two-legs' trailer."

"We have time." With an unconcerned sniff, Johnny squelched through the mud again and studied the angle of the half-buried rear tire. "Lisa?"

"Yeah?"

"Turn her all the way to the left, darlin'."

MARTHA CARR & MICHAEL ANDERLE

"The wheel?"

He pinched the bridge of his nose and squeezed his eyes shut. *When this is over, she'll get a crash course without the possibility of sinkin' my Jeep.* "The wheel. Yeah."

"Okay."

The tires turned, and when he said go, they spun. Mud and water sprayed in every direction and covered the dwarf from head to toe yet again, and he began to push.

CHAPTER NINE

The whole point of going into this backwoods shifter den in broad daylight wasn't so the two investigators would have the upper hand. It was so the shifters wouldn't.

"Do you honestly think they have that much of an advantage at night?" Lisa muttered as Sheila bumped slowly down the rest of the winding, muddy road. They reached the first few outbuildings of the pack's private little community hidden within the swamp, and she peered into the thick shadows of the tall oaks and mangroves that rose all around them.

"Shifters have most of the advantage most of the time." Johnny darted her a sidelong glance from beneath his dark sunglasses—the only thing he'd bothered to clean diligently after being sprayed with mud for the last ten minutes while he tried to get them out of the pothole. "They're hardly ever alone and they heard us comin' from miles away, I imagine. And maybe smelled us too."

"Oh, they smell you now, Johnny," Luther interjected from the back.

"Yeah," Rex added. "Mud stink, dwarf stink, and the wind changed again."

"The toothy bastards might as well be wearin' night-vision goggles when it's dark. The only thing we have goin' for us is that they'll assume we're dumb enough to walk into their den in the middle of the day without tryin' to be sneaky."

"That's exactly what we're doing, Johnny."

"Uh-huh. If that don't catch their attention, darlin', I don't know what will."

Lisa turned her head slightly to study him for a few moments. "Maybe the dwarf who rolls in looking like a swamp monster. That might do the trick."

He grunted. "Then we're two for two."

When the road finally ended and gave way to sparse grass studded across the trampled dirt, Johnny pulled over and turned Sheila's engine off. They were a hundred feet from the first real cluster of buildings—little more than shacks arranged in a half-circle facing the end of the road. Two larger buildings and a shoddily crafted pavilion with a crooked stage filled the center of the half-circle at the back of the den. And, or so it seemed, all the shifters were hiding.

"All right. It's time to get in and start askin' questions." Johnny glanced at the hounds in the rear-view mirror. "Do you have her scent, boys?"

"Yeah, Johnny." Rex poked his snout out of the Jeep and sniffed the air. "You picked the right clothes, that's for sure."

"Totally." Luther whipped his head up and shook it when one of Nina Williams' black heels slipped over the tip of his nose and dangled against his face. "It's crazy, Johnny. Who'd have thought a lady two-legs' shoes would be so stinky?"

"If you pick up on her anywhere within ten miles, y'all let me know." The bounty hunter nodded at Lisa. "We'll find her."

"Oh, I know. Three hounds, a Jeep, and a bounty hunter who looks like he wrestled an alligator in the mud. We're completely prepared."

He rounded the back of the Jeep and opened the door to let all three hounds out onto the dirt road. "We have more'n that, darlin'."

She frowned at him but he simply stretched into the back and popped open a metal lockbox bolted to the floor behind the back seat. From this, he withdrew his handy explosive utility belt, which he strapped quickly around his hips. He shut the back door and joined her at Sheila's front bumper.

She glanced at him and pressed her lips together. "Of course. We have your homemade bombs, too."

"Having a half-Light Elf on the team ain't so bad, either."

"I'll take it. When did you start keeping that in the Jeep?"

"This one's always in the back, darlin'. Do you think I'd have only one of these belts?"

"How many do you have?"

"Enough." The dwarf smirked and adjusted the belt. "You got the phone call and knockin' on Nina's door. I'll do the talkin' on this one."

"Talking." She shook her head slowly. "Right."

They moved forward into the heart of the Everglades' local shifter den. The only sounds were the buzz of the insects, the croaking of bullfrogs, and the occasional splash in the swamp behind the buildings. "Stay sharp, boys."

"You got it, Johnny." Luther sniffed the dirt, then raised his head to sample the scents in the air. "Exactly like these shifters. Talk about sharp—what?"

Both hounds turned to look at the Blue Heeler who padded warily between them.

"No, Boots," Rex said. "He didn't mean sharp like claws and teeth. Even though we have those."

"Yeah. Maybe not as many as a pack of shifters—"

Boots uttered a low whine.

"Great, Luther. Now, she's terrified. Don't listen to him, Boots. He doesn't know what he's saying eighty percent of the time."

"Yeah, but that's only half the time."

"See?"

Johnny snapped his fingers and the hounds ceased their banter.

When they crossed the open center of the half-circle, they had a full view of the shacks' front porches. A shifter woman sat on the top step of hers on their left and her hair fell around her shoulders in a tangled mess. She stared at them as they walked past, her face completely expressionless.

From behind the open, pane-less window in the shack on their right, an old man with folds of wrinkles around his eyes and mouth peered at them. He must have tried to sneer at them when his mouth pulled back into a silent snarl, but there was nothing behind those lips except toothless gums and a gaping black hole.

"How long have they lived out here like this?" Lisa muttered and leaned slightly—and very carefully—toward the mud-covered dwarf.

"As long as I know." He frowned as he thought about it. "And probably before my folks' time too."

"I can't imagine they get out much."

"Sure. They go runnin' through the swamps when the itch strikes." *And come sneakin' into my home to steal Amanda right out from under me. The kid's too good for a place like this. Most folks are.*

A screen door creaked and slammed shut on one of the shack porches up ahead. A six-year-old boy darted into the center of the den's half-circle and froze. He stood in front of the newcomers buck-naked, bent over in a wary crouch. A heron took flight somewhere in the reeds and the boy jerked his head up to stare at it. Without a word, he raced away again across the trampled dirt toward the larger outbuildings at the back of the circle.

"And it would seem no one is around to watch the kids." Lisa forced herself to not reach for her service pistol in her shoulder holster. It was probably the best move in an already tense situation. The boy vanished around the side of the large building on the left and another door creaked open and banged shut.

"They're around, darlin', but they don't wanna be seen." Johnny glanced at the hounds, who'd moved away from their master to investigate the other scents permeating the shifter den. *They'll let me know.* "Come on. I guess we oughta ask around."

"Right. And ask all the friendly faces which one of them kidnapped Nina Williams from her home. It sounds like a plan." When he darted her a glance with his brows raised, she shrugged. "After you."

A dangerously thin woman covered in dirt and with leaves tangled in her hair stepped out of her front door with a basket of dirty laundry in her arms. She walked slowly down her porch steps and stared at the newcomers the whole time before she turned to walk around her home.

Johnny hurried after her. "'Scuse me. Hey."

She turned slowly and glared at him.

"We're lookin' for someone. Y'all seen a Wood Elf around here?"

She scrutinized him intently, sneered, and turned her back and continued to wherever she was taking the laundry.

"I'll take that as a no." Johnny shook his head at Lisa. "The talkin' part ain't gonna be easy."

"Oh, you seriously meant talking."

"Very funny."

They moved from shack to dilapidated, crooked shack and one by one, they were turned away with nothing but hateful glares and the odd condescending cold shoulder. Two more children—another boy and a girl, both also completely naked—raced from two other houses toward the larger buildings at the back of the den.

They're sending their kids out to deliver messages. Somethin' ain't right.

"It looks very much like someone's trying to hide something," Lisa muttered.

"Uh-huh. Boys?" Johnny turned to look for the hounds and almost tripped over Boots who stood at his side. The Heeler gazed at him with wide eyes, her ears almost flat against her head. "All good, good. You stay close. Rex. Luther."

"Nothing yet, Johnny."

"Nothing but stinky shifters and..." Rex snorted. "Well, they're shifters. Bet they don't sit down on a can like you do, Johnny."

"Let's keep lookin'." The dwarf stuck his thumbs through his belt loops and strolled casually down the center of the den's open circle. *It's the first time I ain't been fought out of a place folks didn't want me to be in.*

"Johnny." Lisa stopped and scanned the huge dirt compound. "No one's told us to leave."

"Yep."

"Does that seem a little weird to you?"

"More'n a little. Somethin's—"

A loud crash came from the large outbuildings at the back of the den, followed by a woman's shout of rage. "Don't fucking touch me!"

More shouts rose within the building—at least a dozen voices all clamoring to be heard over the snarls and barks and more crashes.

Johnny and Lisa exchanged a glance, then ran toward the outbuilding. "To me, boys!"

The hounds bayed wildly and raced after their master. "Keep up, Boots!"

"Yeah, shit happens fast now!"

The front of the building facing the compound had no doors or windows, so the bounty hunter darted around the side to find the door the first naked boy had entered. It was easy to locate and didn't seem to be guarded.

The wild shouts of anger from too many voices to make sense of any were louder now. Johnny snatched an explosive disk off his belt and held it at the ready before he strode toward the door.

He didn't expect it to fly open and knock him down the first step he'd climbed. The first little boy, still completely naked, bounded down the steps and barreled head-on into Johnny. He rammed his head into the dwarf's gut and completely knocked the wind out of him.

"Go away!"

"What—"

The boy snatched the disk from Johnny's hand and lobbed it in an impressive overarm throw into the swamp behind the buildings.

"You little—hey!" Johnny turned toward the kid, but he'd already disappeared behind one of the shacks.

Lisa shifted to stare at where the boy had disappeared, then drew her weapon and nodded. "Two other kids."

"Kids are fine." Johnny stormed up the stairs to the outbuilding again and snatched another disk. "The rest of 'em better not be."

He threw the door open and stopped to stare at over a dozen shifters gathered inside. Two of them rolled on the ground in the middle of a fight. They snarled and attacked one another with fists instead of claws and teeth.

"Get your hands off me!" the same woman screamed and struggled against two male shifters who held her tightly by the shoulders and arms.

The others shouted at the brawlers in the center of the ring they'd formed around the battle, all of them wide-eyed and intently focused on the fight.

"Hey!" Johnny yelled.

Everyone but the two shifters engaged in combat turned to the dwarf where he stood in the open doorway. A giant man with a long, tangled black ponytail snarled and strode toward him. "Who the hell are you?"

"I only wanna talk." Johnny spread his arms placatingly. "Where's Nina Williams?"

"Get out!" The shifter raced across the long, one-roomed building lined with shelves and cases of supplies. He leapt at the intruder and shifted in midair.

The dwarf wasn't prepared for the size of the black wolf that careened toward him. Even when he ducked, the shifter's hind legs caught him in the shoulders and catapulted him back down the steps.

With another belligerent snarl, the wolf landed on all fours on the other side of Johnny and spun.

Before he could pounce again, the hounds were on him. They growled and snapped at his ankles, bounded onto his back, and shook him wherever they could clamp their jaws tightly on his flesh.

"Go, Johnny!" Luther shouted. "We got this—"

The wolf threw the smaller hound off with a wickedly agile spin, but Rex lunged at him and took his brother's place. "We totally got him, Johnny."

The bounty hunter scrambled off the ground and saw Lisa racing up the stairs and through the open door.

"Find Nina," he shouted and followed her into the building.

The hounds abandoned the wolf and raced past their master. "Nice try, asshole!"

"You snooze, you lose!"

Johnny strode up the steps after them and hauled the door shut behind him. The black wolf thudded against the outside of it a second after it closed and dented it slightly, but a shifted wolf didn't have hands to open it. He'd shift soon enough, but it had bought them precious moments.

"What is this fucking dwarf doing here?" an older man shouted. Even the guy's missing eye centered on Johnny Walker.

"I'm lookin' for the Wood Elf." Johnny raised the disk in a warning. "That's all I want."

"You don't belong here." The woman held back by the two shifters wrested herself out of their hold. "You're trespassin'."

"And you ain't Nina. Are you?"

"Who the fuck is Nina?"

The hounds snarled and snapped at the dozen-plus shifters who glared at Johnny. Lisa still had her service pistol drawn and now aimed it at the group, although she swept the barrel slowly toward any magical who looked like they were about to pounce.

"The Wood Elf who was taken from her home," the dwarf said and glanced at the two combatants still to defeat each other in the center of the room. "By shifters."

"Man, you got the wrong—"

The door shrieked on its hinges and flew open. Johnny spun toward the shifter with the ponytail, who sneered at him as he stormed up the steps, as naked as the children had been.

"Oh, good. You finally realized what you had to do." The dwarf gazed at the ceiling. "Put some clothes on—"

The man bellowed and surged toward him again, completely ignoring the unwritten rules against grappling bare-ass naked with a stranger.

"What the fuck!" Johnny tried to avoid the huge man's lunged attack, but his adversary barreled into him and he fell heavily. The deactivated explosive disk slipped from his hand and skittered across the floor.

"Aldo!" the man with one eye shouted.

"Move and I'll shoot!" Lisa added.

The hounds snarled and snapped at the large attacker's flailing limbs as the shifter struggled to pin Johnny down. It was no easy feat as the bounty hunter fought best on the ground.

He elbowed his assailant in the gut—which felt like elbowing a brick wall—and used his slightly heavier weight to pin him down long enough to hook his left leg over the shifter's shoulder.

His teeth clenched, he crimped his calf into a tight squeeze around his opponent's throat. He only got one of the huge man's arms pinned, but he grasped it, jerked it back in an arm lock, and paused just past the point of natural resistance. The man snarled.

"Are you done yet? 'Cause shifter arms break as easily as the rest of—"

Before he could finish the sentence, the guy shifted in his impromptu chokehold and uttered a wicked howl. Johnny lost his grasp on the huge arm as it became a shaggy black foreleg, and when the wolf stood on all fours, he swung around the animal's collar like a heavy dwarf necklace.

He landed on his back with a thud and grunted. The black wolf snarled in his face as the bounty hunter scrambled back on his ass. When he had enough space to sit, the wolf tensed to strike. Johnny landed a brain-rattling right hook to the side of the furry head, kicked up against the guy's underbelly, then vaulted on top of the huge magical's hairy, reeking back like he was still fighting a human body.

The other shifters resumed their shouts but now, they were invested in a completely new fight. Even the two who'd tried to beat each other senseless had separated to join the others as spectators but glared at each other intermittently as they wiped blood from under their noses and the split skin around their swelling eyes.

Johnny wound both his thick forearms around the wolf's neck and squeezed. The only thing that kept him in place might have been his knees squeezing against the wolf's sides as the beast lurched and stumbled around the room. In vain, it tried to snap at the dwarf who was too far out of reach.

"Go down easy," the bounty hunter grumbled through gritted teeth, his mouth close to the wolf's ear, "and I won't have to break your windpipe, brother. I said I wanted to talk."

The wolf snarled again and tossed his head uselessly in an attempt to dislodge his tenacious rider. He stumbled sideways and collided with a stack of crates along the wall but continued to struggle as he growled and choked.

"Give it up, man!"

Lisa's service pistol had lowered as she watched Johnny Walker riding a staggering black wolf around the room. *Leave it to Johnny to turn this into a magical rodeo. Jesus. Why hasn't anyone stepped in to get him off the guy?*

"Get him, Johnny!" Luther barked harshly and darted forward toward the wolf and back again, his tail rigid and almost vertical. "Knock his lights out!"

"He's going down, Johnny." Rex snarled at the seething shifter woman who scowled at him. "We might have to worry about the others soon, though."

"Goddammit," the dwarf growled. "It's over."

With a yelp, the wolf stumbled over his forepaws and landed hard. The dwarf squeezed even harder as he felt the beast shift into his human form. He barely managed to hook his ankles around the guy's hips as lupine fur gave way to naked flesh and the thick, furry neck shrank into a slightly smaller pillar of muscle.

The shouts of encouragement from the rest of the pack faded into groans of disappointment. The shifters stepped away from the fight, folded their arms, and shared knowing glances. They didn't look happy about it but they still didn't step in to break up the fight.

By the time the man had shifted completely, he and Johnny both lay on their sides and the shifter's grimacing face had turned an alarmingly dark-red.

"Are you done?" the dwarf asked brusquely.

The guy tapped his forearm and choked his next words. "Get your...fuckin'...boots off...my crotch."

Johnny released him and shoved him away quickly. In an instant, he was on his feet with both hands hovering over two more disks on his belt. He cleared his throat, tried to catch his breath, and turned away from the naked hulk of muscle that pushed slowly off the floor.

With a scowl at the other shifters—who were way less threatening now as they examined a mud-splattered Johnny cautiously and cast exasperated glances at their defeated teammate—Johnny nodded brusquely. "I said I only wanna talk. That ain't so hard to understand."

The man with one eye spread his arms. "Then talk, dwarf. You earned it."

CHAPTER TEN

"Is that right?" Johnny scoffed and lowered his hands from his belt. "I earned it."

"Sure." The man with one eye scratched his chin beneath the graying hair of his scraggly, thin beard and the corners of his mouth turned down in consideration. "It's been a long time since we seen anyone but another shifter overcome one of our own like that."

The dwarf's erstwhile opponent grunted as he jerked on his clothes that someone else had retrieved for him.

"Aldo ain't the best at talkin'," the man added. "It looks like you speak his language too."

"All right." Johnny ignored the angry shifter he'd wrestled into submission as a man and a wolf and turned to the rest of the pack gathered in the building. *I'm not fixin' to add insult to injury. But I'll be as sore as a stuck pig in the mornin'.*

"So why did you come bargin' in here where you ain't wanted, huh?" The woman who was certainly not Nina Williams folded her arms.

"I'm lookin' for the Wood Elf." He stretched his neck from side to side and glanced at Lisa. "Go ahead. I need a minute."

Holstering her weapon, Lisa stepped forward and nodded at the group. "She's local and was taken from her home five, maybe six days ago. By shifters."

"Yeah, you mentioned that." The one-eyed man raised an eyebrow and watched Johnny swing his arm around to get his shoulder moving the right way again. "Don't see why that's our problem."

"And we got enough o' those as it is," added a shorter man with brown greasy hair falling into his eyes.

Johnny studied him carefully. "Like bad hygiene and illiteracy?"

The woman closest to him snarled and stepped toward him.

"Hyla," the one-eyed shifter snapped. "Back down."

She glanced at him and complied, although she didn't try to look any friendlier about it.

Johnny narrowed his eyes. *I thought some other beefy hulk was the alpha down here. There's no way the old guy took over.*

As if he'd known the dwarf was thinking about him, the same alpha shifter Johnny, Amanda, and the hounds had run into on their hunt in the swamps pushed away from where he'd been leaning against the wall and stepped forward. "Bernard said it like it is, dwarf."

"Oh. There you are." The alpha looked less weirdly threatening with clothes on.

"We have our own problems and aren't interested in yours."

"And Nina Williams' ain't one of 'em?"

"I never heard the name," he replied with a small shrug. "Ain't seen no one in our den but our own until you come stormin' in here like you own the place."

"Naw, I own enough swamp. I have no need for the sewers on top of it."

"Johnny." Lisa raised her eyebrows at him.

Shit. Here I am talkin' and it's headin' for another damn fight.

He cleared his throat. "What kinda problems?"

"That's our business," Hyla snarled.

"Well, you're the only pack I know of down here." Johnny pointed at her. "Shifters took that Elf and I'm gonna find her."

"She's not here." The alpha spread his arms and gazed around the room. "You can turn the place upside down if you want to but we already done that. We're lookin' for one of our own."

With a sniff of what might have been disbelief, Johnny darted another glance at Lisa and she shook her head slightly. "Y'all missin' someone too?"

Bernard nodded and his missing eye squinted grotesquely beside the other. "Our bearer. He's been gone seven days from the den and we ain't heard hide or hair of him."

Luther chuckled as he sniffed the baseboards of the room beside the damaged door. "Funny. 'Cause they have hides. And hair."

The old shifter looked at the hound in confusion but decided to ignore him.

"What happened?" Johnny asked.

"Reggie." Hyla stepped forward again, looked at her alpha, and pointed at the dwarf. "He needs to get out. This ain't none of his business and we're runnin' outta time—"

"I'm afraid you're wrong. It is my business."

Every shifter turned to frown at him but he returned their attention with a bland expression and hooked his thumbs through his belt loops.

"What makes you say that?" Bernard asked.

Lisa closed her eyes and sighed heavily.

"'Cause that's what I do." Johnny nodded. "I find people. Magicals. Whatever. It's my business. And it sounds a helluva lot like we might have more than a missin' Wood Elf around these parts. She and your bear or whatever—"

"Bearer," Bernard corrected with a smirk.

"Sure. They went missing around the same time. If he took her—"

"Magnus wouldn't take anyone," Reggie interjected. "That ain't it."

"Oh, yeah? You have your kids runnin' around as naked as the day they were born and you expect me to believe there ain't somethin' fishy goin' on?"

Reggie and Bernard exchanged a loaded glance. "Pups are pups," the alpha said. "But our bearer ain't the kinda shifter who goes stealin' elves outta their homes."

"He is the kinda shifter another pack would wanna kill before his time, though." Bernard nodded sagely. "And that's what we were tryin' to determine before you showed up without an invitation."

Johnny snorted. "That's how you try to find who took your missin' guy? By cheerin' on a fight in your...whatever we're standin' in?"

A small, crooked smile spread across Reggie's lips. "That's how you're tryin' to find this missin' Elf, ain't it?"

"No. I—" He sighed and nodded reluctantly. "Fair enough."

"I think we oughtta sit down and hash it all out, Bernard."

The old one-eyed shifter tilted his head from side to side in thought. "It couldn't hurt."

"Are you out of your goddamn minds?" Hyla shouted. "We can't find Magnus and if he ain't here, we need to find someone to—"

"Watch it," Reggie snarled. "You had your time to get Bill in the ring."

"And the dwarf—"

"The dwarf earned his right as a guest." He nodded at the two other shifters who'd held Hyla back when Johnny and Lisa had first stormed through the door. "Elders stay. Everyone else out."

The two moved toward the woman, who hissed and slapped their hands away. "Don't touch me."

Aldo took the rear and followed the other shifters out of the building. He glared at Johnny as he passed but didn't say a word.

Someone outside pulled the damaged door shut with another squeal of bent hinges, and the two investigators and the hounds were alone in the main storage building with the pack's alpha, old Bernard, and three other elders.

"Take a seat." Reggie stepped toward the middle of the room and sat beside the drying sprays of blood that lingered from the interrupted fistfight.

Johnny joined the shifters and sat. Lisa headed toward them and stopped when a faint scratching came from the door, followed by a low whine.

"Shit, Johnny." Rex whipped his head up toward the door. "Boots."

"Y'all brought more dogs into a shifter den?" Bernard asked, one eyebrow quirked over a curious smile.

"Yep."

"I got it." Lisa struggled to shove the door open but when it finally shrieked away from the frame, Boots raced up the stairs with wide eyes and didn't slow until she reached Johnny's side. She flung herself down and nestled her head between her forepaws, panting heavily.

"Didn't I tell you to keep up?" Luther said as he trotted toward the Heeler. "I told you shit happened fast."

"Dude, maybe she doesn't like to fight." Rex sat a few feet away from the gathered shifters and studied them all with vague curiosity.

"Oh, you're a lover, huh?" Luther lay down so close to Boots that their fur brushed together. "I like that—"

She uttered a low growl and bared her teeth.

"Jeez. Okay, okay." He belly-crawled sideways, stretched his rear legs out behind him, and snorted. "You're sending mixed messages, you know that?"

Reggie raised his eyebrows and nodded toward Luther. "That one has a problem."

"Hey."

Johnny snorted. "Tell me about it."

"The bitch don't belong to you, does she?"

Lisa paused when she finally got the door closed again and stared with wide eyes at Johnny and the shifters seated in a circle in the middle of the room. No one was looking at her, so she relaxed.

"No, she don't." Johnny scratched gently behind Boots' ears. "She belongs to the Wood Elf. This is a little warrior right here, I tell you what."

"Is that so?" Bernard leaned forward to catch the Heeler's gaze and she stared at him without looking away. "Yeah, I can see it."

"Oh, she doesn't like him, Johnny," Luther muttered.

"Come on, now." Bernard chuckled. "If you don't look me head-on, I ain't so scary."

Rex looked at Lisa as she joined the strange meeting. "It's the old guy who smells, Johnny."

"Yeah, like a dead squirrel."

Reggie choked back a laugh before he shared a knowing glance with Bernard.

Johnny slapped his thighs and jerked his chin at the alpha. "So what's goin' on with this missin' shifter of yours?"

"I have no clue. Like I said, Magnus ain't the type to bury his duties right before the pack needs 'em."

Luther sniggered. "Yeah, we bury our doodies too."

Everyone but Lisa stared at the smaller hound, but Luther was too busy licking between the toes of his forepaw to notice.

The agent gazed around the circle and frowned. "Did I miss something?"

"Not even a little, darlin'." Johnny shook his head. "Y'all said somethin' about thinkin' he was taken. Not simply missin'."

"That's our first guess." The female elder with straight black hair and piercing blue eyes despite the wrinkles surrounding them puckered her lips and flicked her gaze toward Johnny. There was no amusement there. "Death or kidnappin'. Those are the only things that would get Magnus to leave his post here."

"You sound real sure of that."

"I am."

"Others have tried to take him from us, sure," Bernard interjected and fixed the older woman with a warning gaze. "Different groups of whatever magicals tryin' to get their hands on what he can do for them. He had more than enough offers that woulda snatched any other member out of our den."

"But Magnus ain't like any other member," Reggie said, raised his head, and straightened his spine. "He's got somethin' different."

"Different in a shifter, huh?" Johnny rubbed his mouth. "I don't get it."

"He's special." The woman hissed disapproval.

"Yeah, we're all special, ain't we?" The dwarf pointed at the ceiling. "We have a whole damn planet full of special on the other side of the damn doorway."

"Gifted, dwarf." Reggie folded his arms. "We ain't talkin' 'bout our rituals to an outsider, but Magnus has that little extra somethin' few of us achieve."

"Few of us even fix our eyes on it before we're dead in the ground," Bernard added.

"And that's why you think someone took him." Johnny looked from face to face, then pointed at the two other male elders seated beside the woman. "Y'all ain't said nothin' yet."

The bald man with cataracts so thick he had to be almost blind opened his mouth to show nothing inside but a few rotting teeth and swollen gums. His tongue, however, had been hacked off at the base.

Johnny raised his eyebrows. "It makes sense. Y'all shifters get into some freaky shit."

"It was bitten off by someone in a rival pack," the woman said, her nostrils flaring. "Then he killed the bastard."

"Huh." With a frown, he pointed at the second elder with a bushy gray beard and an untamed mustache. "Did the same thing happen to you?"

"I merely don't like you." He shook his head, then looked at the alpha. "And I can't understand why we're sittin' down with outsiders when the Glimmering is so close."

"It ain't close enough that we don't have time for this." Reggie nodded at the older man. "And you know that."

"We could be out there lookin' for him, Reggie—"

"No, we'd still be here watchin' the challengers rip each other apart with their bare hands. Bill and Rex weren't nowhere near done when this dwarf showed up."

"What?" Rex raised his head and stared at the shifters. "Who's Bill?"

"Yeah, and when did you get hands, bro?" Luther stopped licking himself to look slowly at his brother. "Where are you keeping them?"

The bounty hunter cleared his throat and nodded at the larger hound. "I have a Rex of my own."

"Uh-huh." Reggie raised an eyebrow at the hound. "Good name."

"Better on a dog than a shifter," Bernard mumbled.

The bearded elder who didn't like Johnny slapped a hand on the floor and snarled as he leaned across the circle. "You ain't got no right to talk him down like that."

"Sure I do. The whole damn pack will be talkin' him down if we don't find Magnus in time."

"He's givin' his life—"

"No, he ain't." Bernard rolled his eyes. "You shut your yammerin' jaw."

"I'll rip yours right off your scabby old face, you back-stabbin'—"

Johnny sat calmly and his gaze shifted to each of the elders as they proceeded to insult the others. *No wonder everyone outside's all tense. They have a shitty location in the swamp, shitty houses, and their top guys can't agree on shit.*

The snarling, high-intensity debate to nowhere continued for another minute before it finally subsided. Bernard turned away from the bearded shifter and smirked. The other guy seethed but didn't get up or try to keep things rolling.

Reggie asked calmly, "Is that it?"

"We're done." Bernard gestured for the alpha to continue.

"Tensions are high and there are too many damn distractions." The alpha looked at Johnny and shook his head. "We need Magnus. Are you truly in the business of findin' magicals?"

"A hundred percent." The dwarf stuck his thumb out toward Lisa. "We both are."

"Dwarf and Light Elf in it together, huh?" The man smirked. "That oughtta work as well as your smaller dog and that bitch lyin' next to ya."

"Excuse me?" Lisa raised her eyebrows. "No one asked for your opinion on anything but your missing pack member. So unless it has anything to do with that, keep it yourself."

Bernard burst out laughing. "She barks as much as ours do, eh, Reggie?"

The alpha sniggered.

"Yeah, I bite too. Watch it."

Johnny twisted slightly to shoot her a smirk over his shoulder that she didn't notice, but he made sure to wipe it off his face when he turned to the shifters again. "So do you have a lead on your...bearer's kidnapper, or am I workin' from scratch?"

"Johnny." Lisa leaned forward toward him. "This feels very much like getting sidetracked."

"They're connected, darlin'."

"Because they went missing on the same day and he happens to be a shifter everyone wants? No one here knows who she is."

"Well, it's a good case, ain't it?"

"Yeah." She glanced briefly at the shifters. "Don't take it for a bottle of whiskey this time, huh? It's worth far more than that."

"Uh-huh." When he turned toward the shifters, they were all staring at him. *And they heard every word a couple of non-shifters whispered to each other. You can't get a lick of privacy with shifters.*

"We think it's the other pack in the area," Reggie said without being prompted. "I'm very sure they took Magnus."

"Other pack?" Johnny snorted. "I would have heard of 'em."

"They're as slippery as all get-out, dwarf." Bernard's smile had faded completely, and his missing eye now made him look like a creature from a ghost story. "It ain't your place to keep an eye on other packs. That's ours. And this one's fairly new."

"It could have been other shifters from a different pack," Lisa suggested. "Why does it have to be someone down here?"

"We ain't had a whiff of any new shifters in our territory." Reggie's eyes narrowed and the corner of his mouth flicked up when he turned toward Johnny. "'Cept for that little pup of yours. Amanda, right?"

"We ain't talkin' about the kid." Johnny brandished a warning finger at the alpha. "Not now and not ever. Got it?"

"Sure. She's outta your hair anyway. Ain't that right?"

"More like outta your reach."

"This new pack's been squeezin' on our territory since they moved in," Bernard added. "Hard. We kept 'em at bay but they went too far with this."

"Bastards." That came from the woman elder and her blue eyes flashed with hatred.

"Damn fancy bastards." The bearded elder nodded. They could all finally agree on something.

Johnny cleared his throat. "Okay, I think I'm missin' somethin' 'cause I ain't never heard of a fancy shifter pack."

"It ain't natural." Bernard hawked and spat. "They came in from the city with all their damn—"

"The city?" The dwarf's hands balled into fists.

"Tampa. They brought in all their shit like they was fixin' to build some kinda condos or some shit." The bearded elder snarled. "Tryin' to take over the swamp with all their high-end city gimmicks."

"That ain't why the Glades are here," Johnny seethed.

Lisa noticed his beard quivering against his chest and prepared herself silently for whatever happened next.

"That's what we're sayin'."

"The last I heard," Reggie added and shook his head, "they were tryin' to build up some kinda business on top of it—a damn tourist site out on the edge of—"

"Oh, fuck no!" Johnny pounded a fist on the floor and pushed to his feet. "I ain't sittin' around while some fancy-ass shifters try to take over my swamp."

Reggie stood quickly, and the others followed as fast as they could—slow for shifters by still spry for their age by human standards. "And they have Magnus."

"Then we're gettin' your special whatever back and pushin' those assholes out."

The woman elder grinned and her teeth flashed in the overhead lights. "I like this dwarf."

"Like me, don't like me. I don't give a shit." Johnny turned and stormed toward the door. "City folk got no business comin' here and claimin' what ain't theirs."

He pounded a fist against the crooked door and almost broke it off its hinges. Without looking back, he took the stairs two at a time and disappeared.

Lisa was the last to stand, even after the hounds and Boots, and for a moment, the room was incredibly silent. She gazed at the shifters, who all grinned viciously now at the thought of storming another pack's den. "I'm gonna go talk to him for a minute."

No one replied, so she turned and hurried across the room, her back tinging under five shifters' gazes. "Boys. Boots. Outside."

"Hey, we don't take orders from her." Luther looked at his brother. "Do we?"

"Well, Johnny didn't tell us to come with."

"He didn't tell us to stay either."

"Better run after your master, doggies." Reggie leaned toward the hounds and Boots uttered a low growl. "We're fixin' to head out."

"Yeah, let's go."

All three dogs hurried out the door.

"Hey, Johnny! Wait up!"

"You can't leave us in there with those guys. They can hear us."

Reggie placed a hand on Bernard's shoulder as he stared through the open door. "Call a gathering in five minutes. That muddy dwarf's gonna need some company."

CHAPTER ELEVEN

"Johnny, wait." Lisa jogged across the dirt to catch up with the irate dwarf. "Are you sure this is—"

"The best idea? Damn straight I'm sure."

She was acutely aware of all the shifters watching them as they hurried out of the den's half-circle of buildings. "This is getting very deep into shifter politics—which I wasn't even sure existed until about two minutes ago."

"This is bigger. No way in hell am I gonna stand by and let some too-good-for-the-city assholes swoop in and turn these swamps into a goddamn tourist trap because they think it'll be good for 'em."

"You don't know—"

"Oh, yes I do. No one moves here from the city with anythin' in mind other than takin' what ain't theirs."

They reached Sheila as all three hounds raced after them across the compound, and Johnny jerked the Jeep's back door open.

"Isn't that kind of what you did, though?"

"What?" Johnny whirled to scowl at her.

"Came in from the city?"

"Darlin', I'm from right here. My swamps. My home. And it ain't for sale, no matter how many highfalutin magicals roll through. They already took Magnus. They ain't takin' my peace of mind." He leaned far forward over the back of his vehicle and fiddled with a hinged latch to pry away an entire section of the plastic floor.

"These shifters don't have any proof of who took him, Johnny. They only—" Lisa stepped aside when the plastic panel hurtled out of the Jeep and landed in the dirt with a thump. "They only want to find their guy, and this is simply another excuse for shifters to start a territory war. That's what they do."

"Well, I'm startin' a territory war too, then." He hauled a thick metal cannon out of Sheila's secret compartment and turned to face her.

"What the hell is that?" She studied it with wary curiosity. "It's almost as big as you."

"Naw. This is the little one." He smirked. "It hurts like a bitch, though."

"Don't tell me you've accidentally fired that at yourself."

He frowned at her. "I meant to fire."

"Oh, good. I think firing missiles at the new kids on the block should be a last resort." Lisa stepped back with wide eyes when he punched the automatic ejection button he'd rigged inside the hidden compartment at the edge of Sheila's open back door. A low whine came from the Jeep before a massive contraption that looked like a nightmare-sized version of one of his spy-bugs unfolded from its hiding place.

The giant cannon clanged against the vehicle's frame before Johnny hefted it and fastened it securely to the weapons mount that protruded from the compartment. He tightened the clamps around the cannon, pulled a foot-long lever on the side of the mount that creaked and clicked before it lodged into position, and gave the weapon a heavy slap.

The swiveling mount turned with a faster series of clicks and the cannon's wide barrel swung three hundred and sixty degrees. When it passed Lisa, she ducked and scurried back. "Or maybe the last resort."

"What, this?" The dwarf held his hand out and the large barrel swung gently into his open palm before it slowed to a halt. He gave it a loving pat. "This is the fun part, darlin'."

"This looks like domestic terrorism."

He scoffed and closed Sheila's back door. It clicked shut three inches below the aiming swivel of the cannon. "The only terrorism I see is what those city shifters are fixin' to do with the Glades."

"And you think you're the one to stop them. With a cannon?"

"Damn straight. And in a territory war like this, if that's what we're callin' it, you gotta put your feelings aside to get the job done." A loud metal bell clanged at the far end of the compound and the pack's shifters responded immediately. They emerged from their huts and hurried to join the gathering at the center of their den.

Johnny counted six naked children this time, all of them running through the adults and completely unaware of the fact that they were most likely the only magicals who could get away with running around unclothed. He scratched his face and frowned at the quickly growing gathering. "Even my feelings about the shifters found down in the swamps."

Lisa folded her arms. "Oh, so the city pack changed your mind about this one, huh?"

"Maybe." He cleared his throat and took a few steps toward the huge ring of the compound. "Maybe these fellas ain't as bad as I thought."

"They were beating each other senseless when we got here."

"Yep. And I wrestled a wolf. Times change, darlin'." He pointed at her. "But you know what ain't changed? The swamp belongs to the folks who know what to do with it. It ain't here to be snatched up and built on and turned all kinds of fancy ways to draw in money and attention and...tourists." He all but spat the last word out. "If the Glades go up like the rest of the damn cities on this planet, Earth ain't even gonna make it another hundred years. Hell, maybe not even fifty."

Lisa stared at him, then cracked a small smile and turned beside him to face the gathering pack. "I had no idea you were such an environmentalist."

"When it's my environment? You bet."

"We looked everywhere, Johnny." The hounds trotted toward their master, Boots close on their heels.

"Sniffed everywhere too." Luther snorted and shook his head. "I smelled things I'll never forget. Do you know where shifters keep their kills, Johnny?"

"No, and I don't wanna."

Rex sat at his master's side and watched the gathering. "Hey, you think they're talking about us?"

"Looks like they're figuring out what they're trying to do with us," Luther added.

From where he stood on the poorly built stage attached to the pavilion, Reggie gazed over the heads of his pack and nodded at the dwarf. Johnny returned the nod and folded his arms. "That's the point, boys. 'Cause whatever it is, we're doin' it with them too."

Reggie spread his arms expansively and his voice carried with surprising clarity across the compound. "It's been six days. We ain't found Magnus yet, even with the Glimmering so close. But we know where he is."

A ripple of surprised whispers passed through the pack.

"That new band of shifters calls themselves a pack out east has him. And now we have a little extra power behind us to get him out."

"Is he alive?" It was Bill, one of the shifters who'd attempted to beat the other inside the main building.

"As far as we know, he is. If he ain't when we get there, that pack's goin' down for good."

A few shifters shouted in agreement and thrust their fists in the air.

"What about the Glimmering?" a young woman asked. "It's days away, and we ain't got no bearer to take up the fang."

The rest of the pack responded with muttered agreement.

"The challenge has been called off for now," their alpha continued. "We ain't choosin' a bearer until we know we ain't got no other choice."

"Man, fuck this." The shifter Rex who'd fought with Bill inside chucked aside the wadded rag he'd held to his still-bleeding nose and glared at the stage. "I would have won that fight, and you know it."

"It don't matter now, brother. You hang tight here, nice and safe, and we'll go get Magnus back. Keep an eye on the pups, huh?"

A few shifters chuckled and jostled the disgruntled Rex. He snarled at them and stormed away from the gathering before he vanished into one of the shacks.

Reggie ignored the other shifter's attitude and continued with his announcement. "I need three more to step up. I'm headin' out to give these assholes a piece of my mind, but I ain't goin' alone. Who's comin'?"

A man with half his face marred by burn scars stepped forward. "I'll go."

The alpha nodded. "You always do, Baron."

"We need Magnus." Another man with mismatched eyes—one green and one gray—stepped forward beside Baron. "I'd rather have him than another challenger."

"Right there with you." Reggie peered over the heads of his pack. "Baron, Mikey, and who else?"

Hyla nudged her elbow into Bill's side. "Get up there."

"What?"

"You're goin' with them."

"Woman, I had my brains beat outta me not twenty minutes ago. I ain't—"

With a snarl, the shifter woman shoved past him, jostled him roughly on the shoulder, and went to join the others. Reggie looked at her in surprise. "Ain't no one else steppin' up. So I will."

The alpha shrugged. "I never said you can't hold your own in a fight. So let's get these bastards."

The pack snarled and howled with human voices, grasped the three volunteers by the shoulders, and jostled them in encouragement. Baron and Mikey endured it as they stared at their alpha, but Hyla slapped the hands away and snarled at anyone who touched her or even seemed to consider it.

"We run here!" Reggie shouted and pumped a fist in the air. "There ain't no one takin' our territory or our people." He threw his head back and uttered a prolonged howl with the rest of the pack.

Lisa leaned toward Johnny and muttered, "Do you know anything about shifter ceremonies?"

"A little."

"So that part about taking up the fang…"

"I have no idea." He scoffed. "I told the kid this and I'll tell you too, darlin'. The shifters down here ain't always right in the head. Maybe never. Whatever they need their missin' shifter for, I don't give a rats ass about it."

"I know. You merely want to keep the tourists out of the Everglades."

"Damn right I do." he slid his dark sunglasses down from his mud-caked hair and nodded. "It's on."

CHAPTER TWELVE

Unfortunately, the mission didn't start immediately or for the next forty-five minutes.

Johnny leaned back against Sheila's rear tire, his ankles crossed and arms folded, as the Everglades shifter pack did whatever they were doing that required so much time.

Lisa sat in the passenger seat with one arm slung over the frame through the pane-less window. "What are they doing?"

He grunted. "I have no idea. But if they ain't out here ready to split in the next ten minutes, I'm goin' on my own."

"Oh, you're ready to take on an entire pack from Tampa, huh?"

"Darlin', we took this pack on by our lonesome and it turned out damn okay, don'tcha think?"

"Beyond all the waiting? Sure."

"Besides, a city pack like those yuppies can't stand up to what we have ready for 'em. Ain't that right, boys?"

There was no reply.

"Boys?" Johnny yanked his sunglasses off and straightened from his slouch against the Jeep's tire. "Rex! Luther!" At his piercing whistle, the hounds returned into the range of their master's hearing.

"Time to go, Johnny?" Luther darted across the open circle of the compound and barked, then spun and lowered his head to the ground, his rear end high and tail wagging furiously. "I don't mind staying."

Two small naked children darted out from between the shacks after him. The younger one couldn't have been much older than two and toddled on his pudgy legs with his arms outstretched toward the hound.

Luther yipped again and raced away.

"Johnny! Johnny!" Rex appeared between buildings and ran toward his master and the huge red Jeep. His eyes were wide, and he kept looking over his shoulder at the three wolf pups bounding after him, close on his heels. "Whenever you're ready, Johnny. We can totally go. I'm ready."

Lisa chuckled at the sight of one terrified coonhound trying to escape admittedly cute pups and the other playing Chase the Hound with naked kids. "This might be the weirdest situation we've found ourselves in."

"Maybe. With a few exceptions."

She leaned out the window and looked at him with a raised eyebrow. "You know what? I don't even wanna know."

Johnny patted Boots' head. She lay beside him in the shade cast by the Jeep and panted with a canine smile. "Heelers are a good breed, ain't they, girl? You bet."

"You know, she doesn't look nearly as scared anymore," Lisa commented.

"'Course she ain't. She had some time to sit back and relax, knowin' she's safe and don't have to be alone anymore. Until we find Nina, that's how it's gonna be."

Rex darted around one of the shacks and raced toward his master. "She doesn't wanna be closer to Luther than she has to—ah! Get it off."

One of the wolf pups had clamped her tiny jaws around the hound's ankle and now snarled and whipped her head from side to side.

"You—jeez! Those teeth! I'm not a chew toy, you runty little…"

"Aw, she's so cute." Luther slowed beside his brother and sniffed the pup's backside. "What's your name?"

"Dude, can we not play fun hound friend while I'm being eaten alive? Shit! Let go!"

The small hound grasped the little wolf by the scruff of her neck and she immediately released Rex's ankle. He dropped her into the dirt and laughed. "I like you."

"You like everyone. She didn't bite your leg."

The naked kids finally reached Luther's side and they laughed and shrieked when he rolled over in the dirt and let them climb on his belly. "You know what, bro? Shifters aren't so bad. We already knew Johnny's pup was cool, but I thought maybe she was the exception—ah! Ah-ha! That tickles. What are you—"

He squirmed frantically and laughed and panted as the wolf pups climbed on top of him beside the kids in human form.

"Great. You can have 'em." Rex snorted and moved toward Johnny and Boots.

"Hey. Hey, Rex!" Luther turned his head to look upside down at his brother, his tongue lolling from his mouth. "Doggie pile. Get it?"

The small wolves growled playfully and pawed at the hound's belly, which made him laugh and squirm even more.

"Rex! I said—ah! Okay, now that hurts. Hey. Little gray guy. Tell your friend to—"

The wolf cubs yipped and growled, the small kids laughed, and Luther lay perfectly still.

"What? What do you mean you're all cousins? Uh…I gotta go." He rolled quickly and stood, scattering naked kids and fluff-ball wolf pups before he trotted toward Sheila. "Johnny. Hey, Johnny."

The dwarf grunted.

"Did you know everyone in this place is related?"

"That's what I heard."

"Oh, ew. Rex, that's like if you and our mom—"

"We don't even know our mom."

"Yeah, but they know theirs."

"That's enough, boys." The dwarf snapped his fingers. Both hounds sat, and Boots lifted her head to rest it on the dwarf's lap for more petting. He couldn't help but oblige with a small chuckle.

"Seriously?" Luther slumped on the ground a few feet away from them. "You like him?"

The Heeler growled softly.

"Yeah, okay. I can take a hint."

"Johnny, weren't we supposed to be doing something by now?" Rex asked.

"Uh-huh."

"So why aren't we—"

"All right. Y'all need to hush up for a minute, understand? Lie down and chill out."

"I don't know, Johnny." Luther whined as he watched the kids and their wolf cousins wrestling each other in the dirt. "Maybe we should get out while we can. I think—wait. What's that?"

Both hounds cocked their heads, and Boots raised hers from Johnny's lap to do the same.

"What?" he asked.

"Lots of rumbling, Johnny."

"Like a big old…huh. Like Sheila."

"Lots of Sheilas."

"Dozens."

Johnny frowned and sat straighter. "There's only one Sheila, boys."

"Yeah, but this one's—"

The rumbling grew loud enough for the two investigators to

hear too as two shifters hauled a massive garage door open on the second large outbuilding at the back of the compound. The bounty hunter grinned and pushed to his feet. "Finally."

Two huge ATVs rolled slowly out of the garage and their engines roared and sputtered occasionally. The tires were massive and lifted the vehicles to a ridiculous height, but it was necessary when the undercarriage of each had been fitted with dangling tanks suspended freely by levered pulleys. The tanks rocked and sloshed beneath the ATVs as they crawled across the compound toward Johnny and his crew.

"What are those supposed to be?" Lisa muttered.

"It looks like they have their own Sheilas. I have no idea why it took so long."

When the ATVs crawled to a stop in front of the bounty hunter, he realized why. Both vehicles had been fitted with an astonishing number of weapons and ammunition—pistols, rifles, a grenade launcher, and something that looked like a jet pack nestled among all of it in each of the ATVs. Johnny gave it all an appraising nod. "Okay."

"Are you ready to ride, dwarf?" Reggie asked from behind the wheel of the first vehicle.

"Is that even a real question?"

"I thought so." The alpha turned and leaned through the window to shout at the compound. "Aldo!"

The giant man with the ponytail—whose scowl hadn't vanished since the bounty hunter had almost choked him—turned away from a conversation with a group of his pack members and nodded at Reggie.

"Get on up here." The pack leader turned toward Johnny with a smirk. "Does your back seat work?"

The dwarf stared cautiously at him. "It depends on why you're askin'."

"We need a fifth. Aldo's it."

Johnny studied each of the ATVs—Reggie and Baron in the

first, Mikey behind the wheel of the second with Hyla in the passenger seat beside him. "I ain't runnin' a taxi service."

"You are today, dwarf, if you wanna find that missin' elf of yours."

Aldo rounded the alpha's vehicle and gazed expectantly at the war party about to leave the den.

"You're ridin' with the dwarf." Reggie clapped the huge shifter on the back, turned the wheel, and rolled the ATV toward the dirt road.

Johnny looked at the guy he'd ridden as a wolf and pressed his lips together. Aldo didn't look any happier. "Come on, boys. We're headin' out."

"All right!"

"Hey, Johnny. Boots says she wants to stay in the Jeep."

"That's fine." He opened the back door and gestured for all three hounds to get in as he narrowed his eyes at Aldo.

"Uh...Johnny?"

"What?"

"There's a giant gun in the back."

"And it ain't on, so get up."

Luther leapt first and thunked his head against the base of the gun mount before he skittered around it. Rex and Boots followed far more nimbly and the back door shut with a bang. Johnny strode to the driver's door.

"Later, wolfy." Luther yipped, his tone smug. "I guess you'll have to wait for the next pack raid to—"

Aldo moved to the rear passenger-side door and glared at Luther. The hound lowered his head and shuffled back until he bumped against the gun mount. "Johnny. Johnny? He's heading to the Jeep."

Sheila's engine started, and the bounty hunter kept his eye on the massive shifter through the rearview mirror. *No wonder shifters don't make friends outside their pack. We ain't makin' nice and bein' buddies after this.*

Aldo slid into the passenger seat and slammed the door shut behind him.

"Watch it," the dwarf growled.

The shifter leaned against the door and said nothing.

"Johnny." Rex sniffed the back of Aldo's neck. "Why are we —hey!"

"Back off," the man growled.

Both hounds moved hastily toward the opposite side of the Jeep as much as they could given the giant gun mount and the swinging cannon protruding from the middle.

"You better say thank you," Rex whispered. "For the ride."

"Yeah, Johnny doesn't let just anyone in this thing. You have to earn it."

The bounty hunter accelerated and turned a wide circle at the end of the road before he set off after Reggie and his two war-ATVs.

It's time to smoke out the tourists. Finally.

CHAPTER THIRTEEN

Reggie led them down a series of winding, twisty roads almost as muddy as the entrance to his pack's den. Fortunately, the ATVs were loaded enough that the massive tires flattened most of the bumps, and Johnny followed closely behind the second vehicle, keeping Sheila in line with the massive treads that packed the mud.

Lisa leaned toward him and had to shout over the roar of the other engines. "Do you know where we're going?"

He glanced in the rearview mirror at Aldo, but the shifter occupied himself by glaring through the window. His massive shoulders jostled over every bump in the road. "I don't even know where we are now, darlin'."

"What?"

"I said—"

"No, no. I heard you." She braced herself with a hand on Sheila's frame over one particularly rough bump and closed her eyes. "You do know how to get us out again, right?"

Johnny smirked at her. "You sure are pickin' out all the negatives today, ain'tcha?"

"Making sure we have a backup plan isn't negative, Johnny. It's necessary."

"We'll be fine. I don't plan on leavin' wherever we're goin' without Magnus, Nina, and both those hunks of metal in front of us."

She gazed at the back of the vehicle in front of them and her eyes widened. "Where will we put them?"

He shrugged. "We can stick 'em in the back. The big guy can ride on top—one of theirs, though. Not Sheila."

Rex and Luther poked their heads out of opposite sides of the Jeep's rear windows and their ears flapped and tongues lolled. "Never been out here before, Johnny."

"Looks like a good place for secret stuff, ya know? Hidden. Out of the way of everyone and everything. No one bothering you with stupid stuff."

"Hey, Johnny." Luther licked his muzzle before his tongue fell out again. "You should get a place like this."

The bounty hunter glanced briefly at his hounds in the rearview mirror and shook his head.

The vehicles rounded the bend beneath a particularly thickly wooded area, and when they straightened out again, the bumps in the unpaved roads suddenly gave way to smooth asphalt. Johnny frowned and peered through the opening in the trees up ahead. They were on another stretch of actual highway now, and he saw the sign for Marco Island as they passed it.

Huh. The damn shifters made their own back roads through the swamp. Not bad.

The wind whipped through Sheila's open frame, and Lisa stared straight ahead when two cars passed them on the two-lane highway. "No one said we were going out in public."

"It won't be public soon enough, darlin'. You have nothin' to worry about."

"Johnny, you're driving down the highway with a cannon mounted in the back of your Jeep for everyone to see." She pointed at the back of the ATV in front of them. "And none of those guns are especially hidden."

"Ain't no one lookin' for trouble out here. If folks ain't part of it, they don't want to be part of it and they'll mind their own business."

She closed her eyes and rested her head against the seat. "I think I'm finally seeing the upside to this new business plan of yours."

"Oh, yeah?" He gave her a crooked smile.

"If this were a federal case, Johnny, I'd lose my job."

"Now you're gettin' it. It's a damn good thing it ain't a federal case."

"Yeah." A surprised laugh escaped her. "A damn good thing."

The ATVs turned quickly onto a side road on the left and they plunged between the trees again. They wove down the road with the swamp and waterlogged banks growing farther away on either side before they shrank in with the curves of various rivers and tributaries around them.

After another twenty minutes, Reggie and Mikey rolled the growling ATVs to a stop and cut the engines. The alpha leapt out of his vehicle and walked down the side until he saw Johnny and nodded. "It's safe to leave 'em here. We're walkin' in."

"Oh." The bounty hunter turned to look at the mounted cannon and scowled. "Are you sure? 'Cause I got this—"

"We're goin' in quiet, dwarf. If that ain't good enough for you, feel free to wait in the car."

Johnny jerked open the door and hopped out, muttering, "It's been too damn long since I used that."

Lisa got out and stared at the four shifters who dug in their vehicles to sling ammunition and utility belts on and hang rifle straps around their necks and shoulders. Aldo went to join his pack members and hauled a massive grenade launcher from the back of one ATV before he settled it over his shoulder.

"Oh, sure." Johnny threw his hands in the air and let them slap against his thighs. "He gets a big one."

Shaking his head, he opened the back door to let the dogs out, then rummaged through the lockbox to shove two handfuls of explosive beads into his pockets. After that came a tiny pistol that looked more like a miniature metal toy than a real weapon. When he shut the trunk and slid the pistol into the back pocket of his jeans, Lisa raised an eyebrow. "In your pocket, Johnny?"

"It ain't that kinda weapon, darlin'."

"Then please tell me what it is so I don't have to worry about you shooting yourself in the ass."

He snorted and patted his bulging back pocket. "That would never happen. I call this here the Whistle."

"Huh."

"Yeah, huh.

"Is there anything I need to know about it before you end up using it at the last second?"

"Only that, darlin'. It's a secret weapon. Literally and figuratively. If I do end up usin' it, you and I are the only ones who don't have to worry about it."

"That honestly doesn't make me feel better."

"Come on." He nodded toward the shifters. "I can't believe I'm sayin' it, but we're followin' their lead."

She drew her service pistol and held it at the ready as the group pushed through the thick foliage, following whatever trail Reggie and his shifters seemed to have found.

Luther looked over his shoulder to where Boots trotted at the very back of the procession, her head low as she peered through the trees. "Hey, I thought you wanted to stay in the Jeep. Oh, right, right. Good idea—wait. You do know how to fight, don't you?"

"Them dogs need to can it, dwarf," Aldo snapped. "They are the noisiest animals I ever heard."

"Oh, this is nothing," Luther replied happily.

"Yeah," Rex added, "you should hear him when he—"

Johnny snapped his fingers. "Quiet, boys."

They moved half a mile through the thick, draping tree branches, then broke through without warning into an open, paved parking lot in the middle of nowhere.

Small, well-kept temporary houses had been built along the outskirts of the parking lot, complete with potted plants on the covered front porches. Some even had large outdoor fans spinning slowly in the muggy heat. In the center of the space was a massive, circular covered pavilion with a podium and built-in seats.

At the far end behind the neat little houses were two portable worksite trailers, one with the door propped open. Two shifters were having a calm conversation within. The women laughed at some joke together and their voices rang high across the paved lot. Someone had hooked up a speaker system in the pavilion and some kind of light instrumental composition floated around the den.

This ain't a shifter den. This is Wanna Be Perfect Town.

No one noticed the five shifters, three dogs, a half-Light Elf, and one explosively armed dwarf.

"Are you sure this is the right place?" Lisa whispered.

"See what I mean?" Reggie snarled. "All their fancy shit. It don't belong down here."

A kid from the rival pack was out taking a spin on his bike. The paint glinted bright blue in the sunlight, and he rang the little bell attached to the handlebar. He skidded to a halt when he saw the intruders standing inside the ring of foliage around the den and stared at them.

"Shit." Johnny turned toward Reggie's shifters when the sound of their raised weapons cut through the silence. "Put those away. It's a damn kid."

"Dad!" the boy shouted. "Dad! Someone is here. With guns!" He kicked off the ground and raced away, looking over his shoulder as he pedaled furiously around the huge lot to disappear behind the pavilion.

Almost instantly, the city shifters stepped out of their tidy little temporary homes and everyone turned to face the intruders. Every single one of them held some kind of weapon.

Johnny grimaced and nodded slowly. "Great. It's a hell of a way to make an entrance, Reggie."

"I told you they were up to no good. Look at this shit."

"I hate it." With a grunt, Johnny stepped completely out of the foliage and scanned the wary gazes of the new pack. "Who's in charge here?"

A large woman in a flowing cotton dress appeared from behind the pavilion and hurried toward them. "You're not welcome here. However you found us, get out. Right now."

"Naw, see, that's where you have things all wrong." Johnny pointed at her. "Ya'll and your fancy buildings and all that shitty music ain't welcome here. That's the problem."

"William!" the woman shouted, her lips pressed together in a firm line. "We have—"

"I see them, Barbara." The man who stepped around the pavilion put a hand on her shoulder and nodded. "I'll take care of this."

He was tall and broad-shouldered and fairly average-looking in every way. The city pack's alpha could have been any other regular guy except for the brand scar in the shape of a claw that peeked from beneath the unbuttoned collar of his lightweight shirt. "Did you folks get lost or something?"

"We know these swamps better than you ever will," Reggie snarled. "They're ours."

"I see." William studied them calmly. "And you're so desperate that you've added a dwarf and an Elf to your pack. Is that it?"

"Where's Magnus?" Hyla snarled. "We know you took him."

"Hmm. Magnus. Magnus…" The city alpha turned to shout to the rest of his pack. "Anyone know a Magnus?"

His shifters said nothing and didn't even shake their heads.

"Well, I guess we can't help you there." William shrugged. "Now, it's time to get off our property before we force you off—"

"Hand him over." Aldo snarled. "And we won't rip you to pieces."

The man threw his head back and laughed heartily. "I'd like to see that very much."

"Okay." Aldo shifted in the blink of an eye and lunged forward to thrust him back with his forepaws. The city alpha shifted before his back touched the pavement and he twisted to move out from under the massive, shaggy black body. In the next moment, the wolves were at each other's throats.

"Sniff 'em out, boys!" Johnny shouted as he snatched two exploding disks from his belt.

The hounds bounded away from their master, baying wildly as they darted between the city pack members who shifted on their front doorsteps.

Boots whimpered and backed into the trees.

"Johnny!" Lisa tried to catch his arm, but the dwarf was already racing into the fray, fueled by his overprotective rage aimed at anything that threatened his swamp.

The local shifters surged across the pavement, shed their clothes, and landed on fur-covered paws before they spun toward the closest city wolf. Teeth and claws flashed everywhere, and the city pack members who hadn't changed their forms tried to aim their weapons at the intruders instead.

Lisa raised her service pistol toward a woman taking aim at Johnny from her front porch and fired two warning rounds into the white posts of the porch railing. "Put it down!"

The woman snarled at her, dropped her pistol, and shifted as she leapt from the stairs. Instead of joining the fray, she targeted Agent Breyer instead.

Lisa's first fireball caught the dirty-white wolf in the shoulder and knocked her sideways. She yelped and shook herself and as soon as she crouched to leap at the Light Elf again, Luther launched himself at her with a snarl and drove her onto her back. They scrambled on the pavement, snapping and snarling.

Rex darted around another house on the outskirts of the den, then spun to face the old, spindly wolf missing patches of fur who'd followed him. "Tell me where you're keeping them!" The old wolf snarled and lunged at the hound, who skittered out of the way and snapped at the magical's hind leg. "You can't kidnap whoever you want."

One of Johnny's explosive disks detonated at the front of the pavilion and scattered splintered wood in all directions. The music cut off with a squeal from the speakers beyond the blast range, and the dwarf nodded. "Fuck that elevator music."

"Johnny, look out!" Lisa shouted and raised her pistol.

Barbara was as big a wolf as she was a woman, and she cast a huge shadow over him when she pounced. He sidestepped her attack and crouched at the ready as she whirled and snarled at him. "Bring it. I already brought one wolf down with my bare hands today, lady. It's simply another walk in the—oof!"

He was flung sideways when a young, skinny gray wolf barreled into him. The dwarf rolled across the asphalt and the small wolf whined and backed away before he darted through the fighting.

"Hey!" Lisa shouted and ran toward her partner. "This isn't helping."

"I don't know, darlin'. It makes me feel a helluva lot better." Rolling his shoulders, he found another wolf to brawl with and hurried after him.

"Johnny!" Lisa gazed at the chaos and gritted her teeth. *We'll never find those two if this keeps going.*

She raised her gun and fired it twice into the air. It didn't make a dent in the massive pack-against-pack brawl that also included a dwarf bounty hunter and two coonhounds.

"Damnit." Frustrated, she turned in a circle, looking for something that might get everyone's attention. Her gaze landed on the tiny pistol that had fallen out of Johnny's pocket. The Whistle, he'd called it.

She darted toward it and stopped to blast a fireball at a red-brown wolf who stalked behind Johnny and prepared to strike. Her attack caught him in the side and the wolf whirled to snarl at her.

Lisa scrambled toward the damn Whistle and snatched it up as the red-brown wolf reached a good running speed toward her. She swept her arm up and pointed the tiny pistol at the wolf, meaning to aim for his shoulder or leg or something that wouldn't kill him outright. Then, she pulled the trigger.

Instead of the familiar jolt of release and echoing crack of a fired weapon, there was…nothing.

The wolf dropped and slid toward her, his eyes clenched tightly shut. He writhed on the ground, flipped onto his feet, and bolted away from her, yelping.

"What?" She studied the tiny gun, then lifted it into the air and squeezed the trigger again without letting up.

Two dozen howls of pain filled the air, rising from shifter throats in both wolf and human form. Those who hadn't shifted screamed in agony and clamped their hands over their ears or dropped to their knees or both. The wolves' howls disintegrated into squeals of agony, and they tried to scurry away from the source without knowing what it was. Most of them fell or ran headlong into the sides of buildings.

Johnny backed away from the muscular wolf he'd been about to tussle with—who now wobbled precariously on his feet, growled furiously, and shook his head. The dwarf turned to see Lisa with the Whistle pointed straight in the air. "Hey, hey! Easy with that."

She released the trigger and looked at him in exasperation. "Your secret weapon? A high-frequency gun?"

"It's convenient in a shifter war, don'tcha think. Gimme that."

The agent pulled the tiny weapon out of his reach and shook her head. "I think I'll hang onto it in case you lose yourself to battle rage again."

He snorted. "That ain't—"

The groans of residual pain and relief pulled him away, and they both looked over the paved city-pack den. Every single shifter had returned to their human form. Most of them sprawled on the ground and rolled onto their backs to take deep breaths and recover from the damage. A few lay curled in tight balls.

One man hoisted himself up by his front porch railing and snarled when he saw the two of them standing there without a hint of discomfort. "What the hell was that?"

Lisa looked at him and shrugged. "The Whistle. Now everyone, listen up."

"Come on now, darlin.'" Johnny extended his hand toward her again. "Hand it over."

"Not until we know a flat-out battle is the only option left." She switched the tiny gun to her other hand to put it farther out of his reach and stepped forward to address both packs. Her calm was challenged somewhat by the need to force herself to ignore more naked bodies than she'd ever seen in one place. "I think we started this on the wrong foot. What do you think?"

Reggie grunted as he pushed up and glared at her. "That damn thing should be illegal is what I think."

"Yeah, well, it would be if anyone knew about it," Johnny snapped in response.

William helped one of his pack members to their feet, then ran his tongue over his top teeth. "What do you want?"

"That's what we were trying to get at." Lisa glanced at the local shifters who'd staged this entire disaster. "We're looking for the shifter Magnus and a Wood Elf named Nina. They're both missing."

"And you thought it was—" William staggered sideways and

pressed his fingers against his temple with a grimace. "You thought it was a good idea to come out here and attack us because you lost a few magicals?"

Lisa opened her mouth, paused, and sighed. "Well, it wasn't my idea."

"Where is he?" Mikey snarled.

"I don't know."

Reggie stormed toward William and thrust a finger toward the other alpha's face. "Y'all been pushin' your way through the swamp like a damn disease. Takin' whatever you want. Settin' up this...fake-ass den and tryin' to turn it into some kind of amusement park."

William scoffed. "What idiot told you that?"

"It don't matter. We know." The other local shifters nodded and glared at the city pack. "And we ain't gonna stand for it."

"We don't have what you want," a city shifter spat.

Low growls rose from human throats all over again.

Lisa thrust the Whistle into the air again and shouted, "Do I need to use this a second time?"

William turned quickly toward her with wide eyes. "I'd prefer it if you didn't. Please."

"Okay. Then..." She scanned the much nicer compound—with the exception of the massive crater blown out of the front of the pavilion—and shook her head. "Put your clothes on and we'll talk. All of you."

Grumbling to themselves and casting her wary glances, the shifters from both packs collected their clothing and exchanged various pieces with one another to get the right ones. Johnny folded his arms and sniffed. "All right. I admit I might have been a little caught up in all that."

"Yeah, maybe we should start with the more peaceful attention-grabber next time."

"Sure." He sighed and nodded. Then, he turned slowly toward her with a smirk.

"What?" she asked, completely deadpan.

"Well, I'd be lyin' if I said I didn't like it when you take charge."

"Oh, jeez." She rolled her eyes.

"What?" Johnny chuckled. "Wrong timin'?"

"Wrong time. Wrong place." She shoved the Whistle into her back pocket and raised her eyebrows at him. "Don't expect it with every case."

"Well, if they keep comin' in like this one…"

Shaking her head, she looked toward the now fully clothed shifters who had gathered in front of the damaged pavilion. "Come on."

CHAPTER FOURTEEN

"Right. Well then." William ran a hand through his light-brown hair and cleared his throat. "I guess you were the one who officially called this meeting, Ms...."

"Lisa." She pointed beside her. "This is Johnny. And the local pack who's missing their bearer and thinks you're stepping on their toes."

The city alpha's green eyes widened. "How did you lose your bearer?"

"We didn't lose him," Reggie snarled. "Someone took him."

"Isn't it kind of hard to take a bearer like the one you have?" Barbara asked. "Yeah, we've heard about what he can do."

"We don't know what happened," Mikey added. "But y'all been takin' more and more from us every day—"

"Taking from you?" a city shifter interjected. "Exactly what do you think we're taking?"

"Our territory. Our dignity."

William raised his chin. "No, I'm very sure that's completely your own fault—"

"You can't simply roll in somewhere you don't belong with all your fancy new buildin' doohickeys and the crummy music and all this…fake," Baron snapped.

"Well, we sure as hell didn't take your bearer."

"Oh, yeah? Why don't we take a look around and see for ourselves—"

"Okay, I'm serious." Lisa took the Whistle from her back pocket again and brandished it in warning. Shifters on both sides ducked away from her and reached reflexively for their ears. "You know I'll use it. And I'm very tired of everyone misunderstanding each other because they're too focused on fighting instead. So let's not."

"Yeah, yeah. Sure." William raised both hands and gestured for her to lower the weapon. "But please, put it away."

Johnny gave her a sidelong glance but didn't say anything.

"So." She pocketed the whistle. "Whether or not your pack's responsible, we still need to find Magnus and Nina Williams, the local Wood Elf."

"We're not responsible," Barbara stated emphatically and folded her muscular arms.

"Y'all have proof of this?" Johnny asked.

Reggie's upper lip twitched. "That's the only way we'll take your word for it."

William opened his mouth to reply but the hounds trotted around the side of the pavilion and spoke before he could.

"Whoa. Johnny." Luther stumbled sideways, righted himself, and shook his head. "Did you hear that ringing a few minutes ago? I think it turned my tail inside out and made my guts fall off."

Following closely behind him in an off-kilter weave, Rex snorted. "And brained your scramble, apparently."

"Y'all okay?"

"Oh, sure, Johnny."

"Better than okay."

"Good thing we weren't closer to that noise. Probably

would've—" Rex sneezed and scrabbled to find his footing again when it threw him off balance. "Died. Anyway, we've been snorting around...snooting aboot...sniffing all...all..."

"Jeez." The bounty hunter sighed and rubbed his forehead. "Now it's both of them with the head problems."

"Naw, it'll wear off, Johnny." Luther sat and panted. "At least, it does for me."

"Tell him what we found, bro," Rex muttered and pawed at his snout.

"What did we find?"

"The smells."

"Oh, yeah. There's no scent of Nina or a shifter who doesn't belong here except for the ones with us. You know, they're much easier to notice here. These city wolfs are decent-smelling for shifters."

The members of both packs looked away from the addled hounds and at each other. William pointed at Luther. "Is that enough proof for you?"

Reggie snorted. "I don't know. I reckon them dogs might not be as trustworthy as you want 'em to be."

Luther whipped his head up. "Wait a minute."

"Trustworthiness ain't the issue," Johnny added. "He merely can't count." *And we'll leave it at that.* "If my hounds say there ain't a whiff of our missing magicals, then there ain't."

"Good." William nodded. "Have they picked up any scent while you guys have been blundering around through the Everglades attacking everyone you don't like?"

The dwarf scowled at him in warning. "Not yet. And it ain't everyone we don't like. Only the tourists."

"Which we aren't," Barbara pointed out. "We live here."

"Not for long."

"Hey!" Lisa leaned forward to give Hyla a warning glance.

The shifter woman flipped her off but stood down from another brewing fight.

"Too bad," William muttered.

"Y'all wanna keep fightin'?" Johnny glanced at all the shifters and spread his arms expansively. "Even after proof we ain't got no reason to?"

"I meant about your dogs and the cold trail." The shifter folded his arms and sighed. "We could've used some extra help from someone who might pick up on the one we can't seem to find either."

Johnny and Lisa exchanged a knowing glance before she asked, "You're missing someone too?"

The city alpha nodded gravely. "For almost eight days now."

Baron narrowed his eyes. "That's about when Magnus disappeared."

"And Nina," Johnny added.

Lisa looked at them with wide eyes. "Okay, if any of you don't believe by now that this is more than pack rivalries in the middle of nowhere, I don't think we can help any of you."

"Naw…" Reggie studied the other alpha reluctantly and gritted his teeth. "I guess it ain't none of y'all's fault."

"Oh, good. We finally agree."

Johnny grunted. "So what now?"

William inclined his head as he considered the alternatives, then thrust his hand out toward Reggie. "Call a stay?"

The local alpha hawked and spat outside the circle of their meeting. "Temporary. That's it."

"Fine."

They shook, and their pack members looked on in surprise.

"So…" Lisa leaned forward. "No more fighting?"

"Not until after we find the bastards who took Magnus," Reggie stated.

"And Cassidy."

"A woman shifter." Johnny shrugged. "Guess crime don't discriminate."

"That's an incredibly callous way of viewing the situation," William said with a sneer. "Even for a dwarf."

"Now hold on—"

"Johnny." Lisa grabbed his arm. "Seriously. Take the high road this time, okay?"

"I always do."

"Fine. The higher road. Let it go."

He rubbed his mouth and waited until she released his arm. "So how do y'all wanna go about the rest of this, huh?"

"So you think these are all connected?" William asked, focused on Lisa now.

"Well, each next step leads to another missing magical, so yeah. I'd say they have something to do with each other."

Hyla scoffed. "They thought our guy took their Wood Elf."

"She's not our Wood Elf."

"Yeah." Johnny nodded. "She's her own magical." When Lisa gave him a confused frown, he shook his head. "Not the right time either?"

She pressed her lips together, turned toward the two packs, and shrugged. "We know Nina Williams was taken by shifters. They damaged her home fairly badly and didn't leave much room for wondering who did it."

"That and the place stank like too many shifters in one tiny little place," Luther muttered. "Hey, no offense."

"Then we'll start there." William nodded. "I assume you have decent trackers in your local pack."

Reggie snorted. "Don't ask stupid questions like that, man."

"So yes. I'll get mine ready and we'll come with you."

"Where?" Baron asked.

"The Elf's place. And maybe we can catch the scent of the right shifter this time."

Not only was William's pack neater, cleaner, and far more polite all round than Reggie's, but they were considerably faster, too. He had his two best trackers rounded up and ready to head out within ten minutes and was even kind enough to offer Johnny's crew and the local pack a ride to where they'd stashed their fully weaponized vehicles. Of course, the offer was declined, but Lisa gave him and his team detailed enough directions to Nina Williams' house and confirmed that they would rendezvous there.

Half an hour later—this time knowing exactly where they were going—they arrived at Nina's trailer to find William's SUV already parked in the front yard and the three city shifters investigating the outside of the house. They looked up and stared at Johnny's cannon-mounted Jeep and the two heavily outfitted ATVs. The late arrivals got out and converged on the front lawn.

"Where's the damage you were talking about?" William asked.

"Inside." Lisa led the way up the front porch and opened the unlocked door before she stepped aside to let the shifters in first.

William whistled quietly when he saw the extent of the damage. "It doesn't look good. That's for sure."

Reggie and his guys followed closely behind. "It looks like shifters fightin' someone else."

"Probably not a Wood Elf," one of William's trackers muttered and moved slowly through the trailer. "It smells like there was wizard magic in here too. Maybe an Atlantean. Or the wizard knew one well enough to bump shoulders with him."

Hyla froze in her inspection of the claw-gouged hallway and turned to stare at him with wide eyes. "You picked up all that? Simply by standin' in here?"

The city tracker shrugged. "Yeah. I could have gotten much more if the place hadn't been empty for…how long did you say it was?"

"We reckon about six days," Johnny said. "Roughly." He turned to look through the open door at Rex, Luther, and Boots sniffing around in the yard. *Long enough for the hounds to miss it too.*

Hyla gave the other shifter a crooked grin. "Damn."

Reggie passed William on his way into the living room and

smacked the other alpha's arm with the back of his hand. "When you said you'd grab your trackers, city boy, you meant it."

The man ignored the hidden insult and met his pack members' gazes. "Yes, I did."

"Hey." The second city tracker had knelt on the other side of the overturned loveseat and now stood, brandishing a cooking knife. "I think I found our ticket." He raised the blade to his nose and took a few quick sniffs, then turned to point at the bloodstain on the carpet. "That's the Elf's blood. But this is definitely wizard."

"No shit." Johnny hooked his thumbs through his belt loops and rolled his shoulders. "Did you smell that from across the room or what?"

"Well...yeah."

"Huh. I thought my hounds had two of the best noses down here."

"I'm sure they do," William said. "For dogs."

"Yeah, until these yuppies decided to take over." Hyla's sneer disappeared when she caught the warning glance her alpha fixed on her.

"We called a stay," Reggie reminded her. "Keep it together."

"Wait." She turned toward the hallway that had been shredded by wolf claws and jaws and dozens of magical burns. "I think..."

Hyla sniffed the walls as she disappeared into the dark hall without bothering to turn the light on.

"It looks like one of your trackers found something too," William muttered.

"Well, we gotta hone our senses down here," Reggie replied and gazed around the room. "We don't get everythin' simply handed to us on a silver city platter."

"Obviously."

"Reggie!" Hyla sounded excited. "I got him!"

"Where?"

The shifters congregated around the mouth of the hallway. "The strongest scent in the bathroom. Magnus was here."

Johnny folded his arms and wrinkled his nose. Lisa stepped beside him and studied his profile. "You look miffed right now."

"Miffed?"

"It was the first word that came to mind."

"Naw, I only… Hell. We can't find a trail or two or three without bringin' in eight shifters tryin' to kill each other."

She slid her hands into her back pockets and felt the Whistle nestled there. "The hounds didn't have Magnus or Cassidy's scents. How would they know what to look for other than Nina?"

"Sure. But they didn't find that knife with wizard blood."

"Johnny, even the shifters were surprised that William's guy found it."

"Uh-huh."

CHAPTER FIFTEEN

After each of the alpha's best trackers hurried down the hall to investigate the bathroom and pick up Magnus' scent from there too, they scoured the house again but didn't catch anything from the city pack's missing member. With no new information, everyone filed out of Nina Williams' ransacked double-wide. Johnny caught up to the shifter who'd found the wizard-blood scent on the knife and clapped a hand on the guy's shoulder. "What's your name?"

The man glanced at his hand and only answered when he removed it. "Steve."

"Steve. Stay right here with that knife for a minute, huh?" He uttered a piercing whistle. "Boys! Get over here."

The hounds bounded across Nina's well-maintained yard with Boots trotting behind them. Luther sneezed and shook tiny purple flower petals off his nose. "Hey, Johnny. What's up?"

"You guys found what you wanted, right?" Rex asked. His tail wagged happily as he gazed at his master but he stopped and lowered slowly when he saw the huge kitchen knife dusted with dried blood in the city shifter's hand. "Johnny?"

"Go ahead and take a whiff of this, huh?" The dwarf nodded at Steve and gestured toward the hounds. "If you don't mind."

The shifter had to bend slightly to extend the blade toward the hounds' snouts.

Rex and Luther both took five seconds to study it with their coonhound senses, then stepped away and stared at Johnny. "Nice knife, Johnny."

"Yeah, real sharp."

"What do y'all smell on there?"

"Uh...metal?"

"Yeah, and Wood Elf."

"Hey, and shifter!" Luther's mouth popped open and he panted in excitement. "Is that one of the missing ones, Johnny? Because shifter was the strongest—oh. Right. Shifter holding the knife."

With a heavy sigh, Johnny glanced at Steve and raised an eyebrow. "You have some nose on you."

"I know." The shifter gave the hounds a wary look before he moved to join his alpha and their other best tracker in scouring the rest of the property for signs of their missing member.

"What was that about?" Luther asked.

"We do something wrong, Johnny?"

"Naw. Y'all did your jobs fine." *I can't blame a hound when only one shifter picks up almost week-old wizard blood.* "Keep lookin' around. William!"

The city alpha turned slowly from the garden bed in front of the porch. "Dwarf."

"Y'all got somethin' of your lady shifter for my hounds?"

William's second tracker went to their SUV and pulled a sweater out of the back seat. He approached Johnny and the hounds quietly and held Cassidy's clothing item out for them to catch her scent.

Rex sniffed tentatively, then backed away and sneezed. "Yeesh.

Never smelled a shifter wearing so much other crap on her. It's all flowers and chemicals."

The bounty hunter folded his arms. *Lady shifters runnin' around dousin' themselves with perfume. That's a new one.*

Luther sniffed next, plunged his face into the sweater, and rooted around. The city shifter looked questioningly at Johnny and the dwarf shrugged.

"He'll get it."

"Ooh, Johnny. This is soft."

The shifter snorted. "Cashmere."

On the opposite side of the yard, Hyla straightened from where she'd bent over to search the hedges and muttered, "'Course it is."

"I like soft, Johnny. Lady shifter has good taste. But I don't—oh. Yep. There it is." Luther whipped his head away from the sweater and almost ripped the article from the shifter's hand and sat. "Got it, Johnny. She smells good."

"Thanks." He nodded, and the shifter went to offer Reggie's pack a hint of Cassidy so they could track her.

"Y'all think you can handle pickin' up on those two?"

"Yeah, Johnny."

"Totally."

"We tracked that 'gator through the swamp, remember?"

"Well, we did have Amanda with us…"

"Yep." Johnny scratched the side of his face. "Stay focused, all right? We're onto somethin' big, and any little bit helps—"

"Found somethin'!" Aldo stood beside a large oak tree outside the back chain-link fence. He held out a necklace on a leather thong and a puffy off-white hair scrunchy.

The shifters of both packs converged around him, and he pointed at a low-hanging branch with its offshoots of smaller leafy twigs. "I found 'em hangin' right here on the tree."

Reggie reached for the pendant and slid it off the shifter's finger. "This is his all right."

William frowned at the scrunchy and held his hand out. Aldo handed it over quietly for the city alpha to take a good long whiff. William glanced at Steve and his other tracker and nodded. "Cassidy."

"So they were both here." Lisa frowned and scanned the yard. "Attacked at the same time?"

"I see absolutely no reason why Cassidy would be out here with a local shifter," William muttered.

"There ain't no reason for Magnus to come runnin' 'round a Wood Elf's house, neither," Reggie added.

Agent Breyer nodded. "Maybe they all knew each other."

The local alpha snorted. "We ain't scuffled with this city pack anywhere but in the swamp."

"Only twice," Steve added.

"Well, there's certainly a connection between Magnus and Nina." Lisa shrugged and studied all their faces to find proof that they were following what she assumed was a very obvious train of thought. "Oh, come on. You said you found his scent in the bathroom?"

"That's right." Hyla folded her arms. "There's nothin' special 'bout the john."

Lisa raised her eyebrows. "In the actual toilet?"

The shifter woman glared at her, then it dawned on her and she rolled her eyes. "Shit."

"He took a piss in the elf's john," Reggie muttered. "What, before or after the fight?"

"Well, it's hard to do it in the middle," Lisa pointed out. "So either he was here when Nina was attacked or he stopped by afterward with Cassidy."

"It don't make no sense," Mikey snarled. "Why the hell was he here in the first place?"

"I want to know why both our shifters left their personal effects on this tree." William pointed at the branch Aldo had indicated. "Those items must have been left there on purpose. That leather thong's still intact, not ripped off your missing guy's throat."

Johnny grunted. "And a hair tie don't simply come off when it's pulled? I assume that's a question for the ladies, right?" Lisa and Hyla both looked at him in exasperation. "What? I ain't used one of those."

The agent shook her head. "It's not only a question for the ladies, Johnny. But no. You'd have to pull on it without getting your hair caught at the same time."

"You would?"

Hyla scoffed. "Well, I guess if you wanna have your whole damn scalp pulled off with it, that's a different story."

"Either way," William interjected, "I think they left these here for a reason. Most likely as a message for us."

Reggie rubbed the side of his clean-shaven face and shook his head. "It don't make no sense. Why the hell would they be workin' together to leave clues?"

"I'm sure it's for the same reason we're working together to find them." William inclined his head toward the other alpha and stepped away from the group. "So let's get to work. If anyone picks up the scent of any missing magical, say the word. Spread out."

Reggie nodded at his shifters and everyone dispersed from the tree to keep sniffing around Nina's property.

"You heard 'em, boys." Johnny pointed at the hounds and nodded across the yard. "We're on the hunt."

"You got it, Johnny." Rex raced toward the chain-link fence to sniff the perimeter. "We'll find them."

"Right, right, right." Luther pressed his nose to the ground and sniffed violently as he wove somewhat haphazardly with his tail sticking straight out behind him. "On the hunt. On the hunt. On the…"

His erratic trail led him over the row of short hedges at the back of Nina's property and he disappeared. Seconds later, the sound of his splashing leap into the swamp made Johnny shake his head.

Lisa leaned toward him as she watched the eight shifters scouring the property. "So now we wait."

"It ain't my favorite part either, darlin'."

"What do you think? Nina and Magnus or Magnus and Cassidy?"

"We're missin' all three, ain't we?"

She smirked and shook her head. "No, I mean the personal connection. Because I can't see how there isn't one at this point."

"Personal as in…" The dwarf's eyes widened. *"Personal personal?"*

"Come on, Johnny. It's not that hard to imagine or to reason out based on the evidence. He used Nina's bathroom. If it was before she was stabbed in her living room, he was there with her, right? If it was after—"

"Then the local pack's bearer is one cold-hearted motherfucker. And…what? You think he was in cahoots with the lady wolf?"

"I have no idea." She turned to study the side of the trailer. "But here's what I don't understand. Cassidy's been gone for eight days. Magnus for seven. And if everything was translated correctly, Nina's been missing for six. Or five."

"It was translated correctly, all right." Johnny turned to scan the yard for Boots, who lay on the well-kept grass of the front lawn. She panted with her tongue out as she watched a whole horde of strangers going through her domain. "But a hound ain't exactly the best at tellin' time."

"Or maybe Boots is better at it than Luther."

He snorted. "There's a real good chance of that, yeah."

"So were they all taken at different times and dragged to the next place until the kidnappers came for Nina? Or were they all here together?"

"I have no idea, darlin'. That's what I aim to figure out when we—"

A warbling, startlingly loud bay came from the swamps behind the property. "Got it! Oh, man. Oh, man, Johnny! I got it —no. Got all three of them!"

The two partners exchanged a glance and raced toward the back hedges. They swiped aside low-hanging tree branches and huge ferns whipped quickly into their faces. When they reached the edge of the swamp, Luther stood in the water, halfway submerged with his tail sticking straight up in the air.

"Right here, Johnny! Right here. All three! Yes!" Luther threw his head back and bayed again.

Rex surged through the foliage and leapt past Lisa to splash in the briny water with his brother. He sniffed and immediately uttered a proud howl of victory. "Found 'em! We found 'em, Johnny. Luther, let's go—"

"Hold up." Johnny snapped his fingers and both hounds froze, stood rigidly in the water, and sniffed the scent they didn't want to lose.

The shifter packs appeared through the trees and stopped at the water's edge beside the dwarf. Steve still clutched the kitchen knife in his hand, and Johnny glanced at it before he looked away again.

"That's it," Steve muttered. "William, I'm getting it too. All three."

"Let's go, let's go, let's go!" Luther shifted in excitement and stirred water, mud, and reeds all around him.

Steve raised the knife and pointed it at Luther. "Your coonhound has a good nose, dwarf. Even I wouldn't have thought to look in the swamp."

"I guess it's 'cause city folk ain't built for the swamp."

The shifter smirked and lowered the knife. "More like it's almost impossible to track a scent across water."

Johnny sniffed. "Yeah, that too."

141

William took a few long sniffs of the air and grinned. "Good work. See if they can follow it."

"What?" Johnny looked at him. "'Course they can follow it."

"Only to see where it takes them. If they end up back on land, we have our trail." The city alpha gazed over the swamp and the scattered pools of shadow beneath the thick foliage. "If it goes farther into the water, though…"

"Yeah, I get it." Johnny whistled. "Go on and chase it, boys. For a short way, ya hear?"

Both hounds uttered warbling bays again and splashed through the water, sniffing madly as they scrambled over moss-covered branches that dipped into the swamp.

The bounty hunter glanced at William, then Reggie, and folded his arms. "They'll find where it leads."

"I sure hope so."

Five minutes later, the air filled with splashing and heavy panting to herald Rex and Luther's return. "Hey, there you are, Johnny."

Rex led the way, occasionally sniffing the air but mostly intent on making it back to his master. "Miss us?"

"What's the verdict, boys?"

"It was crazy, Johnny. You wouldn't believe it! Biggest snake I've ever seen—"

"Luther!"

"What?"

Rex trotted out of the water and everyone stepped hastily away before he shook himself vigorously and flung water everywhere. "The scent goes way out into the swamp, Johnny. Kinda back toward home. But you said only a little way, so we didn't go all the way back."

"Oh, yeah." Luther stepped beside his brother, shook himself, and made Rex shake himself again after being splattered. "Way out, Johnny."

"All three?"

"Definitely." Luther sat and gazed at his master with eager eyes. "So is it hunting time, Johnny? Or snack time?"

"Huntin'. Good work, boys."

"There is only one little problem I see with this," William interjected.

"Same here." Reggie looked unimpressed by the necessity of agreeing with the city alpha. "We ain't trackin' a trail like that through the Glades, dwarf. It don't matter how sure those hounds are of what they found. It's too much of a risk sendin' us all out in the water when we got no idea what we're lookin' for."

"Y'all can trust the hounds. They know what's what."

Aldo folded his beefy arms and grunted. "Not gonna happen."

"It's one thing to trust your dogs," William said. "And we would if we could follow the trail with our noses too."

Johnny looked at both alphas, then turned and scanned the unamused expressions of the other shifters waiting for their next orders. *It ain't about them doubtin' the hounds. The big bad shifters are too good to get their pants wet—and maybe too scared.*

He smirked but removed it quickly by swiping his hand across his lips. "The trail goes back toward my place. I have an easy solution for the rest of it. Y'all can follow Sheila." He uttered another piercing whistle before he trudged through the thick underbrush toward Nina's property. "To me, boys. We're headin' out."

"Yeah, yeah, Johnny."

"On it."

"Come on, lady. Keep up!"

The hounds darted after their master and disappeared behind the branches.

Lisa started to follow but stopped when she realized all eight shifters were staring at her now.

"Who's Sheila?" William asked.

She fought back a laugh and pushed through the reeds. "His Jeep."

CHAPTER SIXTEEN

Behind Johnny's cabin, the shifters stared at the airboat being readied by the dwarf so they could venture into the swamp without anyone having to get their feet wet. William scratched his head and frowned at the vessel. "Ten of us, dwarf. You want to fit all ten of us on that raft?"

"Raft?" Johnny dropped the rope he'd been about to untie from the dock. "This ain't a raft, and don't let me hear you call it that again, understand? It's a flat-bottomed airboat and a damn fine one too."

"Whatever it is, I hope you have a second one."

"Nope." The dwarf bent over again to untie the rope. "Only the one."

"Will it hold us all?" Steve asked.

"Y'all came here to the Glades fixin' to run your tourist business outta your fancy community on cement, and you're tellin' me you don't know how many bodies one of these airboats can hold?"

"It looks very small to me."

The dwarf snorted. "Y'all are killin' me. Sure, she ain't the biggest but this baby seats twelve plus the captain. Let's go."

"And you're the captain?" Hyla muttered and wrinkled her nose at him and the giant fan of the airboat behind him.

"Damn straight. She's my boat, ain't she?"

"I'll stay here." Aldo had moved slowly away from the others gathered at the dock and now stood two feet away from the chicken coop that housed another local's hens. "Someone should watch the poultry."

"Uh-uh. Nope. Get away from them." When Aldo leaned over the tall wall of electric fence to widen his eyes at the plump little chickens that pecked around the enclosure, Johnny growled, stepped onto the dock, and shoved the end of the rope against William's chest. "Hold this. Hey! Big guy! I said—"

A loud zap and a buzzing flash of bright orange light raced around the fence. Aldo snarled and jerked his hand away as the hens fluttered in a burst of feathers and frenzied squawks.

"That's a warnin'." The bounty hunter pointed at the shifter as he strode toward the coop. "And I'll give you one too. Hands off the fence and get your ass on that boat."

Aldo turned slowly toward him and sneered. "What if I don't?"

"Aw, Jesus. Lisa!"

"I'm right here." She stood at the land-end of the dock with her arms folded. "What's wrong?"

"The big guy don't wanna listen to a warnin'. It might be he needs somethin' a little louder."

"You leave that head-splitter gun right where it is," Reggie muttered and placed a wary hand on Lisa's shoulder. "I'm askin' nicely."

She looked at him, then nodded toward the boat. "Then you better get all your shifters on that so we can get out there."

"Aldo! Quit pussyfootin' 'round with them damn hens and get the hell over here."

The giant shifter took one final, longing glance at the chickens, then knocked Johnny aside as he brushed past him and headed to the dock. "What good is a henhouse of fat hens if you ain't gonna eat 'em?"

"They ain't mine," Johnny called after him. He stooped toward the locked box of chicken feed at the base of the electric fence and grabbed two handfuls of the contents to scatter in the front of the coop. The hens clucked appreciatively and pecked at it. *They ain't mine, but I promised I'd keep 'em cooped, fed, and alive.*

"All right. Let's get this show on the water."

"What's that?" Steve pointed at the giant metal hulk of Margo next to the storage shed.

"None of your business. Come on."

The eight shifters, Lisa, and three hounds filed onto the airboat's flat metal dock, and Johnny took his place at the stern in front of the propeller mount. The agent stood beside him, and only when the huge fan whirred loudly and Johnny steered them out into the swamp did she lean toward him and mutter, "It's a good thing your boat isn't any smaller. They'd be pushing each other over the side."

Johnny glanced at the clear division between the local shifters huddled close together portside and the three city shifters with admittedly more room standing starboard. Rex and Luther stood at the edge of the bow, their heads stretched in front of them and tails sticking straight out behind them as they sniffed the air. Boots lay on her belly in the very center of the deck, content to be surrounded by hounds and magicals all looking for her owner. "They'll be fine. We're all after the same thing."

"As long as they can keep that truce until we find our missing magicals."

He gave her a crooked smile.

She leaned slightly away and couldn't help but return it curiously. "What?"

"It's workin' out fine all on its own, ain't it?" Johnny nodded toward the shifters piled onto his airboat. "Less than a week of runnin' our own business and we already have one helluva case stringin' us along."

"You know what? I'll call it a success when it's over and you get paid in something more than whiskey and a temporary friendship with shifters."

"Naw. I reckon that's enough."

"Truly?"

He shrugged and pulled the control throttle toward himself to take the airboat slowly around the bend in the river. "All right. Maybe only the whiskey."

They headed upriver for about five miles before the hounds caught the scent they'd known they'd find out here. Suddenly, tension and excitement suffused the group and Johnny increased the speed of the propeller to get them moving north and away from the coast. He tried as hard as he could to ignore the constant bickering of one kind or another between the local and city shifters so he could focus on taking directions from Rex and Luther, but it finally wore his patience down.

With a growl, he eased the throttle until the fan wound to a halt and they stopped moving forward. They began to drift back on the tide. When the shifters realized the change, they all turned to glare at the dwarf.

"You took us out here in the middle of nowhere on an empty tank?" William muttered.

"Nope."

"Then why did you stop?"

"Yeah, Johnny." Luther's tail whipped against Boots' raised head as he spun toward his master. "The scent's still going that way. Forward."

"And I'd be able to hear that if I could hear myself think." He released the throttle and folded his arms. "The rest of y'all need to shut the hell up so I can do that."

Hyla scoffed and rolled her eyes. "What do you care, dwarf? We called a stay."

"Well how about a stay on talkin'?"

The shifters gave him blank stares.

"Listen, if y'all wanna stay on this boat to find your missin' folks, y'all gotta play by my rules. Or I'll dump you overboard right now and y'all can splash to wherever the hell you think you might wanna go. So quit yappin' at each other's throats and let my hounds do what they do best. Got it?"

Aldo rolled his eyes. "Pushin' us all over the side of this thing? No way in hell."

Steve glanced at the other shifters, then peered over the side of the boat. "It's a big claim for a little guy."

Lisa very clearly moved her hand to her back pocket and raised her eyebrows. "Do you want to make a bet on that?"

Steve and William shared a knowing glance before the tracker turned and stared ahead.

"My guys won't say a word," William confirmed and nodded slowly at Lisa. "We get it."

"How about you, Reggie?"

"We're good." The local alpha nudged Hyla with a fist and nodded for her to turn too. "There ain't nothin' worth talkin' 'bout anyhow. Not until we find the bastards who took Magnus."

"Good." Johnny turned the throttle and kicked the fan up again. It took more speed than he wanted to get them moving smoothly upriver again, but he was satisfied.

Lisa leaned toward him and muttered, "I like this version."

"Of what?"

"A Johnny Walker who can talk things out instead of blowing them up."

"Don't get used to it, darlin'. Or keepin' that Whistle in your pocket."

She grinned and folded her arms as they headed upriver through the swamp. "Too late."

Rex and Luther directed their master and shouted out the change in direction when they reached two different branching tributaries wide enough to fit the airboat. After another hour on the water, they had no choice but to pull the airboat up to shore and tie it off.

"Goes straight up there, Johnny." Luther whipped his head back to look at his master. "We're getting off now, right?"

"Yep." As the airboat coasted to a stop at the bank, Johnny leapt off the deck and grasped the rope to secure it to a thick stand of mangroves. "Everyone out."

Eight pairs of feet jumped and splashed and slogged through the mud. The shifters milled around the soggy shore, searching for the trail themselves before Steve found it.

"There it is." He pointed ahead through the mangroves, then turned to look at Johnny. "Did I tell you your dogs are good?"

"At least once." The dwarf splashed toward the airboat to retrieve his rifle slung around the gun mount by its strap. "It can't hurt to let 'em hear it again."

"He's talking about us, Johnny, right?" Luther paced at the head of the scent trail and sniffed the ground, the air, and the dirt again.

"We already know we're good," Rex added and stood frozen with his nose pointed toward land and his tail out behind him. "You tell us all the time."

"Let's get a move on." Johnny waded onto the shore and nodded. "Get after it, boys. We're right behind ya."

"Yes! The hunt. I love the hunt, Johnny."

"Best part of being a hound. Besides the treats. You get treats, Boots, don't you?"

Rex and Luther pushed into the thick foliage with the Heeler close behind. The shifters followed suit, and Johnny and Lisa brought up the rear.

"Are you good to keep up, darlin'?"

She snorted and easily matched the quick pace set by the hounds. "I've been down here for four months, Johnny, give or take the out-of-state case. I think I've had enough time to learn how to move through the swamp."

He chuckled and hurried after the shifters. "We might make a local out of you yet."

"Yeah, we'll see."

CHAPTER SEVENTEEN

They trudged for at least half a mile along the twisting, water-logged berms and raised land, following the hounds. The anticipation increased noticeably when the shifters caught the full scent of the trail as well, and no one raised a fuss when they had to splash through the rising tide that was now calf-deep in some places to keep moving forward.

Without warning, Rex and Luther both stopped short at the head of the procession and scanned the swamp. The shifters remained focused on the scent, but Steve paused to frown at the hounds.

"What's wrong?" Johnny and Lisa caught up, and the shifter gazed warily around.

"Something's wrong, Johnny." Luther sniffed the ground.

"Don't know what it is," Rex added.

"William," Steve called. "Hang back a second."

The shifters slowed up ahead and turned back. "What is it?"

"I'm not sure." Steve raised an eyebrow at the hounds. "But I'm not about to ignore two dogs who can track this far through water."

"It don't matter if them hounds lost the scent," Reggie said and pointed in the direction they'd all been moving in. "We still got it. Let's move."

Luther sniggered. "Listen to that guy. Lost the scent. Please."

"Then what is it?" Johnny met Steve's gaze and the shifter shrugged.

"Different sound, Johnny." Rex looked up at his master. "Big rumble somewhere."

"Yeah, and a hose."

"A hose." The dwarf folded his arms. "What are you—"

"Shit, watch it!" Steve caught the dwarf's arm and jerked him aside as a thin, black snake slithered across the ground in front of them. It disappeared into the tall grasses, and Luther yelped.

"Johnny! There's more!"

The ground writhed with shimmering black snakes two feet long and dozens of them slithered through the grasses toward Steve, Johnny, and the hounds.

"Stay back," the shifter instructed, then called out to his alpha and the other tracker. "Watch for snakes. I think we disturbed a nest."

"What kind?" William asked.

"I'd say cottonmouths if I had to guess. Very dark ones."

"Damn. Everyone watch your feet." William gestured toward the local shifters. "They're some of the deadliest out here."

Mikey snarled. "Man, what the hell are you doin' tellin' us 'bout the kinda critters in our own goddamn swamp?"

"Johnny…" Luther stuck his snout toward the snake that wove past his paw and snorted. "Wrong kind of snake."

The black creature raised its head to hiss at the hound, and the bounty hunter caught a glint of its glowing red eyes before it vanished into the grass.

"Dammit, you're all wrong. These ain't snakes. They're hair."

"Atlantean?" William asked.

"Unless you know of a different kinda magical that sends their hair out as spies—ah!" Johnny stepped back and kicked at the hair-snake that had latched its jaws firmly around the top of his ankle. "I ain't seen them attack like this—"

"Shit!" Baron stumbled back when another snake clamped onto his leg. The other shifters cried out in surprise and pain when individual Atlantean hair-serpents curled up their legs and bit into their flesh.

Lisa kicked the one that had targeted her and fixed her with its blazing red eyes. It hissed madly and writhed as she hurled it away to splash into the water. "Why are they attacking us?"

"Someone don't want us to find what we're about to find." Johnny ripped the magical reptile off his ankle, hissed at the pain, and tossed it before it could clamp around his hand.

One by one, the shifters took on their wolf forms to better fight the nest of a magical's sentient hair and snarled and snapped at the black, glistening heads.

Then, without warning, every snake turned abruptly and slithered back the way they'd come.

"Dammit, they're headin' back!" Johnny raced forward through the ferns in pursuit.

The wolves snarled and regrouped to focus on the kidnapped magicals' scent again.

Johnny stuck his fingers in his mouth and uttered an earsplitting whistle that made Lisa flinch and slap her hands against her ears. "Forget the damn trail! The snakes were sent to fight us off. Follow them."

She hurried after him, and the hounds bounded behind. The wolves growled at each other as they tried to make their minds up in their present forms. William's huge, shaggy head turned to look at the bounty hunter before he and his two pack members chose to follow in that direction.

Reggie and Hyla snarled and snapped at each other before they finally abandoned the scent and chose to pursue the Atlantean hair-snakes.

Johnny slid to a stop at the edge of the water where the last snake had disappeared. "Shit. Do you see 'em on the other side?"

"No." Lisa shook her head and scanned the opposite bank of the small high-tide tributary that trickled past them. "Maybe we should go back and let them pick up the trail again."

"Easy, Johnny." Luther stopped beside his master, sniffed the ground, and panted. "Whatever trail you want."

"Magicals or magical hair," Rex added.

"Y'all can track the damn snakes?" Johnny stared with wide eyes at his hounds.

"Uh...yeah. They smell like whoever they belong to—"

"Well then, git on!"

The hounds leapt across the water and surged through the thick underbrush.

William stopped beside the bounty hunter in his wolf form and growled.

"It's a different scent. But whoever it belongs to doesn't want us findin' what's out here so it's better than a colder trail." Johnny raced after the hounds and ducked in surprise when William uttered a shuddering howl directly behind him.

The sound was echoed not only by the city shifters but by the local pack too as all eight wolves loped through the soaked underbrush.

Lisa caught up to Johnny, breathing heavily as they ducked beneath branches and climbed over soggy, fallen logs. "What are the chances that the last scent was leading us to a place where someone else happened to be?"

"Naw. Atlanteans don't send those bastards out without a damn good reason. Especially not to attack. Coincidence ain't my thing."

Before they knew it, the entire crew stumbled through a particularly thick wall of cattails and into an open clearing surrounded on every other side by nothing but swamp water and overhanging trees.

"No sign of the snakes, Johnny." Luther alternated between panting and sniffing in the dry grass in the pure Florida sunlight above them. "They were here."

"And now they're gone." Rex turned in a tight circle and tried to find the trail again. "What the hell?"

The wolves joined them and scattered across the clearing. William shifted immediately and turned to stare at Johnny. "You said this was the trail to follow, dwarf."

"And it still is." The bounty hunter clenched his fists. We merely need to find it again."

Steve shifted next and shook a flutter of leaves out of his hair. "It's gone."

"That ain't possible." Johnny stared at his hounds. "How do two coonhounds and eight damn shifters lose a trail like that?"

"Johnny, it disappeared."

"Yeah, we did everything right."

Lisa turned at the light snarl that issued from the cattails behind them. Boots appeared and shook her head vigorously with a glistening black snake caught in her jaws. "Johnny."

"What?"

"Hey! Boots!" Luther jumped toward her. "Good thinking."

"Drop it." Johnny pointed at the Heeler. "Come on, now."

"We should never have followed you out here," William grumbled.

"I know what I'm doin'. Boots. Drop the snake."

She growled and shook her head even more fiercely. Finally, she stopped, looked at Johnny, and trotted toward Lisa instead.

"Huh. I see how it is."

A short laugh burst from the agent's mouth when the Heeler stopped in front of her and wagged her tail. "We're not playing fetch but go ahead and drop it."

Boots spat the writhing snake onto the ground. It flipped, writhed, and slithered across the clearing toward the other side, avoiding human feet and wolf paws as it negotiated a hasty path through the gathered shifters. Everyone watched it return to its unseen Atlantean owner, and when it reached the back of the clearing, it disappeared. Not into a hole or beneath tall grass or behind a rock but instead, through a faint shimmer in the air before the appearance of nothing was restored.

"That ain't right." Johnny took his rifle with both hands and moved slowly toward where the snake had vanished. "Someone has—"

The air rippled again and a shimmer of opalescent light reached six feet into the air. An Atlantean stepped through the illusion, armed with an automatic rifle and with an ammo belt strapped across his chest. The last black snake slithered up the front of his leg until he snatched it and returned it to his head. "I don't know how you idiots found this place, but you need to leave."

"Whoa, Johnny." Luther sniffed furiously. "Snake guy jumps out of the air and now I can smell everything."

"Not only you, bro." Rex lowered his head and uttered a low, warning growl. "Atlantean smell and the shifters, Johnny. Wood Elf too."

"Is that right?"

The shifters had discerned the strong scent of their missing members too. All six of them growled, snarled at the new magical in their midst, and paced the clearing.

"Don't make me say it again." The Atlantean's long black hair-snakes raised their heads and hissed as one at the group of intruding magicals. He aimed the rifle at Johnny and inclined his head, his expression set and cold. "Get out."

"We're looking for someone," William said from where he stood bare-ass naked beside Steve among the six prowling, agitated wolves. "Three someone's, in fact."

"I don't care." The man's rifle swung toward the naked shifters. "You shouldn't be here."

"Then tell us what you're hiding behind that illusion," Steve interjected and his upper lip curled into a sneer as he crouched in a ready stance.

Johnny glanced at them and looked away quickly. *Only shifters could stand there in the nude and still make threats.*

"It's none of your business," the Atlantean retorted coldly.

"Yeah, but the swamps are my business," Johnny added and raised his rifle. "You have serious explainin' to do right now, bud."

The magical turned quickly toward the dwarf and shook his head. The snakes flopped against his shoulders and hissed. "Even if I wanted to, we don't have time. If you don't get the hell out of here right now, we'll all—"

A loud, warbling bellow rose through the swamp—something between a bullhorn and the scream of an enormous animal. The shifters snarled and turned toward the sound. Johnny crouched and spun to search the thick foliage on the other side of the open river that curved around the clearing. "What the hell?"

"It's close, Johnny," Rex said.

"Very close," Luther added. "Like maybe a mile."

The bounty hunter waited for Rex to correct his brother, but when the hound was silent, he merely nodded. *Luther finally got somethin' right.*

"Great." The Atlantean turned toward the last echoes of the creature's bellow and adjusted his grip on the rifle. "Now you've fucked it all up."

"Hold on a minute." Johnny glanced at William and Steve, who both shook their heads. The local shifters didn't seem to have any idea what was going on, and no one else transformed to speak up about it. He turned to the other man instead. "Do you know what that is?"

"No." The magical's eyes bulged in his head as he scanned the water. "But I know what it does."

"I was raised in these swamps and I ain't heard nothin' that sounded like that."

"Then we're all screwed." The Atlantean took a few steps back across the clearing. "I managed to hold it off until you showed up and started making so much—"

The river exploded with another deafening bellow. Massive sheets of water cascaded down the long, thick neck of a sand-colored creature covered in scaly patches of what looked like tan, segmented armor plates. It was as thick around as Johnny's airboat was long, and it continued to draw itself out of the water until it loomed twenty feet above the clearing.

The bounty hunter couldn't make out any eyes beyond all the water that rushed down the creature's head and splashed over the clearing. Still, the gaping mouth lined with huge suckers and three circular rows of shark-like teeth was enough to get the point across.

"Fuck! Kill the bastard!" The Atlantean opened fire on the creature. He aimed at its mouth but was unable to find his target. Bullets ricocheted against the armor-like plates and streaked into the river or the soil of the clearing to trigger sprays of water or dirt and grass.

William and Steve shifted into their wolf forms and howled before they raced toward the beast. The other shifters needed no encouragement and darted past the Atlantean. The man screamed almost incoherently now and fired way too many rounds in a frenzy to be effective against whatever monster this was.

Johnny whipped two disks off his belt and raced forward.

Lisa hurried after him as she drew her service pistol.

The monster bellowed again and reared its head back before it dived below the surface again. Its long, segmented body seemed to roll out of the water and down again behind it for at least fifty feet, maybe more. The ground trembled across the clearing and everyone staggered sideways as they tried to keep their balance.

"What is that?" Lisa shouted.

"The fucking worst." The Atlantean stared at the water, his gaze darting continually to search for the beast. "It's pissed."

"Ya think?" Johnny's thumbs hovered over the top buttons of his explosive disks. "Can it come up on land?"

"It can do way more than—"

The ground erupted in a spray of dirt and clods of earth and even more water. The monster's hard head thrust into the air and thrashed down like a falling tree. Gunshots blasted across the clearing again as the Atlantean fired three times before the massive jaws descended to clamp over his head and cut off his scream. A wet crunch followed, and the beast uttered a deafening hiss. Blood and pieces of broken rifle spewed from its jaws before it surged forward out of the river and onto the shore.

"Shit." Johnny activated one disk and lobbed it at the armored worm-like creature. It exploded against the tough hide with an almost metallic ring and shoved it sideways, but it continued its relentless approach.

The wolves all howled, raced toward it, and darted away from its razor-sharp teeth when it snapped and thrashed in its rush across the clearing. The hounds joined them, and Lisa squeezed off a few shots with her pistol only for the bullets to be deflected every time. She sighed and settled for fireballs instead.

The monster bellowed and raised its head on its segmented body. It continued to rush forward and hissed as it drew into itself and coiled to strike. As soon as it reached its full height, Johnny activated his second disk and threw it.

He dove to the left and landed face-first in the dirt with a grunt as the worm struck. The disk detonated and the huge head lurched sideways and its mighty roar ended in a grating shriek that might have indicated pain. The underside of its head and neck pounded onto the soil and it slid the full length of the clearing before its head splashed into the river again.

"We'll get it, Johnny!" Luther leapt onto its segmented back and scrambled to pull himself up. "It's...whoa! Whoa! Moving fast!"

The hound rode the creature's back while he tried to paw the armored hide loose and snapped between the segments.

"Get under it. Yeah!" Rex raced along the glistening body and lunged at openings between the segments.

Half the wolves leapt atop the creature's back, although only Hyla managed to keep her footing and hold on. The others slid off again and threw sparks where their claws tried to dig into the hide.

"Stay outta the water!" Johnny shouted and snatched another explosive disk as he raced toward the monster's quickly moving scales. The beast was way too big to have stayed hidden in the swamp. *Things like that don't grow to this size overnight.*

Activating the disk, Johnny gazed at the end of the creature's side as it barreled toward him and locked his gaze onto one separation in the segmented armor. He darted his hand out at the perfect moment and wedged the disk in the space, then immediately pulled back with a hiss and looked at the back of his hand. The thick protective layer had sliced across it and the wound now bled freely. "Damn."

"Are you okay?" Lisa asked.

"Well, it ain't a bullet wound to the gut—"

His disk exploded and hurled the last ten feet of the monster's diminishing but still ridiculously thick tail into a wild sideways sweep across the clearing.

"Whoa!" Luther leapt from its back. Hyla held on a little longer but eventually had to jump off too. The ground trembled again and the rest of the creature fell sideways into the swamp with another mighty splash. Huge waves broke against the shore and sprayed the entire party before the river sloshed into its natural shape again.

Everyone scanned the water, searching for any sign of the beast.

"Johnny?" Lisa muttered and summoned a fireball in her palm.

"Yeah."

"You left all your very big guns in the Jeep, didn't you?"

"I have a harpoon on the airboat." He narrowed his eyes and took another disk off his belt. "Although that ain't gonna cut it with this one."

"Probably not."

"Is it gone?" Luther slunk toward his master. "It should be gone. Right, Johnny?"

"It would if the damn grenades did what they were supposed to do."

The wolves paced in agitation six feet from the river's edge.

"Johnny, I don't think you blew it up," Rex told him. "I don't think it left, either."

"Yep." The dwarf swung his rifle out of the way on its strap and retrieved a second disk. "It's merely a matter of time."

CHAPTER EIGHTEEN

The clearing became eerily quiet in the hot, severely humid August afternoon. A white butterfly darted among the waiting group until it paused to flutter above Luther's nose. "Hey, look. I think it—"

The wall of cattails behind them burst apart and stalks and brown husks and cotton fluff scattered in all directions as the monster's gaping jaws lunged across the clearing again. Johnny thumped the top of both disks and threw them before the edge of the creature's mouth pummeled into his shoulder and catapulted him away.

The wolves howled and the coonhounds bayed wildly. Everyone with teeth and claws snapped and leapt and scrambled to find a weak point in the creature's armor as Lisa threw useless fireballs against its side.

"Dammit! How the hell does something like this even exist!" Johnny reached for two more disks and one of his hands came up empty. "And now I'm out."

One of the wolves yelped and darted away when the monster turned in on itself in a tight U and thrust its head across the clearing.

"We have what we need for this!" Lisa shouted and her fireballs grew larger with every attack but still failed to damage the creature.

"I ain't one to run away from a fight, darlin', but I think we're outta options."

"I don't think even the wolves can outrun it."

Johnny grasped his rifle, stepped into the center of the clearing, and aimed at the monster's gaping maw. "Then we keep goin'."

Before he could pull the trigger, a loud hum came from the side of the clearing, followed by an explosion. The air shimmered and a giant metal sphere that might as well have been a cannonball appeared in mid-air and streaked toward the center of the monster's immensely long body. It detonated on impact, rocked the ground violently, and created a massive dent in the side of the worm's organic armor. The creature bellowed and thrashed its mid-section, then reared its head and prepared to strike.

Another giant cannon bomb burst into existence and caught it halfway up its raised neck. A wet, gurgling croak issued from its open mouth with a spray of bloody internal chunks, but it still didn't succumb.

In the next moment, an entire wall of shimmering light appeared and the ends of two wide metal barrels slid slowly through the illusion to emerge into the clearing. They were mounted on something like a tank, although the treads were wobbly and misshapen and had no doubt been intended for some other purpose.

A wizard stood at the helm of the tank's top cannon and gritted his teeth as the machine rumbled across the ground. Five more magicals darted through the illusion on foot, armed with wide, squat firearms that looked more like sawn-off grenade launchers than guns.

"Give it everything!" the wizard shouted and fired another

cannonball. This one struck the monster farther down its back than the last one had as it made another U-turn in the clearing to race toward its attackers.

The other magicals with their strange weapons lined up like a firing squad directly in front of the beast that now careened toward them. The creature's multiple coils that had already looped back on themselves began to draw closer to each other. They tensed and slid inward as the monster bulldozed forward with its jaws wide.

"Hey! Whoa, hey!" Luther yelped and scrambled over the end of its tail to escape being crushed between two separate pieces of segmented armor. Rex and the wolves scurried to get out of the new trap.

A Kilomea who stood in the center of the four magicals shouted, "Now!"

All four fired their weird grenade launchers in rapid succession and aimed at the rampaging beast's open mouth. They all made contact one after the other and slid down the creature's throat. The wizard fired again from the top of the tank with a deafening boom.

The four grenades exploded seconds apart and a glowing plume of dark-blue fire surged from the worm's mouth. As the last one detonated, the wizard's cannonball powered into the side of the monster's head with a deafening crack and the shriek of denting, tearing metal.

More sludgy blood and chunks of the creature's insides spewed from its mouth as its head swung violently toward the river. The armor, though, was only dented and didn't break and was still attached when the massive head fell halfway into the water with a heavy splash. The weight of its head pulled more of its elongated body farther into the river and off the shore before the sharp edges of the armor segments dug into the dirt and stopped its slide.

The monster didn't move.

"Holy shit." Johnny stared at the four magicals who'd all but obliterated the beast's gullet and managed a somewhat rough laugh. "What the hell are those?"

The Kilomea looked particularly surprised to be asked that question, but he lowered the barrel of his weird gun into his opposite hand and shrugged. "Laser bombs?"

The witch beside him snorted and headed toward the tank with the others. "They are better than anything else we could come up with."

The wolves regrouped with their packs and now snarled at the magicals who'd appeared so unexpectedly to save their asses. The wizard climbed off the top of the tank and gave the side two quick thumps with his fist before he frowned at the eight wolves. "This is how you thank the monster-slayers, huh?"

William shifted into his human form and cleared his throat. "Is that what you call yourselves?"

The wizard turned away from the naked shifter and looked at Johnny and Lisa instead. "No. But it's what we did."

"And what those laser bombs did." Johnny scratched his head and stared at the odd weapons as the four strangers joined the wizard. "Lemme have a look at one of them."

"I don't think so." The Light Elf man with closely cropped hair that revealed swirling tattoos around the back of his head scowled at them. "You and your friends should turn back now while you still have the chance."

"We won't go anywhere until we get what we came for." William growled warningly.

"And what's that, exactly?" The wizard gestured toward the worm's motionless carcass. "Because I hope you didn't come looking for that, thinking you could eliminate it with claws and teeth."

Steve, Reggie, and Aldo took their human forms too while the other four wolves crouched and snarled at the new magical faction. "A couple of our folks were taken," Reggie said. "And we tracked 'em here until some Atlantean shithead thought it was a good idea to sic his hair on us."

"Manney." The wizard closed his eyes and sighed. "He said he could handle it."

"Well, now you need to handle it." William swept his hand out toward the rest of the clearing. "Because when that Atlantean stepped out from whatever you have hiding behind that illusion, we picked the scent up again. We know they're here."

The wizard glanced at his fellow magicals with wide eyes. "How many are you looking for?"

"Three," Lisa said as she and the hounds joined the group. "Shifters from the two different packs represented here and a Wood Elf. All of them vanished in the last six to eight days."

"Huh."

"You need to leave." The witch stared at the unmoving worm and though she didn't snarl or shout the order like the shifters, her voice was still a firm warning. "Now."

"I wanna know what the hell y'all are doin' with a tank and all this gear on the other side of that illusion." Johnny nodded toward nothing but thin air from which they'd appeared, but his gaze remained firmly fixed on the weapon in the Kilomea's hands. "And how I can get me one of them laser bombs."

"We should leave them here," the witch said. "They'll kill themselves out of sheer stupidity."

The wolves snarled and snapped their jaws. Lisa folded her arms. Aldo punched his open palm with the opposite fist.

"Hold on. Wait." The Kilomea lowered his weapon in one hand and held the other up for everyone to stop. "Wait a minute."

"Chiron, we have no idea who they are or if we can trust anything they say," the Light Elf muttered and leaned toward the wizard. "I say—"

"I got it!" The Kilomea snapped his immensely hairy fingers

and pointed at Johnny as his eyes widened. "You're the guy from that show."

Everyone but Lisa turned to stare at the dwarf. She snorted and shook her head.

Johnny's mustache bristled as he sniffed with careless indifference. "What if I am?"

"Yeah. You are. Man, I loved watching you deal with those assholes twenty years ago. You know, I saw the first few episodes of the new season too. It's very nostalgic, but you put a whole new spin on—"

"Rick!" The wizard Chiron spread his arms. "What are you doing?"

"Huh? Oh. Sorry, sorry." The Kilomea chuckled. "It's been a long time since I've come face to face with a celebrity."

"I ain't—"

"This is Johnny Walker."

The clearing fell silent and the witch regarded Johnny suspiciously. "Who?"

"Seriously? Dwarf the Bounty Hunter?" Rick looked from each of his clueless buddies to the shifters—both furred and naked—and back to Johnny again. "Wow. I guess I'm the only one who bothers to keep up with what's happening in the world."

"Okay, well, why don't you save the fan-boying for later, huh?" The witch pointed behind them at what looked like empty air at the back of the clearing. "We need to get back before—"

"Yeah, yeah. I know the deal." Rick cast the dead monster a contemptuous glance and hefted the laser-bomb gun under his arm before he nodded at Chiron. "We can trust the dwarf."

"Because of a TV show?" The Light Elf scowled. "Are you nuts?"

"Trust me." Rick winked at Johnny and nodded. "I'm a huge fan."

"I appreciate it." He frowned at Lisa, who could only shrug in reply.

"All right." Chiron clambered up the side of the tank and took his position on top again. "Whoever's with the dwarf can come with us. We'll show you what we're dealing with."

"Worse than that buzzard food?" The bounty hunter jerked a thumb toward the carcass.

The witch snorted and rolled her eyes before she stepped through the illusion and vanished.

"What do you have to say about the shifters?" the Light Elf asked.

Johnny cleared his throat. "Yeah, they're with me."

"Okay." The magical scrutinized the wolves for a moment and glanced at the four naked men who stood and scowled at him. Finally, he nodded. "Hurry up."

Chiron's tank rolled back and disappeared slowly as it passed through the illusion.

"Come on." Rick clapped a furry hand on the dwarf's shoulder and gave him a little shake. "If you're into the laser bombs, you'll love what we have stashed in our base."

"Base?"

The Kilomea shrugged. "Well, kind of."

"Wait for us, Johnny." Rex and Luther scrambled to catch up with their master.

"Yeah, don't leave us here." Luther glanced over his shoulder at the carcass. "I think I heard it breathing."

"Not a chance, boys. Come on." Johnny shrugged out from under the Kilomea's hand and gestured toward the faintly visible shimmer as the other magicals and the front of Chiron's tank disappeared.

"Wait, wait. Where's Boots?" Rex spun and barked sharply. "Boots! Boots, where are you?"

"No, no, no, no." Luther whined miserably. "We had so many plans. Boots!" He added a long, doleful howl to his lament but cut it off when Johnny snapped his fingers.

"Did you happen to see a female Blue Heeler runnin' around before you showed up to save our hides?"

"Oh, she's yours?" Rick chuckled. "She's in here too. You'd better hurry, though."

"Whew!" Luther perked up and trotted after the rest of the procession. "I'm glad we sorted that out."

CHAPTER NINETEEN

The illusion was incredibly advanced and not only because it had masked the scent of their missing magicals until the Atlantean had stepped through or because it drowned out the noise from the other side and now muffled the sounds of the swamp where they'd been only moments before. Mostly, it was the size that made the greatest impact.

"Would you look at this?" Lisa exclaimed in disbelief as she gazed around the so-called base. "It's huge."

"Thanks." Rick glanced at her, then cleared this throat. "Yeah, it took us a while to find the best way to do it but we got it right eventually."

Johnny held his rifle casually with both hands and squinted at the area behind the illusion. It was roughly three times the size of the clearing where they'd stood.

A large diesel truck was parked on the right, its long trailer holding what could have been used as a house or maybe storage. Two sets of folding metal chairs and stabilized card tables stood in the center of the area beside a fire pit lined with large stones. Three more vehicles had been parked in a line on the left. The pickup's tailgate was down to provide access to the giant machine that might have been a communication hub, and the other two were black Humvees with all doors closed.

Stacked behind them, though, were six large black crates. The lids were on but an array of small weapons—handguns, grenades, and a few other gadgets Johnny didn't recognize—had been placed on the lids to keep them close at hand. Another small, raised trailer stood at the far end. The door hung open and the lights inside illuminated two fans that spun slowly in the heat. Beside it, two speedboats had been pulled in on detached trailers.

"Hey, there you are." Luther raced across the grass toward Boots, who crouched under the open tailgate, stared at everyone, and trembled slightly. "How'd you get in here?"

"Like we did, bro. She walked."

"Oh… Maybe say something next time, huh? I thought that giant worm ate you or something." Luther sat beside the Heeler, sniffed the top of her head, and watched the rest of the two-legs walk across the open ground.

Johnny cleared his throat. "So this is base, huh?"

"For what it's worth. The Kilomea shrugged. "There isn't much more we can do with what we have."

"Did you lose power or somethin'?"

"Uh…not exactly."

"I don't like the sound of that," Lisa added. "Do you care to explain?"

Chiron turned with a thoughtful frown. "I'd be happy to explain our situation to you. We might be able to help each other, come to think of it. Jasmine, can you find extra chairs for our guests?" He glanced briefly at the four naked shifters. "And maybe some blankets."

"Don't bother," William said and stopped the witch in her tracks. "We'll be fine."

She studied him with a small, appraising smile until the city alpha shifted into his wolf form. Steve quickly did the same, leaving Reggie and Aldo with no real choice but to follow suit.

"All right, then." Chiron gestured toward the two folding card tables with enough chairs to seat his team and their guests who still had two legs. "Pull a chair up, then."

Johnny and Lisa took the table on the right, joined by Rick the Kilomea. Chiron, Jasmine, the Light Elf, and the fifth member of their team—a dwarf with thick goggles strapped to his face instead of glasses—took their seats at the other.

"So." The wizard folded his hands on the table and scanned the wolves who formed the other third of their odd triangle. "I guess I can start by saying first that unfortunately, we have no idea where your missing magicals are."

Reggie growled and bared his teeth.

He took it in stride. "I'm sorry. If they were taken eight days ago, I'm fairly amazed that you managed to track them this far without any gear at all."

"Well, we do have eight shifters," Lisa said.

"And two coonhounds."

"Right." The wizard shrugged. "Well, we had considerably more than that and it was still rough going for a while."

Johnny frowned and leaned back in the metal chair. "Who are you tryin' to find?"

"Some of our members we think were also kidnapped."

The Light Elf folded his arms. "We didn't think much of it until six of them went missing within a week of each other. Then we ran through the full list of every resource we had and nothing."

"The only thing we had to go on was a kind of...magical burst we picked up on one of our trackers," Jasmine added. "From one of our members. So we packed up and came to find him, hoping the others would be in the same place."

"Y'all are still here," Johnny said, "so I'm guessin' you never found 'em."

"Not yet, no."

"Sorry." Lisa leaned forward and folded her arms on the table. "Members of what, exactly?"

Chiron shrugged. "Our own private…organization."

"Like a club." Rick nodded contentedly. "You know, like a chess club or a sports club. Only ours is for tinkering with magic and tech put together. For weapons, mostly."

Johnny's eyes widened. "You don't say."

"Yeah, it's awesome." The Kilomea's eyebrows drew together. "At least, it was."

"Listen to that, Johnny." Lisa nudged his arm. "A weapons club."

"Naw." He scoffed and sat again. "I do fine on my own. Where did y'all say you're from?"

The Light Elf kicked his legs out in front of his chair and crossed one sneaker over the other. "Philly."

"No kiddin'. And y'all picked up a magical message from one of your members all the way down here?"

Chiron gestured toward the control machine resting in the open bed of the pickup. "That's what the STACK is for. Don't ask me what the letters mean. It was named before I even got here."

"You ain't the leader? Or president or whatever?"

The weapons-club magicals exchanged pained glances. Rick lowered his head and rubbed slowly between his eyes.

"No." Chiron slid his hands off the table and into his lap. "I've only been a part of it for the last few months. But we all volunteered to come out here and try to get in touch with our missing members."

"And it's not like they simply got bored with what we were doing and ran away without saying anything," Jasmine added. "These guys were seriously dedicated. They arrived early and stayed late to clean up. That kind of thing."

"Did you find them?" Lisa asked.

"We came close." The Light Elf gestured toward the beginning of their illusion. "And then we got stuck here."

"Stuck?" Lisa raised her eyebrows. "If it isn't a power issue—"

"It's that damn worm," Rick grumbled. "It has appeared every single time we tried to leave the camp to search for our guys."

"It did considerable damage," Jasmine added and nodded slowly as she stared at the tabletop.

"Huh. It don't look like y'all had that much cleanup to deal with."

Chiron focused on the dwarf and cleared his throat. "There were eighteen of us when we got to Florida, Johnny. We were six this morning, and then you and your shifter friends arrived. Now, we're at five."

"Damn. I'm sorry to hear it."

"Yeah, so are we."

"I know it doesn't make the loss of your members any easier, but at least you finally killed the beast," Lisa said. "It must have taken a long time to find the right combination of weapons."

Rick sighed heavily and squeezed his eyes shut. "We had the right combination from the very beginning and it didn't help us at all."

"What?"

"We worked out how to kill it," Chiron explained, "but it doesn't actually die."

"You're kiddin'." Johnny snorted and fixed them with a doubtful smirk. "I watched y'all put four laser bombs and three explodin' wreckin' balls in its hide. Or whatever it's made of. It was pukin' blue fire and blood. That giant bastard ain't movin'."

"It will." Jasmine shot him a warning glance. "Because that's what it always does. Rick, what's the count up to now?"

"Twenty-three."

"See? We've been here for almost a month. It likes to attack fairly regularly."

"That don't make sense." Johnny rubbed his mouth. "Ya'll killed it twenty-three times and can't get on outta here?"

"It heals itself, from what we can deduce," Chiron said. "And that only takes about half an hour, so if you guys want any chance to leave, I suggest you move now."

"Are your missing members still in the area?"

"No. We lost the signal early this morning."

"Uh-huh. So you ain't comin' with us why?"

"Are you kidding?" Jasmine snorted. "We can't leave our gear here. I don't know if we'd ever be able to find our way back, honestly, and some of the equipment we have here is invaluable."

"Your lives are supposed to be invaluable." The bounty hunter grunted. "Ditch the gear. Y'all can make more."

"That's...no. No way." The witch shook her head. "I can't do it."

"That's the only way you'll get outta here in one piece." He glanced at the gathered shifters, who hadn't said a word but were now missing two of their number. After a moment, he located the others sniffing around the gear in the makeshift camp, exploring every inch around the vehicles and even inside the back of the diesel and the trailer. *I assume that's the city trackers. They still all look the same.* "Listen. Y'all found a dead end. So did we when the scent we've been trailin' ended here with you."

"I wish we could help you more than that," Chiron said with a shrug, "but we—"

"Yeah, I ain't buyin' it. Hey!" Johnny turned in his chair and nodded at the closest wolf. "Did you find anythin'?"

Hyla shifted and tossed her hair out of her face. "Nothin'. The three we're lookin' for were out in that clearin'—the real one. But they weren't never brought back here like us."

"Good. It's proof that you're innocent." Johnny slapped the table and looked at the wizard. "So now we know you ain't lyin' about kidnappin' our magicals and I aim to help get the five of y'all outta this camp trap and back into the real world."

"And we have to go home to Philly completely empty handed," the Light Elf grumbled. "No members and no gear. Talk about returning with your tail between your legs."

Rex's head popped up above the table beside Johnny's chair and he snorted. "Hey. "He can't say that, Johnny. He doesn't even have a tail."

"Y'all got any portable trackers you can slip in a pocket or pack or somethin'?" Johnny stood from the table and headed toward the vehicles to see what they did have.

"Small ones, sure." Jasmine stood as well to keep an eye on the dwarf going through their things. "But the range isn't nearly as long as the STACK's."

"Y'all can worry about the range later. If your missin' folk brought you here, I assume there's some kinda connection between them and ours—maybe even the same assholes doin' the snatchin'. And we ain't lettin' up until we find our two shifters and the Wood Elf. So take what you need and let's get on out."

"We can't." Rick shook his head. "Every time we put a boat in the water or start one of the cars, that creature whips after us and takes a bite out of whoever we have left."

Lisa pointed at the wizard. "I thought he said it stays out for half an hour."

"When we keep quiet, yeah. I don't know. I guess boats and truck engines are on its list of top ten biggest pet peeves or something."

"It don't matter." Johnny set a small hand grenade on top of the black trunk. "I have an airboat tied up about a mile south of here. It ain't that far so y'all don't need boats or engines. As long as you can stay quiet while you walk."

"And go where?" Chiron asked. "We have no idea where we are other than that we almost found our missing members."

The dwarf shrugged. "My place, to start. We can decide on the rest of it from there."

"What if that monster follows us?" The Light Elf shook his head. "Don't get me wrong. It's been hell stuck out here for a month. But I don't want to be responsible for the deaths of a group of magicals who didn't sign up to track our guys in the first place."

"We ain't dyin'. Not while I'm steerin' the boat. So get the hell off your asses and collect the gear you wanna keep."

No one moved.

The dwarf grunted. "Wow. A month in the swamp and y'all can't tell when someone's offerin' to rescue you. Let's go!"

Slowly, the weapons-club members rose from their seats, shared a knowing glance without saying a word, and moved quickly to gather their things.

"There ya go. Get ready to head out, boys. We're movin' at top speed after this."

"Johnny." Rex trotted toward his master. "I don't wanna hunt that giant worm."

"We ain't huntin', Rex." He snorted and allowed himself a small grimace of dissatisfaction. "This time, we might be the ones bein' hunted so we'll have to be faster than the regeneratin' hulk of…whatever the hell that beast is."

"Oh." The hound stepped back and turned to watch the magicals gathering their tech and weapons and the wolves rising to their feet, preparing to move. "I hope those other guys know how to run."

"I can run, Johnny," Luther said beneath the open tailgate and finished with a sharp yip. "Boots, you can run too, right? Yeah, Johnny. She can run too!"

"Great."

CHAPTER TWENTY

They were out of the illusionary camp and moving swiftly through the swamp toward the airboat five minutes later. Fortunately, the magicals from Philly did know how to move quickly and quietly. Without having to track a scent or fight off misinformed Atlantean hair-snakes, the large group reached the airboat with little noise. Everyone focused on moving as fast as they could while still listening for sounds that the armored worm had resurrected.

All fifteen of them piled onto the airboat and Johnny kicked them away from the shore before he started the fan. They gained considerably more speed now that they were headed downriver and toward his cabin.

"Are you sure we'll make it...well, anywhere on this?" Chiron asked and grimaced at the narrow space between his seat on the deck and the edge of the boat.

"'Course I'm sure." The bounty hunter squinted downriver and spared a glance at the crowded deck. "Are we a little over capacity? Yeah. But if I can haul game on this baby, I can haul... shit. Fourteen magicals and three hounds."

"It sounds like far too many when you say it out loud," Lisa muttered.

"Yeah, well, at least the shifters managed to huddle together this time."

They crossed a branching tributary that fed into this river and broke off again another half-mile south. He turned the throttle control stick slowly to keep them centered on the water.

"All right. It ain't more than forty-five minutes until we get to my cabin, so y'all sit quietly and try to—" The whir of a speedboat engine rose over the roar of the giant fan behind him, and Johnny turned to squint through the rotating blades. "What the hell kinda idiot comes up on an airboat like that?"

"Maybe he's in a hurry," Lisa suggested.

"There's more than enough space on the river for—"

A gunshot cracked across the swamp and was immediately followed by a telltale metallic ping as the bullet ricocheted off the propeller's frame.

"Aw, shit."

The passengers turned and tried to find the source of the shot. They peered over the sides of the hull but were unable to move from where they'd found what space they could.

"Is someone shooting at us?" Chiron asked. "Seriously shooting at us?"

"Y'all make weapons and you've never been in a shootout?"

"We're usually the ones doing the shooting," Jasmine replied and flinched when another bullet struck the base of the propeller mount. "Before we came out here, it was only target practice."

"Well, now's your chance to get a little more practice under your belts." Johnny turned the throttle to the airboat's highest speed and gritted his teeth. "Does anyone know how to shoot a harpoon gun?"

"I could take a shot at it," Rick offered.

"You're on the wrong side of the boat, man. You'll throw half the passengers off gettin' to the—"

An automatic weapon fired behind them, although whoever was shooting at them seemed to not know how to aim and steer at the same time. "Dammit!"

Hyla shifted into her human form, crouched on the deck, and stared at the mounted harpoon gun. "I'll do it."

Johnny grimaced at her nakedness and looked hastily directly ahead again. "Yeah, okay."

"Great." Lisa turned from peering through the spinning fan blades. "There are two boats now. Coming up fast."

"Yep." Without taking his hand off the throttle control, Johnny whipped the strap of his rifle over his shoulder with the other hand and offered it to her. "Try to take out the engine first if you can."

"Johnny, I have my own gun."

He gave her an impatient glance and frowned. "Yeah, mine's better. How close are they now?"

"I don't know. Maybe fifty feet."

"Hyla, you fire that when I say so, understand?"

The naked shifter woman grasped the handles on the gun mount and turned it almost all the way around to point at the stern of the airboat.

"Jesus—no! Straight starboard."

"What the hell you talkin' 'bout?"

"Right. Point it straight out to the right!" Johnny grunted and turned toward Lisa. "You lean out to the left and fire a few rounds with that pistol."

"I can't hit them around the giant fan."

"That's the point, darlin'. We need to get 'em to move the other way so the shifter mannin' that harpoon gun can hit 'em."

"Right." The agent balanced herself against the fan base, took a deep breath, and leaned as far as she could over the portside edge of the hull to fire three shots from her pistol. The speedboat drivers returned fire. Bullets pinged off the propeller frame and into the water but weren't any deadlier than that.

"Who gave those idiots guns?" Johnny grumbled.

"Isn't it better that they can't aim?" Lisa shouted.

"Sure. But it makes ya think, you know?"

The speedboats raced closer, and the next shot gouged a chip out of the starboard hull at the stern.

"Shit. Get ready to fire the harpoon."

Hyla tightened her hold on the weapon now aimed correctly to the right of the airboat and grinned.

"If you can hit one of 'em in the process, great. But aim for the boat farthest out."

"Farthest out of what?"

"On the damn starboard side!"

Lisa fired two more shots around the port side to direct the speedboats where she wanted them, then Johnny cut the throttle completely.

The passengers lurched forward in their seats and braced themselves with nothing but hands against the smooth wooden deck.

"Whoa, whoa, shit!" Luther almost toppled headfirst over the bow, but the dwarf with the goggles seated behind him reached out with incredible speed and caught a handful of fur and flesh at the scruff of the hound's neck.

The speedboats raced toward the starboard side, and the second Johnny saw the first glint of another bow under the sun, he shouted, "Now!"

Hyla fired the harpoon gun at the hull of the farthest ship. The barbed point sliced through the frame with a crunch and stuck. Half a second later, the second speedboat raced between them, a sneering Kilomea at the helm with a pistol aimed at the airboat's passengers.

The weapon spun from his outstretched hand when the harpoon rope caught him in the neck and hurled him off the boat and into the river with a strangled choke. Hyla leapt off the airboat with a snarl and landed in the speedboat before it had a

184

chance to lose its speed. Steve had already shifted and reached out with lightning-fast reflexes to catch the pistol. He stared at it in surprise and jumped when Lisa shouted, "Shoot him!" and gestured at the Kilomea in the second boat.

The pistol flipped immediately in the shifter's hand and he only fired one shot. The large magical screamed and fell, clutching his hip. His weapon plopped into the river and vanished.

Hyla uttered a shrieking whoop in the speedboat and kicked it into high gear again to circle and return to where the first Kilomea floundered in the water.

The second speedboat slowed immediately and jerked on the harpoon rope. The gun mount swiveled and groaned when the rope drew taut, and Johnny eased the throttle to make the tug he knew was coming a little less intense. It didn't make much of a difference.

The airboat's hull yanked to the starboard side and twisted them slightly toward the speedboats before the rope slackened again. The shifters and random magicals somehow managed to stay on board through all of it, and he wiped the sweat off his forehead before he turned the throttle slowly to get them up to speed again.

"Make sure he stays there," he told Steve. "Shoot him again if he tries anythin', but try not to kill him."

The shifter kept the pistol aimed at the Kilomea's body barely visible now in the bottom of the speedboat that was dragged behind them.

Hyla raced up portside and whooped again. "Does anyone wanna hop out the sardine can, or what?"

Two wolves leapt immediately out of the airboat and rocked the other vessel when they landed and shifted into Mikey and Aldo. Johnny looked away quickly and shook his head. *I'm sure naked boatin's against at least one law around here. Maybe two.*

He pointed up ahead and shouted without taking his eyes off

the water. "I'm down here a ways. If anyone else shows up behind us, y'all can take it from there, yeah?"

Hyla grinned as she kept the speedboat level with his craft. "And we don't even need guns."

"Great."

CHAPTER TWENTY-ONE

No other random magicals attacked them on the river before they drew up to the dock on Johnny's property. The airboat thumped lightly against the wood, and he nodded at whoever managed to step off first. "Someone grab that dockin' rope, will ya?"

"Got it." The goggled dwarf took care of it as the five remaining wolves and four other Philly magicals practically ran onto the dock to get off the water. Rex, Luther, and Boots bounded down the wooden planks and yipped and snapped playfully at each other.

"You saw him, right, Boots?"

"Yeah, Johnny knows how to steer."

"Johnny knows how to do everything! He—hell yeah, I'll chase you!"

With the airboat tied off and empty, Johnny hauled on the harpoon rope to pull the speedboat toward the shore. The Kilomea inside groaned and his eyes fluttered in his hairy face. A decent-sized puddle of blood had pooled around him already.

Hyla and her two pack members slowed to a rough stop not at the dock but against the bank of Johnny's back yard with a thump and screeching scrape against the hull. They all scrambled out and headed into the yard like it was no big deal to jump out of stolen boats and strut around someone else's property in the nude.

Johnny grunted and tried to reach the bleeding Kilomea's collar to haul him out.

"I got it," Aldo said from behind the dwarf.

"Jeez! You—don't sneak up on me like that, man. And put some clothes on."

"I left 'em out in the swamp." Aldo splashed into the water and pulled the Kilomea over the side of the speedboat with surprising ease, then dragged the guy by his hairy hands up onto the bank and the sparse grass of Johnny's back yard.

"Fine." The dwarf joined Lisa at the head of the dock and shook his head. "I'm tryin' to run a business here, not a nudist colony."

She pressed her lips together to hold back a laugh. "I'd offer to find them some clothes but I don't think anything of yours will fit."

"Naw. One shifter runnin' around in my things was enough. Maybe give them some towels or somethin'."

Lisa scanned the yard that now milled with naked shifters and five Philly magicals who pretended to be interested in anything but the nudists. "Do you have eight towels?"

"I don't count my towels, darlin'. Take some sheets if you have to."

With a low chuckle, she headed toward the stairs to the back door. "I'll see what I can come up with."

"Aldo." Johnny nodded at the huge shifter. "Go ahead and drop him there."

The Kilomea's head and arms thumped immediately onto the dirt and he groaned.

"All right. Let's see if we can't get this asshole to come to and tell us somethin' useful."

It took five minutes for their prisoner to finally open his eyes and become lucid enough for a little chat. Johnny already had his wrists and ankles zip-tied by the time he struggled to rise. He squatted in front of the captive and rested his forearms on his bent knees. "It didn't turn out the way you wanted it to, huh?"

The Kilomea sneered and revealed crooked yellow teeth as he exhaled the stench of a dying animal. "That's what you think." He spat at the dwarf but couldn't get the distance he wanted and only managed to spit on his own chest instead.

Johnny wrinkled his nose, stared at the flecks of spittle, then seized the Kilomea by the shirt collar with both fists and hauled him off the ground. "Who sent you after us?"

The stranger chuckled. "Yeah. You're trying to puzzle out so many pieces, aren't you?"

The dwarf's open hand smacked fiercely against the prisoner's cheek and made his head whip back until Johnny buried his fist in the guy's shirt again. "There's far worse than that for you if you don't start talkin' right now."

"I won't tell you anything."

He drew his arm back and made a fist this time, but the Kilomea's agonized scream made him stop. He looked down to where Aldo's bare toes pressed into the bullet wound in the captured magical's side. Another trickle of blood oozed from the hole, and the magical went slack in Johnny's grasp.

"Hey, hey." He shoved Aldo's calf away. "I appreciate the extra muscle, man, but we don't need him to pass out again so we can start all over."

The shifter grunted and stepped back. "He'd better talk."

"Yeah, he will."

The other shifters and Philly magicals began to gather around the non-violent interrogation and glared at the attacker who'd tried to gun them down in their escape from a much bigger threat.

"I got this. Y'all back away."

"He don't need space to be questioned," Reggie said with a sneer.

"Yeah, well, I need it to do the questionin'. Back away."

They did as they were told but not by much.

The bounty hunter cleared his throat and returned his attention to the questioning. "Who's waitin' on the other side of this to hear you and your buddy eliminated a dozen magicals in the swamp, huh? Gimme a name."

The Kilomea responded with a phlegmy cackle. "There is no name for us, dwarf. Unless, of course, you're looking for the names of those no longer trapped within their pitiful existence."

That caused more animosity among the spectators than Johnny needed.

"What the hell does that mean?" a shifter asked. "Did he kill them?"

"No way this guy and his pal could kill Cassidy and another shifter."

"We're missing six!"

"Shut up," Johnny snapped at them, then smacked the victorious grin off the Kilomea's face. He gritted his teeth and shook his hand, which now screamed painfully from the worm armor cut, the saltwater, and this asshole giving him the runaround. "I know you didn't kill the magicals we're lookin' for, so don't even try to convince me otherwise."

"Kill them? No. But we set them free." Their prisoner sneered again and gazed at the angry magicals surrounding him. "It's cute, truly, that you got two moronic shifter packs to kiss and make nice. If they're not careful, they'll lose anyone who's worth anything in their tiny little packs."

This has somethin' to do with shifters in particular. Johnny shoved the Kilomea to the ground and stood. "All right, Aldo. Have fun. He's all yours."

"And you think everyone's here to help you?" The Kilomea laughed where he sprawled on his back. "We're not buying it."

"Wait, we?" Johnny spun toward the prisoner, but Aldo had already pressed his toes into the guy's hairy, bullet-torn side. The large magical shrieked and muttered something quickly and without pause under his breath. "Hold up." Johnny drew Aldo back again. "What the hell do you mean by 'we?'"

"Doesn't…matter." The Kilomea coughed and swallowed thickly. "The connection's lost already and you'll never find what you're looking for. It's—"

A shudder wracked his body and his eyes flashed with a crimson light before he started to foam at the mouth.

"Shit. Roll him over." The dwarf knelt at his side, but the Kilomea's quick, violent bucking stopped instantly and he didn't move again. "Did y'all see him bite something? I know a cyanide capsule's old-school, but he couldn't aim for shit, either."

"It was a suicide spell," Jasmine muttered and stared at the foam that dripped down the side of the dead Kilomea's face and stuck to his thick fur. "That's what he was whispering to himself."

"Aw, come on." Johnny turned toward the witch, his expression openly skeptical. "Does that exist?"

"Oh, yeah." Her eyes were wide and for the first time, she looked like a month trapped in the swamp had finally gotten to her. "Becky did the same thing during our first week fighting that armored beast."

Lisa stepped toward the group when she heard that and offered the witch an empathetic frown. Jasmine shrugged and turned away. "It looks like another dead end."

"Naw." Johnny snorted and backed away. "He said somethin' about a connection. Who's ever heard someone talk about themselves as a 'we?'"

No one had an answer for that, but his mind had already raced far beyond that snippet anyway. "'Lose anyone who's worth anythin'.' In the packs—he was focusin' on the shifters. That's what this is all for."

"What about Nina, though?" Lisa asked.

"Only two of our guys are shifters," Chiron added. "The other four are three witches and a gnome."

"William." Johnny waited for the city alpha to step through the gathering of mostly naked bodies around the dead Kilomea and glanced briefly at the sky. "Your shifter. Cassidy."

"Yeah."

"Is she special in any kinda…special way?"

The Light Elf snorted. "Very precise."

"She's one of our best trackers along with Steve and Mario." William didn't have to look at his shifters and they both nodded. "And she has an uncanny skill with numbers."

"Numbers?" The bounty hunter wrinkled his nose. "Like math?"

"Like high-level accounting."

"Yeah, that probably ain't the reason she was taken." He turned in a slow circle and scratched his head. "But both y'all's packs would say Magnus and Cassidy were up there in terms of importance, right? If not the best, then damn close?"

"Without a doubt." William nodded.

"You already know how important Magnus is to our pack," Reggie added, unwilling to say anything more about their special bearer in front of even more outsiders.

"What about y'all's?" Johnny pointed at Chiron and his three club members.

"Well, we're all completely involved in what we do, man," the Light Elf answered with a shrug. "But yeah. The magicals we're looking for were ridiculously skilled."

"We might as well call them geniuses," Chiron added. "They were working on next-level ideas before they disappeared and even had a few patents pending."

"Naw, I don't think it's about what they can do specifically." The bounty hunter tugged his beard and scowled at the dead Kilomea. "This one didn't seem all that special, though."

Aldo grunted and kicked the body in the side. He sniffed the air quickly and paused. "Somethin' ain't right."

"Yeah, no shit."

Ignoring Johnny's quip, the hulking shifter squatted in the grass and grasped two fistfuls of the Kilomea's shirt before he ripped it open down the middle. The weapon-makers sucked in sharp breaths and the shifters snarled and hissed. Lisa grimaced and uttered a queasy groan.

The bounty hunter grunted. "I wasn't expectin' to find that."

The fur on the Kilomea's chest had been recently shaved down to his mottled brown skin. A fresh burn mark filled the shaved flesh, still raw and swollen and crusted with leaking fluid in a few places. The guy had been branded on his chest.

The hounds raced around the side of the house and darted between all the two-legs to investigate. Luther reached the Kilomea first and sniffed intently across the ground.

"Whew. What'd you do to this guy, Johnny? Smells like something died in his—" The hound's nose bumped against the dead magical's thigh and he whipped his head up and shook it quickly. "Oh."

"Smells like he was already dying, Johnny." Rex turned to look at Boots, then gazed at his master. "Boots thinks so too."

The bounty hunter leaned closer for a better look, then tilted his head to the left and the right and tried to get a better angle. "What is that? I know I've seen it before."

"It looks like the symbol for one of the dark wizard families," Lisa said and pinched her nostrils shut. "I can't remember exactly which one."

"I wasn't aware that the wizard families branded their Kilomea servants," William said. "Or any of their servants for that matter."

"I don't think that's what this is." The Light Elf stepped toward the body and squinted at the branded symbol the size of two large hands. "It looks the same but that's because of this top part here. My Oriceran's a little rusty—"

Johnny snorted. "Yeah, that happens when you leave the planet for decades."

The Light Elf spared him a glance, then gestured toward the top of the brand. "But if I recall correctly, this aspect up here means unity."

"Dark families sure are as united as shit," Reggie hissed. "With themselves."

"That'd explain the 'we, ourselves, and us' part." Johnny nodded at the Light Elf. "What's your name?"

"Eddie."

"Oh, yeah? Small world. All right, Eddie. Do you have any clue what the rest of this nasty-ass burn's supposed to mean?"

"No. Sorry."

"I don't think it's only for show." William peered at the body over his folded arms. "It's not like a tattoo or a brand someone put on themselves willingly. And yeah, I've seen a few magicals do it for fun. But this is different and not well taken care of at all."

"It could've been from a boss," Johnny suggested. "Or owner if it's like a cattle brand."

"He said he lost the connection." Lisa looked at no one in particular and frowned in concentration. "What if it's some kind of communication spell? That would have shut itself off if whoever was on the other side of the connection knew he was about to end his own life."

"Huh." The dwarf stepped away from the body. "I rarely say go with the modern tech, but shit would've been much easier for the guy if he'd stuck with a cell phone."

"Or it might be it's all part of tryin' to throw us off," Baron commented. "Yeah, he sounded like he knew an awful lot about packs and shifters. Maybe he wanted to push the right buttons and make us force him into checkin' out early."

"This is far bigger than we thought." Lisa rubbed her nose and finally lowered her hand when the stench of the Kilomea's festering brand wound had faded to a more bearable level. "I want to know how this guy and the one in the other speedboat even knew where to find us."

"Yeah. That's the tricky part, ain't it?" Johnny clapped briskly and stepped away from the group gathered around the dead body. The chickens clucked hungrily when he passed the coop, but he barely heard them. "How many of y'all have phones?"

"Um…" Jasmine glanced around. "Probably all of us."

"Anyone ain't got one?"

No one volunteered an affirmative answer.

"I'm guessin' shifters leave theirs at home when they know they're gonna be out shiftin'?"

William nodded. "That's a good assumption, yeah. Sorry, what is that?"

Johnny thumped a hand against Margo's sleek metal shell and a hollow gong sound resulted. "It's somethin' I've been wantin' to use for a hot minute. Y'all…uh, make yourselves at home or whatever. As long as you stay outside."

"Do you want me to ask around about this?" Lisa called after him.

"You might as well, darlin'. It ain't a federal case but gettin' a second opinion from the feds ain't exactly a bad thing at this point either." He disappeared around the side of his new machine and stepped through the dark doorway.

CHAPTER TWENTY-TWO

Lisa pulled her phone out of her front pocket and dialed Tommy's number. She paused when she felt thirteen pairs of magical eyes on her. "If he said make yourselves at home, he meant it. I also wouldn't try to go in the house. This'll only take a few minutes."

She pressed the call button and held the phone to her ear.

Tommy picked up after the second ring. "Oh, now you decide to call me back."

"Yeah. Tommy, listen—"

"It's been six days, Lisa. I can't imagine you and Johnny are so swamped with his new PI work that you can't answer your phone."

"That's exactly what's going on right now."

The other end of the line went completely silent for five seconds. "Are you serious?"

"Yeah. And we're in a tight spot with information on a case, so will you listen and at least try to help us?"

He cleared his throat. "What do you need?"

"Have you had anything come across your desk—or at least

heard of anything—involving a weirdly large number of magicals going missing? Mainly shifters."

"Lisa, we're the FBI. People go missing all the time. Magicals go missing all the time. We both know you don't have to phone in to ask a question like that."

She sighed and tried again from a different angle. "Okay, well what about magicals with huge brands on their chests reminiscent of dark-family symbols? Maybe even talking about themselves in the first-person plural."

"The what?"

"We and us, Tommy?"

"Weird. Uh…I can't say I've ever heard anyone talking like that."

"Well then, what about the brand?"

"Sorry, Lisa. Nothing we've come across so far. Okay, sure, the number of missing shifters across the whole country might've gone up in the last month or so, but that doesn't necessarily mean anything."

"I don't know. It might." she bit her bottom lip and stared at the drying grass beside the chicken coop's electric fence. "Is there even a hint of a connection there?"

"Why would there be? They're spread too far apart. A couple of shifters in Lincoln, Nebraska. A few more from some town I can't even remember in Maine. Don't even get me started on how many magicals are reported missing on the West Coast and end up dead within the week—"

"Yeah, I don't need to hear about everything else you're dealing with right now. I have enough on my plate."

"Are you okay?"

Lisa ran her hand through her hair, turned to stare at the weirdly spaceship-like metal hunk on the other side of Johnny's back yard, and shrugged. "Yeah. We're fine. If anything comes to mind, though, give me a call."

"Sure. So the business is—"

She hadn't meant to hang up on him, but she hadn't expected him to try to keep making small talk after he'd provided her with another dead end. With a grimace, she shoved the phone into her pocket and skirted the naked shifters and clothed weapon-makers to join Johnny inside Margo.

"Hey." Eddie jerked his chin at her and slid his pack with his few emergency belongings off his shoulders. "Do you know what that is?"

"It's a secret project." She turned and walked backward, spreading her arms vaguely. "Emphasis on secret. This is off-limits too."

He looked at the top of the sectioned dome and snorted. "Awesome."

When she rounded the corner, she stopped beside the open doorway and knocked twice on Margo's outer wall, which still sounded like striking a gong. "Johnny?"

"Yeah."

"Can I come in?"

"Whatever you want, darlin'."

She stepped slowly into the strange contraption and found it up and running way more than it had been earlier that morning. The bounty hunter stood at the control panel on the far end and typed on the keyboards. "Wow. Didn't you say this wasn't ready to turn on yet?"

"Naw, she's been ready since she got here. I didn't get to finish settin' her up the way I wanted her to be. She ain't perfect yet but that don't make her useless." He poked a finger down on the final key and spun around to face her. "What'd Nelson say?"

"Basically nothing."

"Surprise, surprise."

"Nothing with the symbols, at least. Or the weird connection making magicals talk like they're more than one person. There are numerous missing magicals, though."

"It's not unusual."

"I wouldn't have thought they could be connected either, but now we have a whole group here from Philly with the same problem of missing members. Only a day before Magnus disappeared, too, and they end up barricaded in the one place where all three trails lead?"

"Like I said, darlin'. I don't do coincidences." Johnny pointed at the five monitors over the control panel. "If there's anythin' to find, Margo will find it."

"Yeah… You still haven't explained that part."

He smirked, then laughed and it settled into a wide grin. "I have a piece of Big Brother in my damn back yard. Can you believe that?"

She wrinkled her nose and studied the monitors scrolling with information way too quickly for her to read. "I'm trying."

"Satellite communication." He patted the control panel. "That's only part of it, but it's the part I got runnin' right now. I set this baby to scan cell phone data, texts, phone calls, Internet searches, emails…Tic-Tac. Whatever the hell's out there, Margo's siftin' through the whole bang caboodle right now."

"Okay, no. I can't believe the Department would hand over a tool like this and certainly not to you."

"Is that supposed to be an insult?"

Lisa grinned at him. "No. Merely the truth."

"Uh-huh." He laughed and moved across the contraption toward her. "I'll have you know they didn't simply hand it over. I told you this was part of the negotiation, didn't I?"

"Negotiation?"

"Sure. The whole Bureau tried to tell me I was insane and I said, 'Try me,' and we both walked away with what we wanted."

"That's certainly one of the more colorful definitions I've heard."

"Either way you cut it, darlin', I got half the US intelligence agency manpower right here next to my shed and I'm puttin' it to use." Johnny set a hand on her lower back and guided her out of

Margo and around the corner toward the rest of the yard. He didn't remove his hand until they came within sight of over a dozen magicals and one dead one lurking on his property. "Dammit. Y'all still ain't covered up, yet? She brought the damn towels."

He thrust a hand toward the stack of towels and sheets Lisa had placed on the edge of the small back porch.

The shifters barely spared him a glance.

"You got somethin' against bodies the way nature intended?" Reggie muttered and smirked at his pack members.

"Nature didn't intend for me to have a horde of naked shifters partyin' in my back yard." Johnny shook his head and stared out into the swamp instead of at so much bare skin. "If y'all can't hide what needs hidin', go ahead and get on home."

"What?" William frowned at the dwarf. "Don't tell us you're giving up."

"'Course I ain't." He turned toward Lisa and cleared his throat. "We ain't givin' up. But we have no other lead right now, so this might take some time."

Hyla snarled and strode across the yard. "We ain't got time. The Glimmering's almost—"

"Not here," Reggie snapped. "We focus on one thing at a time, got it?"

The female shifter glared at the other three from the city pack with undisguised contempt before she stormed toward the side yard to make her way out front. "This is bullshit."

"Don't you have anything for us?" William asked. "Even with your...whatever that is?"

Johnny leaned toward Lisa and scowled at the magicals in his yard. "Did you tell 'em about Margo?"

"What is there to tell? I still don't know what it does beyond the little you told me."

"All right." He nodded and hooked his thumbs through his belt loops. "Correct. I have nothin' for ya. That's for right now. If y'all wanna leave phone numbers or whatever, do that. I'll let you know when I hear somethin'."

"You mean if you hear somethin'." Aldo scowled belligerently.

"Nope. I mean when. It's been a long day, fellas. Go on home and get some rest while you can. I'll reach out."

The shifters grumbled amongst themselves but didn't have anything concrete to argue about. Reggie and William approached Lisa to give her their numbers. She saved them in her phone and forced herself to not look at the two naked men who stood way too close even though she'd already told them to back off.

Finally, the city and local shifters headed out front together to return to their respective vehicles and their dens.

Lisa turned to glare at Johnny as she slipped her phone into her pocket.

He returned her look with a smirk. "What?"

"I told you I'm not your secretary."

"Aw, come on—"

"I did it this time because I didn't want them here without their clothes any more than you did. But it's not my job to take numbers."

The bounty hunter shrugged and shook his head. "You did it before."

"When it was my idea and my initiative. Next time you want contact info, you take it."

"Well damn, darlin'. If I knew it was that big a deal—"

Chiron cleared his throat and they both turned toward the Philly magicals seated on the lawn. The wizard spread his arms. "What about us?"

"Uh…" Johnny turned and scanned the back yard, Margo and the shed, and the back of his cabin. "Y'all can camp here. It's similar to where you've been the last month, only with less…worms."

"Yeah, okay."

WHAT THE DWARF

"Thanks." Jasmine folded her hands in her lap over her crossed legs and nodded. "It's good to be out of there and know we can get out. You know?"

"I bet." Lisa took the stack of towels and sheets off the deck and brought them to the four displaced magicals. "You can use these for now. I'll go see if Johnny has anything a little more comfortable for when it's dark."

"Great. That sounds good." Chiron took the stack of linen and set it beside him before he and his club members engaged in a private, muttered conversation.

She headed toward the porch steps and looked pointedly at Johnny on the way. "Do you have better blankets? Sleeping bags, maybe?"

"They ain't gonna need sleepin' bags, darlin'. It ain't swelterin' at night, sure, but it's still warm enough to sleep naked."

"I think I'm done with naked strangers for today." She snorted and ascended the stairs. "What about food?"

"Sure, I have plenty of that."

"Food!" Rex skittered around the side of the house, raced up the stairs, and almost knocked Lisa over to get past her and through the dog door.

"Come on, Boots! Yeah, of course we'll share. Are you kidding?" Luther pranced toward the foot of the porch stairs as he panted and whipped his tail happily. "Oooh. Bitches first."

The Heeler didn't need any further invitation and simply raced nimbly up the stairs and through the dog door.

"Ha-ha! Watch, Johnny." Luther pranced up the stairs, his head held high. "I'm gonna beat you to it if you don't hurry."

"Beat me to what?"

"You know…" The hound disappeared through the dog door. "Hey, Rex. Stay away from Boots!"

With an exasperated sigh, the bounty hunter opened the back door and held it open for Lisa. *The damn hound's tryin' to one-up me with a Heeler who don't even like him.*

That night, all three hounds snored soundly on the area rug and Lisa snuggled in Amanda's old room, but Johnny couldn't get to sleep. He tossed and turned for a while, then finally gave up and went to the desk in his bedroom. From the center drawer, he retrieved the small black service box he'd made a month earlier—one for him and one for Amanda—and pressed the small button on the side that sent an alert signal to its twin.

Before he could change his mind, he picked his phone up and texted the shifter girl living it up at the Academy of Necessary Magic.

Just checking you're okay. Someone's snatching shifters around here. Reply ASAP.

He sent the text and growled at himself. *I probably sound exactly like all her drill sergeants at that damn school. I should've gone with friendly concern.*

With another sigh, he sat on his mattress, stared at his phone, and waited.

She's safe there. She has to be. But she's not exactly a low-profile shifter either, which is exactly what these kidnappers always seem to want.

Amanda's text came through, and he squinted in the darkness to read it against the incredibly bright backlight.

Not kidnapped. Everything's good. Go catch the bastards.

She finished off the well-rounded message with a smiley face and that was it.

Johnny chuckled in surprise and rubbed his gruff, beard-covered cheek. *Yeah, she's fine. There ain't nothin' to worry about.*

Ten minutes later, he was asleep.

CHAPTER TWENTY-THREE

The next morning, Johnny stood outside over the body of the dead Kilomea and snapped a few pictures with his phone from various angles. The Philly magicals watched him quietly as they finished their simple breakfast. Lisa stepped onto the porch with a cup of coffee in hand and paused to frown at him. "What are you doing?"

"Collectin' evidence."

"Huh. Normally, that wouldn't be a weird thing to hear on a case but it's fairly off-putting coming from you."

"Thanks." He slid his phone into his pocket and looked at her with wide eyes and a tight smile. "Are you ready?"

"For what?"

"Oh. I guess I've been too busy linin' it all up to remember to say anythin'." He cleared his throat and hooked his thumbs through his belt loops. "We have a flight takin' off in an hour and a half."

"What?"

"So pack whatever you need for...eh, call it twenty-four hours."

She glanced at the Philly magicals, who continued to chew their last mouthfuls and watched the business-partner drama unfold in front of them. "Where are we going?"

"Right outside Sedona."

"Arizona?"

"Yeah. Have you been there?"

"No, but it's the only Sedona I know of." She narrowed her eyes at him as she sipped casually from the coffee mug. "Go on. I know there's more."

"Ah. I have an old friend out west right around there who deals in this kinda stuff. Old-school ritual symbols and the like."

"And we have to fly to Arizona because…"

"Well, he's worse than I am."

"Oh." Lisa nodded and laughed wryly. "That doesn't narrow it down very much."

"I meant with technology, darlin'. If you think I'm bad, Otis don't even own a cell phone. And he won't do business unless it's in person."

"How fun."

"Yeah, that's what I thought too."

She didn't bother to tell him she was being sarcastic. "Okay. Twenty-four hours. And you get plane tickets and a hotel room and everything."

"Sure."

"On your dime, Johnny?"

The dwarf scratched the back of his head and gazed around the back yard. "Not exactly."

"Things usually tend to go a little sideways when you say things like that."

"It's taken care of, darlin'. So go on and gather your things. You don't need much for twenty-four hours, right?"

"Nope." With a raised eyebrow, she glanced at the camped magicals again. Jasmine responded with a tight-lipped smile and nodded. Lisa returned the gesture before she returned to the house with a confused frown.

"All right." Johnny pointed at the dead Kilomea. "Do any of y'all know how to deal with this body?"

"Um…" The Philly group shared wary glances. Eddie sighed. "Get rid of it?"

"Yeah. That's a start. I have a chainsaw in the shed over there if you need it. Don't go inside Margo."

"Who?"

"The big metal shell. You can't miss it." Johnny grinned at them. "It's very convenient out here if you ask me—no drivin' and no draggin'. Cut him up and toss him off the dock. The 'gators'll get him real quick and if they don't, somethin' else will."

"Wow." Jasmine swallowed her last mouthful and turned slowly to look at Chiron. "He's serious."

"Do we have to cut him up?" the other dwarf asked.

"No, uh… What's your name?"

"Les."

"All right. No, Les, you don't have to cut him up. It's not likely that he'll float with all that fur, but if he does, that's on you. 'Cause by the time you get that body into the water, I won't be here anymore."

Eddie sighed, pushed to his feet, and headed toward Margo and the shed. "I'll get the chainsaw."

"Attaboy, Eddie." The bounty hunter pointed at him and pumped a fist in encouragement.

"Seriously?" Jasmine called after the Light Elf.

"Hey, we spent a month trapped in the swamp by an unkillable monster who ate all our friends in front of us. Cutting up a dead body that we didn't kill seems tame in comparison." Eddie disappeared behind Margo, and Johnny rubbed his hands together.

"The elf has a point."

"Wow."

"He's right, though," Les added with a shrug.

"Hey, before I forget. Y'all feel free to stay out here until we get back. We won't be gone long but don't go in the house."

Chiron frowned. "So we should...forage for food out here or..."

"Fine. Eat what's in the fridge if you have to. But that's it."

"What about the shower?" Jasmine asked. "I could use a shower right now."

"Sure. The outdoor shower's around the side of the house. And don't forget to feed the hens, huh. The box of feed is right here." Johnny kicked the side of the feed box gently. "It's an electric fence, so don't touch it. And Boots has to be fed too."

"Boots?"

"The little Heeler runnin' around here somewhere. I don't think she's cut out for so much flyin' and trekkin' in such a short time. She seems to like the hounds' food so, yeah. That's also inside. Any questions?"

The magicals stared at him, and Eddie reappeared from the shed with the chainsaw in both hands. "Any suggestions for how to do this?"

The dwarf smirked at him. "Turn it on and start slicin', man. Hey, uh..." He pointed at the laser-bomb gun in Chiron's lap, which the wizard had finished polishing and was now halfway through reassembling again. "Is there any chance y'all have a spare one of them—"

"Nope."

"Sure. Sure. So...don't break anythin'. The workshop's off-limits too. And make sure the animals don't die."

"Twenty-four hours?" Jasmine nodded. "I think we'll all make it."

"Yep." He stared at the magicals, who returned it with neutral expressions and he grimaced. *This is why I don't do house sitters.*

Fortunately, Lisa saved him from having to say anything else when she stepped through the back door with her overnight bag slung over her shoulder. "We have a plane to catch, right?"

"Right. See ya."

"Have fun in Arizona." Jasmine wiggled her fingers and gave them an exaggeratedly huge grin as the two partners headed down the side yard.

Lisa waved in response before they disappeared around the corner of the house. "What was that about?"

"That? Nothin'. Are you all set to head out?"

"Yep."

Johnny whistled. "Rex! Luther! Let's get a move on, boys."

The hounds raced across the yard toward Sheila. "Yes! Ride time!"

"The best time, Johnny. Where are we going?"

"On another plane."

"Ooh! We get treats this time, right? Right?"

"Yeah, we'll see." He opened the back door and sighed when he saw Luther pause to circle Boots with a low whine. "Come on, boy. She'll be here when we get back."

"You wait for me, Boots. Got it? Yeah, I'll be back. Duh. And when I do, you and me—hey." Luther stopped circling and snorted.

Rex burst out laughing and jumped into the back of the Jeep. "Told you, bro."

"Shut up." Luther took one more sniff of Boots' backside before he trotted away. "Don't forget about me, bitch."

"Aw, Jesus." Johnny closed the door behind Luther and moved to the front of the vehicle.

"Is everything okay?" Lisa climbed into the passenger seat and buckled up.

"I think it's about damn time we got ourselves outta here and took a little breather."

"You do?" She smirked at him and didn't even think about bracing herself this time before Sheila lurched into gear and hurtled down the gravel drive. "Johnny Walker's ready to get out on the road. Imagine that."

"It ain't somethin' I enjoy, darlin', but we'll make the most of it."

CHAPTER TWENTY-FOUR

"A jet, Johnny?" They stood on the tarmac of Florida International with the private jet's engines whirring in front of them as the flight attendant waved them up the rolling steps. "You bought us a flight on a private jet."

"Not quite."

Lisa's eyes widened. "You bought a private jet?"

"Ha. Almost. Come on." Johnny strode toward the stairs and she had no choice but to follow him into the aircraft.

Once they were settled in their seats and the hounds lay stretched out in theirs, Lisa turned toward him and narrowed her eyes. "This looks like the jet we took to Baltimore."

He nodded at the flight attendant, who went to get him his Johnny Walker Black, and shifted in his chair. "That might be 'cause it is the jet we took to Baltimore."

"What?" A surprised laugh escaped her. "I thought the point of this whole 'Johnny Walker independent bounty hunter' business was so you could get out from under the department's finger."

"Yep."

"But you didn't get out from under anything if they're still paying for your private jet flights."

"Oh, yeah. They paid for it, all right." He accepted his drink offered by the flight attendant and took a long sip as the captain prepared for takeoff. "But that was a one-time purchase, darlin'."

"No."

"Uh-huh." Johnny tried not to smile and failed as he took another drink.

"They bought you a jet. This jet."

"It's part of our arrangement. Hold on. We'll have us a little toast."

Right on cue, the flight attendant returned with a gin and tonic for Lisa and a syrupy sweet smile for the bounty hunter. "Anything else, Johnny?"

"This'll do fine, darlin'. Thank you."

The agent stared at the drink in her hand and couldn't think of anything to say.

"To the business." He raised his glass toward her.

She laughed and raised hers too. "Hell yeah."

They clinked and drank, and the dwarf cleared his throat as he leaned toward her and stared up the center of the jet's single narrow aisle. "That's a double by the way."

"Great." She took another long sip, then nestled in the seat and closed her eyes. "I'll be nice and comfy when we land in Arizona."

"That's the ticket."

They landed at Sedona Airport a little before noon where a rental car waited for them at the airport. Of course, Johnny drove, and the journey was far longer than she expected. She didn't put two and two together, however, until they passed the exit signs for the city of Sedona and continued toward the open, empty desert.

"Johnny."

"Lisa."

"You said Sedona."

"I said outside Sedona, darlin'. It ain't that far."

An hour later in the middle of nowhere, he pulled the rental onto the shoulder and cut the engine. Lisa stared at him. "No."

"Hey, I don't like it any more than you do, but this is how we get our answers."

"Do you honestly know where we're going?"

"Sure." He leaned forward and pointed through the windshield on her side. "Right up there in them hills."

"Those are mountains, Johnny."

"That's what I said. We'd better get a move on, though. Otis don't like folks stayin' longer than nightfall."

"Wow."

"Yeah, I know." He let the hounds out, and Rex and Luther raced across the parched, baked, cracked earth toward the so-called hills.

"Oh boy, oh boy, oh boy, Johnny!" Luther ran at full speed in a wide circle around the two partners as they started their trek into the mountains. "I've never been out here, Johnny! Look at all this space. All the sky. I think...I can't..."

Rex trotted at his master's side and paused occasionally to sniff the dry, brittle spikes of some desert bush Johnny didn't even want to try to name. "It's hot, Johnny."

"It ain't nothin' new, boys. We do hot all the time."

"Not like this, Johnny. This feels like that electric fence but all over."

Lisa pulled a sun hat out of her overnight bag slung over her shoulder and settled it on her head.

Johnny snorted at her and couldn't look away no matter how hard he tried. "Real cute."

"Yes. My top priority is looking good in the desert, Johnny."

"No, honestly. I mean it."

"Thanks." She glanced at his black duffel bag with the skull and crossbones embroidered on the side. "You brought one too, right?"

The dwarf scoffed as they started up the relatively steep incline. "Naw. I don't do hats."

"Suit yourself."

Over an hour later, Johnny hoisted himself up the last boulder on their route and sat on the edge of the rocks. Lisa turned when she heard him grunt. "Johnny, we took a break only twenty minutes ago."

"Yeah, and I need another. It's damn hot out here."

"Told you, Johnny." Rex sniffed his master's duffel bag. "You have more water, right?"

"Yeah." He took the water bottle out and splashed some into his hand for Rex to lap, did the same for Luther, then tipped his head back and poured even more into his mouth and over his face and head and neck. "Damn. How anyone survives livin' in an oven is beyond me."

"You get used to it."

"Nope. Gimme a hundred percent humidity at ninety degrees any day of the week, darlin'. It's a miracle anythin' even grows out here."

"So how far are we from this friend of yours?"

With a massive sigh, Johnny rose to his feet again and pointed to the next crest ahead of them. "About another ten minutes."

"Well now, you've had your break." Lisa caught his hand and pulled him up the dry, baked and barely visible trail as it wound through dry shrubs and cacti and lichen-covered rocks. "We'd probably be there already if we hadn't stopped."

"You're tryin' to kill me, ain'tcha?"

She snorted and released his hand when he increased his pace and passed her to lead the way. "If I wanted to kill you, Johnny, I can think of at least three other ways that would be much more satisfying than letting you shrivel in the desert."

"Oh, you been thinkin' about the ways, huh?" His chuckle turned into another grunt as he started the next steep incline. "I suppose that means things are gettin' serious between us."

"If you say so."

"Do you wanna fill me in on these top three ways to kill your favorite dwarf?"

"Nope." She laughed when he turned to stare at her. "Oh, come on. If I tell you I have to come up with three completely different ways and these are good."

"All right. I ain't askin' anymore questions."

"Oh-ho! She got you good, Johnny."

Rex sniggered with his brother as they bounded up the hillside. "Burn, as a funny insult and literally, Johnny. Too bad you don't have fur on your face like we do."

The bounty hunter touched his cheek gingerly above the line of his beard and winced. "Shit. Lisa, did you bring that—"

She already had the bottle of sunscreen out of her bag and extended it toward him when he turned again. "I don't have to say I told you so."

"Naw, you don't."

"But I told you so."

"Thanks." He tried to look pissed-off when he took it from her, but a short laugh escaped him all the same. *Now she has me all worked out. I'm screwed.*

He'd miscalculated the distance to Otis' home buried in the Arizona mountains, and it took them another twenty minutes before he recognized the large pillars of red stone that served as his old friend's front gates. "Finally."

"Oh, good. I had begun to think we might be stranded in the desert overnight."

"Naw. I knew it wasn't far. As long as we head down with enough daylight left it shouldn't be an issue."

They crested the final rise of the hill before it descended into a low valley. A wooden shack was set against the exposed stone face of the next rising peak and looked barely big enough for one person to live in comfortably. "That's where your friend lives?"

"Yep."

"It's smaller than your shed."

"That's what it looks like, ain't it? You'll love this." He didn't give her any further explanation before he proceeded into the valley.

The hounds darted in front of him and sniffed at the rare greenery growing in the small narrow valley oasis that got less than half the amount of sunshine as the rest of the desert.

"Plants, Johnny. Real plants. Not those spikey things that make it impossible to take a good— What is that?" Luther spun to face the wooden shack built against the side of the mountain. "Johnny?"

"That's where we're headin' boys. It might be y'all need to stay outside while we have our chat with Otis. But if he does let you in, don't keep runnin' around like a couple of idiots. All right?"

"Hey, that's easy." Rex trotted at his master's side and sniffed the much greener grasses along the valley floor. "There's only one idiot here."

Luther's giggle cut off abruptly. "Wait."

Johnny stopped in front of the slanted wooden door and knocked carefully so he wouldn't dislodge it from the crooked frame. The entire front of the shack trembled under the gentle pressure. "Otis. Johnny Walker."

A slow shuffle sounded on the other side of the door and a dark shape moved clearly between the gaps in the wooden boards. "And?"

"Lisa Breyer, plus two coonhounds. I'll vouch for all of 'em."

Otis sniffed his door heavily and grunted. "Are they house-trained?"

"Is he talking about us, Johnny?"

"Yeah, why would that matter? The dude lives in a shack."

"Since the first week I took 'em in," the dwarf replied. "I know it's been a while but I'm hopin' you might help us with—"

The door creaked open to reveal nothing but a gaping black hole on the other side. Otis' raspy voice sounded like it came from very far away—farther back than his tiny hut warranted. "Don't just stand there, dwarf. You came to do business. Let's do business."

Johnny raised his eyebrows at Lisa and gestured for her to step inside first. She pursed her lips and shook her head slowly. "Yeah, all right."

The hounds squeezed through the narrow door after their master, and the agent cast a last look over her shoulder at the shady valley before she brought up the rear. As soon as she was inside, the door slammed shut behind her and a cloud of dust flurried through the front of the shack.

A fiery glow burst to life ahead and illuminated the inside of Otis' home.

Her eyes widened. "You live in a cave."

"What's wrong with that, huh?"

"Nothing. I only—"

"You thought the crazy old shaman hiding in the desert would be content to live in a shack the size of your bedroom closet. I get it." The hunched figure shuffled past the coffee table and the three cozy armchairs set around it as he cleared his throat and waved them inside. "I'm a recluse, Lisa. Not a monk. And no, technically, I'm not homeless."

Johnny leaned toward her and muttered, "I'll take the rest of this one, huh?"

"It's fine with me."

"Come in, damnit." Otis sat in the center armchair and flicked his wrinkled brown hands to adjust the cuffs of his lightweight, flowing, long-sleeved shirt. "You came all this way, which means you want something. No one gets anything in this life by waiting around for someone else to give it to them. Johnny, sit."

His lips pursed, the dwarf moved toward one of the two empty armchairs and lowered himself into it. Otis stared at Lisa until she took the chair on his other side. His eyes morphed from black to blue to purple and then to black again every time his

MARTHA CARR & MICHAEL ANDERLE

gaze shifted. The hermit's stark white hair stood up in ruffled clumps from his head covered in age-spots, and his puckered lips gave him a toothless look until he grinned at her to reveal two complete rows of perfectly white, perfectly straight teeth. "I like you."

"Thanks."

"You have no idea what you're doing here."

She laughed and gestured across the coffee table at Johnny. "No, but he does."

"Yeah, Johnny always thinks he knows what he's doing. What do you want, dwarf?"

The bounty hunter snapped his fingers and pointed at the floor beside his armchair. Both hounds obeyed immediately and sat where he indicated.

"It smells weird in here, Johnny." Luther licked his muzzle.

"Like magic. Way too much magic. I don't think it's his."

Johnny raised an eyebrow at the hounds and muttered. "Quiet. Stay."

"What?"

"Why are you talking in one-word sentences all of a sudden?"

There's no way in hell I'm tellin' Otis about those collars. That'd be the end of this meetin' and any leads for this case.

He turned away from his hounds and shrugged "We have a little problem, Otis."

"No shit. Why else would you fry your face like that trying to reach my front door?" The wrinkled magical leaned forward in the chair and squinted. "I thought I told you last time you were here not to fuck around in this desert without sunscreen."

Lisa stifled a laugh and lowered her head to hide her smile when Johnny glanced at her.

"Yeah, you did."

"And you haven't gotten any smarter in the last twenty years. Well, hey. At least you haven't gotten uglier, either."

Rex looked at his master and chuffed. "What's up with this guy, Johnny?"

"I think your dog wants something, dwarf." Otis nodded at the hound. "Boy, if I'd known an animal like that could look so confused—"

"He's fine," Johnny muttered.

"Okay, okay. Great." Otis spread his arms expansively and clapped. The sound echoed harshly around the cave, and the fire-light in the lanterns mounted along the stone walls blazed brighter for half a second. "Let's see what you got."

CHAPTER TWENTY-FIVE

Here goes nothin'.

Johnny tilted his head and shifted slowly in the armchair. "I brought my phone with me—"

"Aw, Christ, Johnny."

"It's only so I can show you a picture. Maybe two if you need a different angle 'cause I got no idea what this is and there are many lives on the line. Are we good?"

"Well, don't sit there all afternoon, man. Show me the damn picture."

The bounty hunter drew a deep breath through his nose and took his phone from his back pocket. *I don't remember him being this rough around the edges last time. Or maybe I'm a little smoother than I was twenty years ago.*

He unlocked his phone and pulled up the images of the magical brand on the dead Kilomea's chest. Without a word, he leaned over the armrest and held the phone toward Otis as far as his arm would allow.

The wrinkled old hermit leaned so far forward, his backside practically hovered over the chair's cushion. When he squinted at the screen, his eyes flashed rapidly between their myriad colors as if to indicate careful scrutiny of the image. "So?" he asked finally.

"Do you know what that symbol is?" Lisa asked.

Johnny looked warningly at her.

"Of course I know what it is." Otis slumped in his chair and pointed at her. "I still like you but you ask stupid questions. Next."

Johnny sighed and slid his phone into his pocket. "What is it?"

"There you go. You know, I haven't seen that one in a long time, Johnny. And I mean a very long time." He winked at Lisa and flashed his weirdly perfect teeth in a wide grin. She wrinkled her nose and leaned away. "But I never forget something I've seen before."

"So it's nothin' new."

"Nope." Otis pointed at the dwarf, examined him in an apparent search for the cell phone, then shrugged. "That is a super-old, super-power sigil used by some of the shittiest magicals I can think of."

"Great."

"They used it often on Oriceran way back before your time, Johnny. Almost before mine but not quite."

Johnny stared at the hermit and forced himself to remain silent. *He'll get to the point eventually. I only hope it's before he kicks us out.*

"Ass-backward communities of magicals, if you catch my drift. I remember the year it died out at home. Or maybe lost its popularity with the masses. Who knows?" Otis sniggered and glanced at each of his guests. When neither offered much of a reaction, he shrugged. "And now it looks like someone decided to bring it back for another round but on Earth. Exactly like fanny packs. Right, Johnny?"

The dwarf tsked. "Those ain't never comin' back."

"Never say never." The hermit leaned back in his chair, folded his arms, and crossed one bony knee over the other. His bare foot with grotesquely long toenails bounced up and down as he smiled pertly.

I hate this game.

Johnny took another deep breath. "And what does the sigil do?"

"Oh, that." Otis scoffed and gave the dwarf's question a dismissive wave. "It's a command sigil using high-frequency transmutation magic set to rewire the individual consciousness and convert it into one overarching thought process spread across multiple subdivisions of emotional, mental, and some-times physical sensitivities."

The cave fell silent.

Luther uttered a low whine. "Can we go now, Johnny?"

The bounty hunter exhaled slowly and tried to hide his frustration. "You're gonna have to dumb that down for me, brother."

"I will? Eh, well, I already said you haven't gotten any smarter. Here's the idiot version. That sigil, when burned into someone's flesh, assimilates that magical into the collective consciousness of a hive-mind. Better?"

"Wait." Lisa frowned and squeezed her eyes shut as she tried to put the pieces together. "You're saying this Kilomea wasn't operating under his own free will but...what? The orders of someone else?"

"Whew, you two make a perfect dummy pair, don't you?"

"Otis." Johnny gestured in irritation.

"No way. That Kilomea was most certainly operating under his own free will, which happened to be the free will of the entire hive-mind into which he'd been assimilated. How hard is that to understand?"

"Wow." She shook her head and studied her hands in her lap. "The whole 'we' and 'us' makes more sense now."

"So who else did you kill besides that hairy beast with the giant teeth to get this far in the puzzle?" Otis grinned at Johnny. "How many?"

"No one. We're trying to find a number of magicals snatched up without warnin' and taken away to…who knows where."

"Uh-huh."

"That Kilomea came after us, tried to stop us, and when we flipped the script on him, he said we'd never find what we were lookin' for. Then, he offed himself."

"And?"

Johnny rolled his eyes. "I give up."

"If this hive-mind were recruiting new magicals," Lisa began, "would there be any reason for the missing magicals to come from farther away from each other as opposed to all in the same place? Like the same city?"

"Uh, yeah." Otis scoffed. "The hive-mind draws way less attention if they're spread out all over the place. People can't pick up on how weirdly these guys are acting if they only see it in one magical once in a blue moon."

"That would explain Philly, at least."

Johnny scooted to the edge of his armchair. "What about shifters?"

"What about shifters?"

I can't believe I never wrung his scrawny neck. He gritted his teeth and forced himself to speak calmly. "These magicals—the hive-mind, if we're callin' it that—have focused on bringin' more shifters in than any other kind. At least that we know of."

"It makes perfect sense to me." The shaman nodded. "Shifters are the easiest sell."

"What?"

"Come on, Johnny. Use your brain. Hell, your head's already big enough. There's a large amount of concentrated magic in a shifter. They don't need illusions and they live in two bodies. It makes them ridiculously powerful, right? Of course, I wouldn't say shifters are the best at casting spells per se, but they already spend their lives operating under a pack mentality. So you have super-strength and shifter-whatever abilities on one hand." Otis held out one wrinkled hand to demonstrate, then the other. "And on the other, you have super-easy-peasy indoctrination because they're already primed to take it where it hurts. Think about it. Why wouldn't a single entity with a few thousand tiny little minds swarming over a planet want a hefty helping of shifters in the mix? It's always good to have one of them on your side."

"Sure." Johnny snorted and frowned at the coffee table. "Unless it's a side gearin' up for somethin' very big and very bad."

"Nah." The hermit waved him off. "It died out on Oriceran. It'll run its course here too."

"How long did that take the first time?" Lisa asked.

Otis took a moment to think about it. "A few thousand years."

"Yeah, that's not something we can let run its course." She caught Johnny's gaze and raised her eyebrows.

Yep. It's worse than I thought too.

"Is there anythin' else you wanna add to that bright ray o' sunshine before we head out?"

The old shaman glanced from one to the other, then shrugged. "Nope."

"Is there anything else we should know?" Lisa clarified.

"Ah!" He pointed at her and gave her his widest grin yet. "I knew there was a reason I liked you. You're catching on, little half-Light Elf. The answer's still no."

"Thanks for your time, Otis." Johnny stood from the chair and extended his hand toward the hermit. "We appreciate it."

"I know." He clapped his hand around the dwarf's forearm instead of making a normal handshake but didn't stand from his armchair. "Whatever you do, Johnny, don't let the bastards stick that brand on you. The world could use more big heads like yours. Both worlds could come to think of it."

"Good tip."

"Oh, hey. And maybe invest in a Polaroid camera before coming back here, huh? I hate even sitting in the same room as a cell phone. You know that."

225

"If I can find one, sure. We'll see ourselves out."

"Yes, you will." Otis sank into the armchair until his narrow frame rested at a forty-five-degree angle and slapped his hands onto the armrests with a contented sigh. "Yes, you will."

The hounds cast the hermit wary glances as they hurried after their master. "That's the weirdest guy we've met, Johnny."

"Yeah, that two-legs has some serious issues."

"And he smells weird."

"And he talks like a hound but makes even less sense."

Johnny pushed the wobbly front door of the fake shack. As soon as it opened, the lantern light in Otis' cave winked out and nothing but complete darkness yawned behind them again.

They stepped out into the valley, blinked fiercely, and shielded their eyes against the suddenly blinding intensity of the sunlight. Luther yelped when the wooden door slammed shut again, knocked against his tail, and made him skitter across the scrubby dirt.

"Well." Lisa pulled her aviator sunglasses off her head and slid them on before she put her hands on her hips. "That was more insightful than I expected."

"It always is with him." Johnny flipped his sunglasses open and put them on one-handed. "If you can get past the parts that make you wanna kill him first."

"Old Oriceran sigil magic. Hive-mind kidnappings. Johnny, this feels way bigger than I thought it would be. It's like stumbling onto something like the Red Boar all over again. He was everywhere too."

"I hear ya. The good thing is I ain't got a personal vendetta against whatever asshole's runnin' the show with this." Johnny frowned and gazed at the sun-drenched peaks in front of them. "It should be easier to stay focused this time around—on track. I aim to find one of these hive-mind suckers, snatch him up, and keep him from killin' himself like the last guy."

"To...what? Interrogate someone else who will simply laugh in our faces again?"

"Naw. But I think I can find a way to get into one of these brainwashed magical's heads and pick out a few key pieces on my own."

She wrinkled her nose as she considered this. "That's a tall order."

"I like a challenge." He headed toward the mountainside, then paused and turned to point at her. "And you know what? I still have a couple of leftover potions from this one time I was out in New Orleans and had to interrogate a group of..." He only realized how deep he was digging himself in again when he noticed her slowly widening eyes. "Never mind. It don't matter how I got 'em. What's important is I got 'em."

She let it go and turned to frown at the fake shack-front built against the stone side of the mountain. "You know, I couldn't work it out and I usually can."

"What's that?"

"What kind of magical is Otis, exactly?"

Johnny chuckled. "I've been tryin' to find that out for the last fifty-odd years, darlin'. I simply had to accept the fact that he ain't never gonna say, either."

"Huh."

"Time to go, Johnny. Come on." Rex trotted up the mountain rise in the direction from which they'd come.

"Yeah, let's get outta here." Luther snorted and shook his head. "Creepy two-legs left a bad taste in my mouth."

"I think that's only your mouth, bro."

"Maybe. Maybe not."

The dwarf headed after the hounds and paused to offer Lisa a hand up the next set of stones embedded in the mountain that were almost as climbable as a staircase. She gave him a playful frown but took his hand anyway and let him pull her up. "So what now?"

"Now? I think we make one more stop after this."

"Uh-huh. You had this whole thing mapped out before we left Florida, didn't you?"

"I wish I could say I did, darlin'. Honestly, everythin' was ridin' on this get-together with Otis. But now I know exactly where we're headin'."

"And that is?"

"Wyomin'."

"Oh, come on, Johnny."

He laughed and continued his steady trek up the hillside after the hounds. "There's no reason to get all twisted about it. I said a twenty-four-hour trip and I meant it."

"Yeah, but three states in twenty-four hours?"

"Lisa, the FBI bought me a private jet. We could make it to every state on this side of the country if we wanted."

"Nope. Wyoming's fine."

CHAPTER TWENTY-SIX

Around dinnertime, they pulled up in their second rental car of the day at the gated entrance of a massive ranch in Cody, Wyoming. The intricately crafted wrought iron gates opened slowly inward, and Johnny smirked as he pressed the accelerator and rolled through.

Lisa stared out the window with a smile of disbelief. "First a crazy hermit of indeterminate race in the desert mountains. And now, a cattle rancher in Wyoming. I had no idea you even knew your way around places like this."

He chuckled. "It's been a while, sure, but I have friends almost everywhere, darlin'."

"Yeah, I'm starting to see that. So why are we here?"

"Well, to start, Grady ain't a cattle rancher. That's his sister's business and she's doin' damn well for herself by the looks of it."

"And Grady is a…"

"Tinkerer."

She laughed. "Are you serious?"

"Absolutely. We toyed with a few things together when we were first startin' out. You know, discovering our own invention style."

"Oh, you did, did you?"

"Laugh all you want, Agent Breyer. That'll stop as soon as you see what this guy's capable of."

"Hmm. Why don't you tell me? Otis was enough of a surprise."

He cleared his throat as they passed the main house and continued down the road toward a long narrow building half a mile down. "Fine. As I bet you already noticed, my specialty is in weapons—different Boom levels and gettin' the most bang for a buck I ain't gotta spend."

Lisa snorted. "Go on."

"Grady here does the same kinda tinkerin' with whatever already exists. Sometimes, he comes up with something from scratch, but his best work is also in improvements. Only this guy's been doin' some wild stuff with syncing tech to living consciousness."

"Um…" She took a sharp breath. "Did you use the word syncing in the correct context?"

"Yeah, I know what it means."

"Tech and consciousness?"

"The sentient mind, darlin'."

"Wow."

He pulled their car to a stop in front of the long building and shifted into park. "That's right. Here's a fun little fact for ya. Grady invented virtual reality."

"What, like the games?"

"Uh-huh. The only problem was that it was way too ahead of its time when he had it all hooked together. He had to dumb it down so humans could stomach it 'cause they weren't ready to dive all-in."

"How long ago was this?"

The dwarf unbuckled his seatbelt and raised his eyebrows at her. "1962."

Lisa laughed and sat there even after he exited the car and opened the back door for the hounds. "That's impossible."

"Say that again when you see his shop."

She finally pulled herself together and got out of the car, then stopped to take in the full expanse of the building that stretched in front of them. "I didn't know ten-car garages existed."

"Oh, sure. It ain't for cars, though. Come on." Johnny strode to the door at the very end of the building and knocked briskly. A camera lens opened in the top of the door and swiveled until it settled on the dwarf, the half-Light Elf, and the two hounds. "Hey, man. It's Johnny."

A lock slid noisily before the door handle turned on its own and the door swung open.

"That's a neat trick." Johnny pointed at the hounds. "Y'all touch anythin' and you'll wait out the rest of this outside."

"Why would we wanna touch anything, Johnny?"

"Yeah. The place already smells like wires and melting plastic."

The bounty hunter pushed the door fully open and stepped inside.

The garage was one massive room, open from this side to the other, although the far end was impossible to see. Filling the space were rows upon rows of tables scattered with machine parts, robotic limbs, and gadgets for every conceivable purpose. Johnny scanned the warehouse-workshop with undisguised curiosity. *How many grenades could I make in a workshop this size?*

"Grady?"

Lisa peered into a clear plastic bucket on the closest table, which was filled halfway with tiny metal hands. "Wow. What are these supposed to—"

"Please don't touch." The voice came from everywhere and echoed across the garage.

She flinched and spun reflexively, but of course, no one was there. "Sorry."

"It's fine. I know it's curiosity. I like curiosity. Without it, where would we be right now? I'll tell you where—grunting and huddling around a fire in a cave, ignorant to the word fire or the fact that we control our destiny. Or dead. Then again, curiosity can kill us too. But not in here."

She glanced at Johnny and grimaced. "What?"

"Come on back, Johnny." The eager voice echoed from speakers in the ceiling. "All the way to the end. It's a fair walk, but there's nothing wrong with exercise. Ha-ha. When you can get it."

"Yeah, okay." Johnny nodded for everyone to follow him, and the walk down the massive garage seemed to take much longer when they had to skirt piles of discarded parts, multiple open boxes of tools, and a rumpled tarp spread over something in the shape of a U with the words *Do Not Step Here* printed on it in large black letters.

As they wove carefully through Grady's experiments and contraptions, a soft, rhythmic click and hiss grew louder. When they reached the other side, Johnny sucked in a sharp breath.

"Hey, Johnny." The other magical sounded way too chipper for his current circumstances. "Yeah, yeah. I know. It was a surprise for me too, but what can you do, right? I started giving out years ago and then I found a way."

Lisa turned in slow circles, scanned the walls and shelves, and even bent over to search under the closest tables. "Johnny…"

He caught her hand and squeezed, then nodded ahead toward the far wall of the garage.

"Oh," she whispered and swallowed thickly. "My God."

Grady the gnome—or what used to be a gnome, at least—hovered in front of them. Very little of his original body was visible beneath the thick net of wires, cables, tubes, and nanotech mesh that held him suspended four feet off the floor. He could have been floating in a stasis tank full of fluid given how animated he was, which was not at all.

Johnny gritted his teeth and tried to decide how to approach this. "It…uh, looks like you stepped it up a notch with the organitech, Grady."

"I know you don't mean that as a compliment, Johnny, but

thanks anyway. Who's your friend?"

"Lisa," she answered quickly. "Did you build all this...stuff for yourself?"

"Oh, you're interested, huh? The short answer's yes. I knocked my body around a few too many times working out how to shovel my consciousness in and out of...hell, basically whatever I want. And then, you know, more problems mean more necessary solutions, which by default create more problems. So here I am."

"And here."

"And here."

"And down here. Oh. Hey, doggy."

Luther backed away from the ten-inch robot that rolled toward him on treads beneath its metal feet. Its eyes flashed blue and white in rotation. "Johnny? What kinda trick is this? I don't like it."

"Hey, don't be scared." Grady's voice came from everywhere at once again, which included the speaker on the robot's face where a mouth would have been. "Wanna fetch? Here."

The robot raised its jointless metal arm and the end folded away in tiny segments to reveal a built-in cannon. A small red bouncy ball launched from its barrel-hand and bounced under the table.

Luther snorted. "I'm good."

"Huh." The robot turned smoothly and rolled away. "That usually works."

"I assume you got my message about a small...update I'm fixin' to make on my end."

"Yeah, Johnny. I got it. I was surprised to hear you wanted to get your hands on any of my work, though."

"Well, it's for a good cause. That's the whole point, right?"

"You bet. Always looking for ways to be bigger, faster, stronger." When Grady—or his consciousness—laughed, it sounded more robotic and far less alive than anything he'd said so far. "Anyway, it's over here."

A metallic arm descended from the ceiling and rummaged in one of the shelving units below it before it withdrew a simple black box. Johnny grimaced and strode toward the robot hand that held out his newest gift from the gnome who was no longer much of a gnome. "Thanks. What do you want for this?"

"What do I want? Nothing, Johnny. Come on!" That last part shrieked deafeningly through the speakers. "I wouldn't be where I am right now without you—relatively speaking. You go kick some ass and save some lives, huh? Hey, don't forget to send me observations, though. It's the only way anything gets done around here. Constant vigilance and always experimenting."

"You got it, Grady. Good…seein' ya."

"Yeah, you too. Even though your increased temperature and heart rate tell me you don't mean it."

"Hey. Stay outta my vitals." Johnny turned and gestured for Lisa to follow him down the long garage so they could get the hell out of here.

"Feel free to try it on yourself, Johnny," Grady called and his voice echoed from each speaker in front of them as they moved. "You got the best updated version. It'll blow your mind."

When they all scrambled into the car, the bounty hunter shoved the black box into the center console and started the engine.

"You know, you could have said more about your friend Grady the gnome cyborg," Lisa muttered.

"I didn't know he'd gotten that bad, all right? It's been at least twenty…twenty-two years since I seen him, darlin'. And he went way downhill."

"You don't say. I think I prefer Otis, honestly."

"Uh-huh." He shifted into gear and pulled away from the garage to move down the long drive toward the estate's front gates. "See? That's why I ain't a fan of all that fancy shit every-one's callin' 'modern tech.' You saw what it did to him. I'll take old-school over that any day of the week."

CHAPTER TWENTY-SEVEN

Early the next morning, Johnny woke in his bed in the Everglades and rolled out quickly, feeling fairly optimistic despite everything they still had left to do. He shuffled into the kitchen to make a pot of coffee, careful not to make too much noise and risk waking Lisa in Amanda's room.

Sure, we had a few late nights. It's better to let her crash here than try drivin' to that hotel in the middle of the night. He leaned away from the counter and peered across the hall at the closed door of the second bedroom. *Yeah, all right. Dammit. I like her stayin' over.*

The coffee started its burbling, hissing trickle into the pot and Luther whimpered in his sleep on the living room floor between Boots and Rex. He whipped his head up with a sharp bark. "Johnny! Someone's coming!"

"Shh!" The bounty hunter grunted and strode through his workshop and into the hallway. "Do you wanna wake up every damn magical on the property, boy?"

"What's the big deal? They'll be up anyway."

Boots raised her head and growled.

"Yeah, yeah. Pipe down. It's the shifter pals, Johnny."

"Dammit. I told them to wait for a call."

Rex snorted, lifted his head, and allowed himself a massive yawn. "Maybe they were too excited to see you, Johnny."

"Yeah, right." He snatched the coffee pot up before it finished brewing, poured himself a cup, and took it with him as he stormed through the front door.

Thirty minutes later, the shifters from the local pack and the city pack stood outside with Johnny, Lisa, and the Philly magicals.

"So that's what we discovered and now, we're lookin' at the next steps to get this whole business wrapped up best we can." Johnny shrugged, raised his coffee cup to his lips, and grunted when he found it empty.

"And now you want to hook a hive-mind magical up to your fancy machine with a fancy new gadget that'll...what?" William squinted at the dwarf. "Read its mind?"

"Sure. Why not?"

"Where will we find someone who's a part of the hive-mind?" Eddie asked. "The Kilomea's dead."

"And disposed of, I noticed." Johnny gave the Light Elf an exaggerated wink and a quick thumbs-up. "I reckon we'll be able to find us another one soon enough. The Kilomea was tryin' to gun us down, after all."

"Wait." Lisa shook her finger in the air and frowned in thought. "We found that clearing, fought the worm, and met you guys."

Chiron folded his arms. "Yep."

"And the monster was still down when we made our escape. It hadn't regenerated yet. So the Kilomea and his buddy, whoever they were, targeted us instead."

Jasmine's eyes widened. "Do you think they knew where we were because of the monster?"

"It makes sense. If that worm is part of the hive-mind too, it could have sent some kind of message or something to everyone else. That it was down for the count but had been attacked by us —a new threat."

Johnny grinned at her. "Darlin', that's brilliant."

"Thank you."

"And I think it's worth a shot." He folded his arms and nodded at the magicals gathered in his back yard. "So who's ready to go for another hunt?"

"Wait. Hold on a minute." Les held his hand up and shook his head, his eyes even larger than usual behind his thick goggles. "We can't kill it."

"That's why it's perfect. And we don't need to kill it, man. All we gotta do is find it, beat it up enough to haul it back here with us, and hook it up to Margo."

"Margo?"

"The big metal contraption over there." The bounty hunter snorted. "I thought we'd been over this."

"Do you honestly think that damn worm has thoughts enough for your new mind-reader doohickey to pick up on?" Reggie asked. "Assumin' we get that far without havin' our guts chewed out first."

"Well, I don't know, Reggie. But we ain't gonna figure that out by standin' here and debatin' every single tiny detail. I thought y'all wanted to find your missin' folk."

"We do." William nodded. "I won't speak for anyone except my guys, Johnny, but we're in."

"All right. The rest of y'all better hurry up and decide what you wanna do 'cause I'm fixin' to head on out after that beast in the next twenty minutes. Hey." Johnny pointed at Chiron and wiggled his eyebrows. "How many of those laser-bomb guns y'all got on ya right now?"

"All of them."

"Great. We'll take those with us too."

As it turned out, Reggie's pack didn't want to be left out of the action either. Fortunately for the large group of magicals who were all determined to work with Johnny and Lisa on the case, two speedboats were docked next to the airboat. While the two partners had been away, the group had made hasty but water-worthy repairs to the one that had been damaged and they were able to take full advantage of the extra craft.

The bounty hunter was particularly happy about the extra opportunity to use the massive cannon he'd previously rigged to the self-deploying mount in Sheila's secret compartment. With a few quick modifications, he managed to secure the weapon ready for action on the airboat's harpoon-gun mount. He grinned like an insane dwarf and couldn't stop admiring his handiwork as he steered the airboat carrying the Philly magicals, Lisa, and the hounds north through the swamp.

The shifter packs, of course, segregated themselves in the speedboats but overall, everyone had far more space. In addition, there was much less potential for unnecessary fights to break out before they could even get the job done.

They didn't reach the clearing where the weapon makers had set up camp and didn't need to. The giant armored worm had resurrected and attacked again, this time forsaking the element of surprise in lieu of darting agitatedly along the river in front of the clearing.

It's like it knows they can't help but come back for their belongings.

Johnny held his free fist up and cut the throttle with his other hand. The airboat slowed to a light drift along the river and the speedboats quieted their engines as well. "Y'all know the plan," he said but only loudly enough for everyone to hear. "Aim for the spaces between the armor plates with whatever you have. As soon as this bastard's out for the count, we'll tie him up and haul him outta here."

Eddie sneered at the huge sand-colored worm that thrashed on the bank of the clearing and cracked his knuckles, one hand after the other. "Blasting that bitch apart never gets old."

"That's the right headspace, Elf. Let's do this."

The Philly magicals readied the few explosive weapons they'd managed to escape with, although each one of them held the short, squat laser-bomb guns as well. The shifters snarled in their prospective speedboats. William and his members untucked and unbuttoned their shirts in preparation for transformation. Reggie and his team showed no consideration about what happened to their clothes as long as they were able to sink their teeth into the giant armored bastard that simply wouldn't die.

Johnny stepped toward the harpoon mount that now held his specialized cannon and winked at Lisa. "Are you ready, darlin'?"

She smirked at him. "Shoot the damn thing."

"Yes, ma'am." He grasped the swiveling handlebars and cranked the mount toward the restless monster that flailed along the shore. It sprayed water and bellowed in frustration and impatience. Once he had the gnarly, tooth-filled maw within the crosshairs of his sight, he squeezed the thick trigger of the cannon gun and fired.

The cracking boom of the weapon as it launched its first attack triggered an actual vibrating ripple that raced away from the airboat across the river. The cannon burst streaked toward the clearing and pummeled the worm halfway down its midsection. The monster lurched with a scream and folded in on itself for two seconds before it launched into the water and raced toward them, faster than either of the speedboats.

"Get ready for it!"

The shifters thumbed the tops of the first round of exploding disks Johnny had given them. All eight of them found their intended targets within the thin, exposed spaces between the armored segments. The Philly magicals raised their laser-bomb guns and steadied themselves on the deck of the speedboat. Lisa slid the bolt into place on Johnny's crossbow and aimed. She glanced briefly at the bright-red tip of the bolt—a Boom Six.

The worm bellowed again and lurched in a jerky zig-zag

motion across the river, increased its speed, and almost emptied the riverbed with the dragging force of its massive wake.

"Take it down!" Johnny fired the cannon again and the huge projectile filled with dozens of mini explosives rocketed toward the monster's gaping mouth.

A second before the ordnance made impact, the worm darted to the side and dove beneath the water. Its violent wake swept over the bows of all three crafts.

"What the fuck!" Johnny scanned the river for his target and ignored the explosion of his perfectly aimed cannon shot when it detonated on the riverbed instead of in a giant hive-mind monster's gut. "That ain't the way this plays out."

The shifters who'd already detonated their explosive disks held on as long as they could before they threw them uselessly upriver. They exploded in quick succession with a severely anti-climactic splash.

"What a waste," the dwarf grumbled.

"Hive-mind," Lisa muttered and turned slowly to scan the opposite side of the bank and farther upriver. "It's not operating on its own anymore."

"Damn."

"So now what?" Hyla snarled. "We wait for it to attack us again? If it knows how to duck and dodge now, we're screwed."

"Not necessarily." Chiron steadied his grasp on the laser-bomb gun in his hands. "This monster has—"

The airboat lurched forward when the beast surged from the water behind the vessels. Everyone shouted, turned, and aimed their weapons at the toothy, bellowing jaws that descended toward them with incredible speed.

Johnny swung the cannon on the mount and fired. At such close range, he barely had to aim. The shot pounded into the underside of the worm's jaw, which snapped shut against its upper jaw with a splintering crack. The creature reared, propelled by the force of the blast, and a spray of what looked like shattered teeth exploded from either side of its mouth.

"It's now or never," William shouted and lobbed a new explosive disk at it.

With a deafening hiss, their massive adversary rocked forward and plunged below the water again. The other shifters threw their disks and managed to lodge half of them between the armor plates through nothing more than sheer luck. They detonated one after the other, sent huge ripples across the river, and made the worm's body shudder. Unfortunately, that seemed to be the extent of the effect.

Johnny pointed at the laser-bomb guns. "Do those do any damage to that armor?"

"Nope." Les shook his head as he searched for the monster again. "Trust me. We've already tried and more than once."

"Well, shit. Now the fuckin' thing decided to get smart on us—"

The beast's head reared from the river on the port side this time. It rocked the airboat violently before it plunged into the water and submerged itself. The segmented body raced in a constant arc with an odd ripple-like movement almost too fast to see until the end of its huge tail whipped out of the water and arced toward the city shifters' speedboat.

All three of them leapt overboard simply to get the hell out of the way. The weight of the monster's tail pounded into the side of the speedboat and launched it across the water toward Johnny and the cannon. Everyone but Les saw it coming and ducked. The goggled dwarf, however, was caught completely off guard and had nothing to grasp hold of as he flailed his arms and tried not to fall over back into the water.

He toppled, however, despite his frantic efforts.

The bounty hunter lunged toward him and tried to catch hold of the other dwarf's shirt or arm or something, but it was too late.

"Les!" Jasmine raced toward the side of the airboat and searched the river desperately for her friend. "We have to get him out of there. That bastard could snatch him up and we'd never even see it."

"It's comin' back," Johnny muttered when he noticed the tell-tale movement beneath the surface of the river that looked like nothing more than a breeze ruffling the surface. Except, of course, that there was no breeze.

"Les!"

"Hey—there he is!" Chiron took Jasmine by the arm and pointed to the other side of the boat. Les bobbed in the water where he sputtered and waved his arms over his head. "No, no. Don't do that, buddy. We'll come and get you."

"Swim as calmly as you can," Eddie added.

The dwarf began to comply before his eyes widened behind his water-streaked goggles and his mouth fell open.

"Everyone off the boat," Johnny snarled and snatched the laser-bomb gun out of Jasmine's hands. She didn't protest even slightly.

Lisa leapt toward him. "We can—"

"You too, darlin'. Now!" Without thinking, he shoved her roughly over the side of the airboat and heard her shout of surprise and the splash as she landed in the water. "Out, boys!"

"You hit it first, Johnny!"

"We'll rip it apart after that!"

The hounds bounded over the side with the rest of the Philly magicals as the worm reared out of the water to a height of a full thirty feet above the airboat.

The bounty hunter switched the safety off on the laser gun and braced the stock against his hip as he aimed up with both hands. He gritted his teeth and stared into the open, razor-lined maw of the monster. "Finally. Fuckin' bring it!"

CHAPTER TWENTY-EIGHT

The worm powered down onto Johnny Walker as he fired a laser bomb into the monster's hissing, reeking mouth. Somehow, the airboat emerged unscathed and dipped below the water until the creature spun away, then bobbed up again and drifted toward the opposite bank.

All the magicals in the water—plus Reggie and his shifters still in the boat—stared dumbfounded at the empty, drenched airboat. Two terns soared over the river to head across the swamps and nothing else moved.

"Johnny!" Coughing on half-seawater, Lisa swam toward the side of the airboat and spun frantically in the water. "Johnny!"

"Oh, shit, man." Luther whined incessantly and paced in agitation along the bank where he and Rex had swum to shore. "Shit, shit, shit. This wasn't part of the plan!"

"Johnny!" Rex barked repeatedly but remained in one position while his brother pawed the ground, whined, and called for their master. "Not a funny joke, Johnny. Come on!"

"Oh, my God." Fighting to catch her breath, Lisa thumped a hand on the edge of the airboat and turned to look at the other magicals. "Anything?"

No one said a word. It seemed no one could see anything either.

Come on, Johnny. Her heart pounded in her ears. *This is not how you go out. I never said it was okay.*

Rex and Luther howled so violently that their front forepaws lifted off the ground. "Johnny!"

"Johnny!"

"Shit. Get ready for another one," Reggie said and pointed across the river at the clearing. "That motherfucker's gonna try again."

The other shifters lifted more exploding disks with grim expressions and readied themselves. Lisa blinked through the saltwater stinging her eyes—or maybe it was her tears—and tried to focus on the huge ring of bubbles that churned and rose increasingly higher on the opposite shore. She gritted her teeth, placed her hands on the deck, and pushed out the water to scramble awkwardly toward the cannon on the swiveling mount.

"You're going down, asshole," she snarled through clenched teeth. Everyone waited for the worm to make another appearance.

As soon as it emerged from the water, the agent uttered a terrifying battle cry and fired the cannon. She realized immediately that it wasn't the worm slithering out of the river but Johnny. "Shit—"

Fortunately, the dwarf made an especially small target from that range and her shot went wide by five feet to the left. He slogged out of the swamp only to be knocked aside by the blast of the cannon as it drove into the earth.

"Johnny!" She made a running leap over the bow of the airboat and swam like hell across the river.

"Ah! Ah!" Luther yipped and howled and darted along the bank. "He's alive! Johnny! Johnny! Johnny—"

Rex's splash into the water pulled his brother from his frantic shouting and Luther hastened after him to doggy-paddle to their master.

Reggie started the speedboat's engine and headed toward the dwarf, and the Philly magicals helped one another climb onto the airboat before Les frowned at the throttle control stick and shrugged. "It can't be that hard, right?"

Eddie stared directly at where the bounty hunter pushed himself off his back and the half-Light Elf woman threw herself at him. They both toppled onto the dry grass. "I think anything goes at this point, man."

"Yeah, okay." In the next moment, Les steered Johnny's airboat toward the shore, his jaw set in grim determination as he leveled the propeller.

"You're alive!" Lisa barreled into Johnny and threw her arms around him. His grunt was cut short when she kissed him fiercely and didn't let up for a full five seconds. Finally, she lurched away from him and wiped her mouth vigorously. "Oh... oh, my God. Ugh. What is that?"

He licked his lips and grinned at her. "Worm guts."

She laughed and threw her arms around him again but avoided the kiss this time and settled for a very tight, incredibly relieved hug. "I thought it had killed you, Johnny."

"It must have been hard for you."

"Shut up." She shoved him away again with a scowl, but the dwarf only laughed.

"What? I'm serious, darlin'. The last thing I wanna do is break your heart."

"Well, too late." She stood quickly and smirked at him as she blinked more tears away and reached to offer him a hand up. "But I'm very sure I'll be fine."

"Johnny! Johnny!"

"Holy shit. You're not dead!"

The hounds raced onto the bank and leapt at their master to knock him down again and lick his face exuberantly.

"All right, boys. Come on now. I was gone for all of thirty seconds. Maybe forty."

"It felt like you were dead forever, Johnny."

"Yeah, and you—hey. What's this?" Luther licked the worm guts mixed with swamp water that covered his master from head to toe. "Johnny, you taste weird."

"That's to be expected." He pushed up again in time to nod at the other magicals who steered the speedboat and his airboat to rest against the shore. On the other side of the river, William and his shifters finally got situated in theirs again and came to join the others.

"Now what the hell was that?" Reggie asked gruffly, although he couldn't hide the tiny smile that snuck through.

"Yeah, we—" Les burst out laughing. "We watched it eat you, man!"

"It tried." Johnny shrugged. "It's a good thing I got my hands on one of those laser-bomb guns, huh? Although I'm not sure exactly where it went. Things got a little messy in there. Hey, but next time I ask to hold one of those things—"

"I'll hand it over right away. Yeah, I got it." Chiron nodded vigorously. "Goddamn."

"I'm just sayin'."

"What about the worm?" Hyla asked.

The bounty hunter grimaced and flung off chunks of the worm guts that still clung to his clothes and beard. "Sorry, folks. It was me or the worm this time. I think we'll need to find another hive-mind to tap into."

"I…wouldn't be so sure about that." William studied the swamp water along the bank of the clearing. It bubbled, churned, and rose feet into the air like it had when Johnny emerged.

Everyone on land backed away from the commotion, and Luther yelped when the worm's massive head slid out of the water and thumped onto the bank with a hiss. "What the hell?"

"It regenerates." Chiron stared at it in disgust. "Even when it's been blown to pieces."

"Yeah, that ain't natural." Johnny sniffed and immediately hawked up what was already in his nose—which he'd rather not think about—and spat. "Well. It looks like we have our half-hour window after all. Y'all still got the rope and hooks?"

William nodded and Steve turned to retrieve the two huge coils of rope they'd stashed in the speedboat.

"Let's get this fucker to my place."

Towing the monster from three points—the airboat and both speedboats—was far easier than they'd anticipated. They did worry briefly about it waking up again and causing problems before they reached Johnny's property, but it seemed regenerating from a thousand tiny pieces took far more energy and effort than resurrecting from the creature's previous temporary deaths. It snorted a few times and uttered low moans but did nothing for them to be concerned about.

Finally, with the entire team working together, they hauled the massive worm onto the shore and stretched its huge length across Johnny's back yard until its head lay five feet from Margo. The dwarf retrieved the black box from Grady and returned to hook the creature up to Margo's central system. He had to rig two connected extension cords to get the electrodes on Grady's device out the door, around the metal hull, and to the motionless captive's head.

"What is that?" Les asked and adjusted his goggles.

"The mind-sync." Johnny slapped a hand on one side of the worm's head over the electrode, then the other—way harder than necessary, but it sure felt good. "I told y'all bout this part, didn't I?"

"Yeah, but it's—"

The bounty hunter stood and looked at the magicals who stared skeptically at the felled monster. "It's what?"

Les scratched the side of his chin. "I don't know. It's a little—"

"High-school science project?" Jasmine offered.

"Yeah. It looks like something someone set up in their garage for trial runs, not the tried and tested device you made it sound like before."

"Huh. Well, if I had a garage, Margo would be in it, probably." Johnny shrugged, strode around his massive satellite communication network machine, and disappeared inside. His voice came through Margo's exterior wall somewhat muffled and with a tinny ring to it. "Y'all let me know if anything weird happens."

"Oh, yeah. Sure." Eddie scoffed and stared at his fellow weapon-makers. "How are we supposed to tell the weird stuff from the normal stuff anymore?"

Lisa chuckled and nodded over her folded arms. "You don't."

"Oh. Nice."

"Go ahead, Johnny," she called and winked at the cautious magicals who stared at her, then Margo, and finally at the worm as they shuffled nervously.

"All right, darlin'. You're gonna get a text. The link in there will let us hear whatever she picks up 'cause I ain't lettin' y'all climb in here with your soaked shoes drippin' water all over Margo's clean floors."

Steve turned toward William and raised an eyebrow. "He's still covered in worm guts, right?"

"As far as I know."

"Huh."

Lisa hurried across the yard toward the back porch and snatched her cell phone up as it dinged with an incoming text. She opened it and was about to click the link but paused. "Johnny?"

He stepped around the corner of his metal contraption and nodded at her. "What's up?"

"Where's your phone?"

"I left it inside. You get the text?"

"Uh-huh. Now I'm wondering how I got it."

"Um…" He puffed his cheeks out and gestured toward Margo. "Giant satellite comm unit straight from the federal government, darlin'. With upgrades. It shouldn't be that surprisin'."

"And that shouldn't be able to find my phone number."

"Yeah, I reckon that's what they all say. Are you ready?"

Raising her eyebrows, Lisa looked at the dwarf in disbelief. When she realized everyone was staring at her again, she sighed and returned to the group gathered around the beast's monstrous head. "Let's see what we find, then."

"Open the link. I have Margo savin' all this on a private server, but I thought it would be more fun to listen to it like this." Johnny winked at her. "Make a show out of it."

"Sure." She clicked the link and turned the volume up on her phone as high as it would go.

Nothing but static crackled for the first few seconds, then faint voices began to filter in.

"…got three out in Oregon ready to be transported…"

"…Nexus is gonna want to see those shifters…"

"…five. We said five! You can't even bring in the right number, you moron. We're gonna have your head…"

"…much time left before the doorways close. So we want to make sure we grow as much as we possibly can. It's gonna be a wild…"

"…don't care if the magic is pulled out of this body. It's only a physical form, Carl. What we're about to do is so much bigger…"

"…keep the doorways to Oriceran open forever…"

The voices continued and switched in and out at various points in hundreds of different conversations scattered across the United States. Johnny peered over Lisa's shoulder and tapped another link on her phone, which pulled up a map of the US and pulsed red dots for every place Margo had located a conversation.

Or maybe it ain't Margo doin' the mappin'. It might be she's only the amplifier.

MARTHA CARR & MICHAEL ANDERLE

He narrowed his eyes at the worm's head and its gaping mouth. The creature's slow inhale and exhale was a soft background noise to all the voices exploding from Lisa's phone. "Y'all heard that, right?"

"Yep."

"Uh-huh."

"I truly wish I hadn't." Les folded his arms and grimaced at Lisa. "Because it sounded like whoever's at the center of this hive-mind is trying to collect as much of everyone else's magic as they can to—"

Chiron glanced at his dwarf friend and wrinkled his nose. "Can't you say it?"

Les shook his head and turned away to get some air.

"Then I'll say it." Hyla pointed at Lisa's phone. "It sounds like those bastards wanna break the doorways down and keep them from closin' every cycle, which doesn't make any goddamn sense."

"It would if this...Nexus person had a plan to draw magic from both worlds simultaneously," William mused. "But needed more time than the current travel window, I imagine."

"That's insane." Johnny snorted and shook his head. He paced between Lisa and Margo's outer wall with a scowl on his face. "What kind of idiot would ever think that's a solid plan?"

"I don't know, Johnny." Lisa gave him an apologetic shrug. "We've been up against any number of idiots. Most of them are idiots."

"Naw, I can't draw that line—"

A loud, harsh static filled the air and cut all the voices off in Lisa's phone. The worm stirred.

"Aw, shit." Reggie snatched an explosive disk from the loan belt the bounty hunter had given him and stalked toward the monster's head. "If this thing wakes up, I ain't waitin' for it to attack a second time. And we ain't in a river anymore."

"Hold on." The dwarf headed toward the worm's head instead

and raised a hand for the shifter to wait. "Give it a minute. I wanna see what's happenin'."

The local alpha snarled but lowered the inactive disk to his side.

The beast slowly opened its mouth even wider and Johnny leaned down it and turned his head to listen.

"Maybe that's not such a good idea, man," Eddie muttered. "It already ate you once."

"Shh." Johnny squinted and strained to hear what came out of the monster's mouth.

It struggled again where it lay, and a ripple of movement rushed down its body to the tip of its tail that dangled in the swamp. The static in Lisa's phone cut off entirely and suddenly issued from the worm's gaping maw, amplified a hundred times. The bounty hunter reeled away from it with a snarl. "Jesus!"

"Wait, wait, wait." Chiron rubbed his eyes with one hand, then stared at the monster. "Is it a radio?"

"I have no clue," Johnny muttered. "But I—"

"Congratulations, all of you!" The voice that boomed from the unmoving mouth sounded like a game show announcer.

"What the fuck?" Johnny staggered back again, then raced toward Lisa to study her phone.

"I'm not doing this, Johnny."

"Then where the hell is it coming from?"

"You've finally discovered the truth," the unknown voice stated, followed by a jovial laugh. "You know our secrets and we know yours—namely that you endeavor to hunt us and stop us from achieving our victory before it's too late."

"Damn straight." Johnny clenched his fists at his side. "And I think I could get it done right."

"But we have a better idea," the speaker continued. It was impossible to tell whether or not he could hear them on the other side or merely discovered what they were doing and continued to talk in the hopes of reaching his unexpected audience. "Instead

MARTHA CARR & MICHAEL ANDERLE

of trying to stop us, why don't you join us? Come and be a part of the greatest party you'll ever know, huh? Share what we share. Feel what we feel. Then you'll truly see that what we're doing is for the common good of all, even you."

Mikey clamped his hands over his ears and bared his teeth. "Ain't there a way to turn this fuckin' thing off?"

"So think about it, huh?" the man continued. "We sure could benefit from bringing in a few magicals as smart as Johnny Walker and Lisa Breyer."

"Holy shit." The dwarf's mouth dropped open.

The agent swallowed. "Yeah, I'm getting a new number."

"We can't wait to welcome you both with open arms," the stranger continued with another laugh. This one sounded slightly more sinister and far more insane. "There's an underground warehouse in Gallup, New Mexico. Don't worry about the exact address. You'll know it when you see it. We're not on a time crunch or anything—yet—so feel free to think about it if you need to. But don't wait too long because we've been waiting for you for long enough."

Another deafening hiss of static burst from the worm's open mouth. The monster writhed and bucked on the ground and its head shuddered as its mouth opened and closed by a fraction of an inch, almost as if it attempted to shut its jaws to drown out the sound. A massive pop preceded a spray of blue sparks that erupted from the worm's maw, and it fell completely still.

"Uh…Johnny?" Lisa reached slowly toward him, staring blankly at the now very dead creature stretched across his entire back yard.

He slipped his hand around hers and gave it a reassuring squeeze—one meant to reassure them both. "Yeah. We need to get to New Mexico."

"It's a good thing you have a private jet on standby."

"Yep."

"And I'm gonna call Nelson."

"Yeah, I think that's a good idea."

"Okay." She turned slowly to meet his gaze, then moved toward the back porch. Her fingers slipped out of his and Johnny's arm fell limply at his side.

"Wow." William squeezed his eyes shut. "That was the weirdest thing I've ever heard."

"The bastard didn't say anythin' about our missin' shifters, though," Baron grumbled. "How do we know this is real?"

"Because we had to put all the pieces together first." Johnny rubbed his mouth and exhaled a long, slow sigh. "If that worm ain't part of this damn hive-mind, I'm throwin' in the towel right here and now."

Both alphas nodded at their pack members and with no little hesitation, the shifters stepped toward the worm and congregated around its head.

"I'd try one of them plates right beneath the jaw," Johnny muttered. "They won't be nearly as hard to pull off now."

"How do you know that?" Jasmine asked.

"'Cause it's truly dead now."

No one argued with that.

The shifters worked together to pry the closest segment of armored hide away from the worm's body. It finally peeled away with a wet smack and trailed strings of slime behind it that smacked against the monster's actual flesh when the shifters tossed the plate aside.

"Ooh, hey. What's that?" Luther trotted toward the worm and Johnny snapped his fingers.

"Y'all stay back. That ain't for you."

"Not even a sniff, Johnny?"

"Nope."

"Aw…"

"Yeah, that's it, all right." Steve pointed at the symbol branded into the gooey, slimy flesh of the armored worm.

"It has the same damn smell too," Aldo added with a scowl. "You were right, dwarf."

"Yep." Johnny turned away from the worm and tried to shake the damn happy-slappy announcer-type voice out of his mind. *Lisa was right. This is way bigger than anythin' else either of us has come up against. And we're about to walk smack-dab into the middle of it.*

CHAPTER TWENTY-NINE

When Lisa finished her phone call, she stepped around the side of the house, her lips pressed tightly together in a grim line.

"What did Nelson have to say?" Johnny walked toward her and glanced over his shoulder at the magicals investigating the dead worm and whatever secrets it had hidden under the damn armor.

"The location checks out." She nodded slowly, her expression distant and entirely too preoccupied but with good reason. "And he even has an address."

"For the underground warehouse?"

"Uh-huh. It seems the FBI has two other agents there already."

"You gotta be shittin' me."

"They're investigating something completely different, Johnny. At least, that's what Nelson said. He wouldn't tell me what the actual case is out there, but he said he'd let them know we were coming."

"Undercover?"

"Yeah, they are right now."

"All right." The bounty hunter scowled and sighed heavily. "Then I reckon it's a good thing we'll have help down there."

"You mean because we'll be walking into what might be the most dangerous building on the entire planet? Or for some other reason?"

They stared at each other for a moment before they broke into tense, disbelieving laughter.

"Yeah, darlin'. That and any other reason that might come up in the next few days."

"Right. Yeah, I agree. It'll be good to have backup."

"It ain't much."

"Well, we didn't have much to work with when we started down this road. It shouldn't take that much more to finish it, right?"

"We'll finish it."

"And we're coming with you." William stalked toward them with his fists clenched at his sides. "Cassidy's out there in New Mexico being brainwashed by these...these..."

"The hive-mind?" Lisa offered.

"Yeah. And I can't sit here and hope that things work out so we're coming too."

"Sorry, brother." Johnny reached out to clap a hand on the city alpha's shoulder and frowned in sympathy. "Shifters are the single easiest target for that brand and the brainwashin'. That's why Cassidy and Magnus were taken. I ain't got a clue about the Wood Elf but at this point, I reckon these assholes are an equal-opportunity assimilator. I can't put you at that kinda risk."

"You ain't." Reggie joined them and nodded grimly. "We're puttin' ourselves in it, dwarf."

"Nope." Johnny turned and headed to the back porch steps.

"You can't simply cut us out of this because a worm radio called you by name," William shouted.

"Sure I can." Johnny stopped at the top of the stairs and gestured toward the magicals in his yard and the massive worm carcass he didn't want to ever think about again, let alone see lying in his grass. "We're goin' this alone 'cause we're the ones with an in."

"Well, you gotta give us somethin'," Eddie said and gestured in agitation.

"Do you wanna help out while Lisa and I go after these bastards?"

"Absolutely."

The other magicals nodded and stared at Johnny, eagerly awaiting his next order.

The dwarf grimaced and stared at the railing of his porch. *If anyone saw this from the outside, they'd think I was startin' a cult.*

"Fine. Y'all can keep an eye on my property and that little Blue Heeler who started this whole thing 'cause she was missin' her owner."

The eagerness to be a part of the mission faded quickly from the other magicals' faces.

"Come on, darlin'." The bounty hunter waved Lisa toward him on the back porch and turned to open the back door. "We have packin' to do and a jet captain to call."

Hyla snorted and folded her arms. "That's it? Watch your house and take care of the damn dog?"

He rubbed his mouth for slightly longer than usual and pointed into the yard. "No. Don't forget to feed the chickens."

The threat from the hivemind runs deeper than it initially appeared. Just how deep? Johnny and Lisa are going to try and find out in *DWARF IT ALL*.

THE STORY CONTINUES

The story continues in book six, *Dwarf It All*, coming soon to Amazon and Kindle Unlimited.

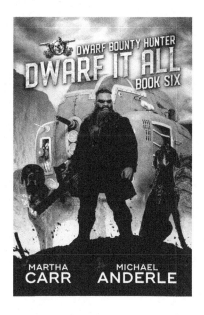

Pre-order your copy today for delivery at midnight on March 8, 2021!

Get sneak peeks, exclusive giveaways, behind the scenes content, and more. PLUS you'll be notified of special **one day only fan pricing** on new releases.

Sign up today to get free stories.

Visit: https://marthacarr.com/read-free-stories/

AUTHOR NOTES - MARTHA CARR
JANUARY 18, 2021

I hail from Chicago, by way of New York, Washington DC and Philadelphia. Moving to Austin was like leaving the city behind with just enough high rises to make it feel like home. My idea of living in the country. Bonus, there's real countryside just a few miles away with longhorn steer and a donkey or two.

But, unlike all those cities there's not much in the way of seasons unless your seasons are warm, hot and what happened hot. It's January right now and it's in the low seventies a lot of the time. Heavenly and the start of spring around here. Winter was last month for a few weeks.

I miss the change of the color in the leaves and snow. Normally, I could go visit both those things, get my fill and return home. Of course, last year made that impossible and my anticipation for seeing both has been building. It was looking like anything like that would have to wait for the next fall and winter seasons.

However, last week something really odd happened. It snowed. Just getting a few flakes of snow in Austin is weird, but this was legit, fat, fluffy flakes, coming down all day, snow. The sky was overcast all day and the scenery was filled with those flakes falling to the ground. It wasn't long before there were a few inches.

Of course, we all lost our minds and went hunting for anything that could be employed as a sled. I saw a grown woman using a ski as a sled and a few people were using trays. Snowmen were created, snow angels were made, mostly again by the adults. Kids managed to elbow us out of the way some of the time.

Even better, by the next day it was gone and the temperature was back in the sixties. No mounds of ice. No piles of snow growing dirty and taking up parts of the road. Nothing to scrape off the windshield while you wait for your car to warm. It was perfect and for all of us who hail from colder climates, a nice replay of childhood memories in a time that's been tough.

May you all be finding pockets of joy and fun, running outside to greet the neighbors from a safe distance. Forgetting for just a little while everything else and enjoying something as simple as snow. More adventures to follow.

Thank you so much for not only reading this latest book in the *Dwarf Bounty Hunter* series but these author notes in the back as well.

Now, I'd like to turn these author notes over to Robin Cutler, who recently joined LMBPN in a role that allows me to spend more time creating stories in my new role as CEO and Chief Creative Officer.

If you missed the announcement, you can find it here:

https://www.prnewswire.com/news-releases/lmbpn-hires-robin-cutler-to-lead-publishing-division-301197109.html

Now, here's Robin….

Hello Everyone—

You may have heard that I recently joined LMBPN Publishing as President so I wanted to introduce myself today by telling you a little about the path that leads me here today. From my earliest memories that mirror the literary themes of both *Oliver Twist* and *Peter Pan,* I have been educated, entertained, and nurtured by books. It began when, as a 7-year-old girl, I walked into a small, dusty library in rural South Carolina and my imagination caught fire. Today, nearly 60 years later I have traveled a direct and remarkable path paved by, in my estimation, nearly a million books. If destiny is foretold the way some people believe, surely my destiny is and always has been, firmly anchored in the book world.

My first big job out of college was as the Design and Production Manager at the University of South Carolina Press. Over the next 12 years, I moved into other roles there as Marketing Manager and finally Assistant Director. From there I founded Summerhouse Press, publishing some 50 titles including the best-selling book, *The Forest of Love* by the Academy Award-winning actor, Jack Palance. How I came to be Mr. Palance's publisher is a story that makes no sense except to chalk it up to *divine providence.* I'll share that story another time but suffice it to say, Jack Palance was a wonderful author and artist and I greatly enjoyed working with him.

Summerhouse fed my family for years, but I was soon lured back to academic life, working for a private college and then at the University of Wisconsin where I served as Executive Director of University Relations from 2000 to 2004. Being responsible for the news, publications, events, conferences, as well as the television and radio stations on a college campus is a 24/7 job that never stops. I loved it and would probably still be on a college campus if family responsibilities had not required me to move back to South Carolina. Looking for a job there, I posted my resume online and it was found by a recruiter at Amazon.com. I was hired to be part of a team that took a startup that Amazon had just bought, eventually turning it into CreateSpace, Amazon's precursor to what is now, KDP. During my six years working for CreateSpace/Amazon, I learned much and worked hard. Coming from the protected and predictable university bubble, I found Amazon both exhilarating and scary as a new company with stratospheric growth. I remember that first year, I had a gnawing feeling of uncertainty, not feeling entirely sure of what I was doing. The uncertainly diminished when I figured out that I might not have all the answers but neither did anyone else because we were building something entirely new in the history of publishing. There is a joke that working at Amazon should be counted in dog years. So, after six (42 in dog) years when I was offered another position, I opted instead to leave Amazon and move with my husband to Nashville for his new job.

My intention, once we settled in Nashville, was to leave publishing for good and to crawl back into the campus bubble. But surprisingly, someone told the president of Ingram, the world's largest book wholesaler/distributor that I was in the area and that he should hire me. He eventually tracked me down and talked me into joining the company. A year later, I began the hard work of creating Ingram's self-publishing platform, which we named IngramSpark, that was launched to much fanfare in 2013. I directed that program through incredible growth each year along with garnering industry awards until my retirement this past November 2020.

When the announcement was made of my retirement, I was satisfied that I had fulfilled what seemed to be my destiny of enabling hundreds of thousands of authors and publishers to make their books available to the world through the work I had done at both Amazon and Ingram. But little did I know that there was more to come in my publishing journey when just two days into my happy retirement, Michael Anderle called and asked me to take over his role as President of LMBPN so that he could focus on the creative side of the business. I have been on board now for about a month and over these past weeks, I've been impressed with the professional team that Michael has in place along with the quality content that LMBPN produces. How I got here isn't anything I predicted or even asked for, but it's been an interesting career that is still being played out. I am very grateful and frankly astonished that the book world is not quite done with me. And I'm very happy to be a publisher once again.

--Robin Cutler, President, LMBPN Publishing

robin.cutler@lmbpn.com

Solve a murder, save her mother, and stop the apocalypse?

What would you do when elves ask you to investigate a prince's murder and you didn't even know elves, or magic, was real?

Meet Leira Berens, Austin homicide detective who's good at what she does – track down the bad guys and lock them away.

Which is why the elves want her to solve this murder – fast. It's not just about tracking down the killer and bringing them to justice. It's about saving the world!

If you're looking for a heroine who prefers fighting to flirting, check out The Leira Chronicles today!

<u>AVAILABLE ON AMAZON AND IN KINDLE UNLIMITED!</u>

THE MAGIC COMPASS

If smart phones and GPS rule the world - why am I hunting a magic compass to save the planet?

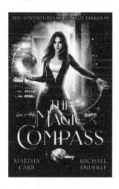

Austin Detective Maggie Parker has seen some weird things in her day, but finding a surly gnome rooting through her garage beats all.

Her world is about to be turned upside down in a frantic search for 4 Elementals.

Each one has an artifact that can keep the Earth humming along, but they need her to unite them first.

Unless the forces against her get there first.

AVAILABLE ON AMAZON AND IN KINDLE UNLIMITED!

CONNECT WITH THE AUTHORS

Martha Carr Social
Website:
http://www.marthacarr.com
Facebook:
https://www.facebook.com/groups/MarthaCarrFans/

Michael Anderle

Website: http://lmbpn.com

Email List: http://lmbpn.com/email/

Social Media:

https://www.facebook.com/LMBPNPublishing

https://twitter.com/MichaelAnderle

https://www.instagram.com/lmbpn_publishing/

https://www.bookbub.com/authors/michael-anderle

ALSO BY MARTHA CARR

Other series in the Oriceran Universe:

THE LEIRA CHRONICLES

THE FAIRHAVEN CHRONICLES

MIDWEST MAGIC CHRONICLES

SOUL STONE MAGE

THE KACY CHRONICLES

THE DANIEL CODEX SERIES

I FEAR NO EVIL

SCHOOL OF NECESSARY MAGIC

THE UNBELIEVABLE MR. BROWNSTONE

SCHOOL OF NECESSARY MAGIC: RAINE CAMPBELL

ALISON BROWNSTONE

FEDERAL AGENTS OF MAGIC

SCIONS OF MAGIC

Series in The Terranavis Universe:

The Adventures of Maggie Parker Series

The Witches of Pressler Street

The Adventures of Finnegan Dragonbender

OTHER BOOKS BY JUDITH BERENS

OTHER BOOKS BY MARTHA CARR

JOIN MARTHA CARR'S FAN GROUP ON FACEBOOK!

OTHER LMBPN PUBLISHING BOOKS

To be notified of new releases and special promotions from LMBPN
publishing, please join our email list:

http://lmbpn.com/email/

For a complete list of books published by LMBPN please visit the
following pages:

https://lmbpn.com/books-by-lmbpn-publishing/

Made in the USA
Coppell, TX
05 August 2022

81008121R00157